Lea

THE THREE
Heirs

by

Monique Desrosiers

*Love always finds
a home.*

Monique Des___

A Wood Dragon Book

Other books by Monique Desrosiers

The Cartwright Men Marry

THE THREE

Heirs

by

Monique Desrosiers

A Wood Dragon Book

The Three Heirs

Copyright © 2023 Monique Desrosiers

Cover art: Callum Jagger
Inside design: Christine Lee
Pen graphic: Celine Peter

Published by:
Wood Dragon Books
Post Office Box 429
Mossbank, Saskatchewan, Canada S0H3G0
www.wooddragonbooks.com

ISBN:
978-1-990863-22-6   eBook
978-1-990863-21-9   Paperback
978-1-990863-20-2   Hardcover

Contact the author at:
Email: authormjd58@gmail.com
Website: www.moniquedesrosiers.com

Dedication

For my eight siblings
You have inspired me more than you know.

Prologue

Emily and Lilith walk across the great hall toward the study, aiming for the man standing in front of the open door. The women had been informed that they were two of three heirs named in a Will and had travelled from Delton, Michigan the previous afternoon for the official reading.

January 21, 1868 is a typical Philadelphia winter day with a brisk wind and a sullen grey sky, yet inside the mansion, the inhabitants are cocooned and protected from the weather. The Neustat House is famous for its stunning workmanship of wood and Italian marble. The grand staircase dominating the great hall is brilliantly lit by table lamps, wall sconces and candle chandeliers. The walls are adorned with wool and silk tapestries of European scenes purchased in France.

After a thirty-seven-year absence, Emily is exhilarated to be back in Philadelphia and that the day to hear the mysterious Mrs. Neustat's Last Will and Testament has finally arrived. Still slim at age fifty-four, Emily has a diamond-shaped face with delicate features and a dimple on her right cheek. Her hair is beginning to show strands of grey, but most of them can still be concealed by her blond tresses. She picks up the skirt of her crimson dress, her blue eyes dancing with anticipation as she nears the older gentleman.

Lilith, Emily's daughter-in-law, is a step behind. Her heart-shaped face, featuring a perky turned-up nose and clear hazel eyes, is crowned with thick, blond hair.

"Good morning to you ladies. Mr. Trolley, Lawyer, at your service. This way please." He motions with his right hand for them to move passed him and into the study.

Inside, a large oak desk is flanked by bookshelves. On the far left of the desk are tall book-laden cabinets that obstruct a view of comfortable high-back chairs, tables and lamps clustered together around a fireplace.

At the door, Lilith immediately becomes agitated when she recognizes Graham Lestor, standing in front of one of the three chairs facing the desk. She fights her instinct to flee and moves to claim the chair on the right, as far away from him as possible. She asks herself, *What is **he** doing here?*

Graham had stood when he heard the lawyer greet the women but now his stomach does a flip as Emily and Lilith enter the study. His eyes can't help but follow Lilith. He thought he would never see her again. With longing, his brain registers how her new hairstyle, pulled up into a riot of curls, compliments her sweet face. Her emerald dress makes the amber of her eyes sparkle. She appears agitated and he knows his presence is the cause. He casts his eyes down as the embarrassing memory of their last rendezvous replays in his mind and he feels fresh regret.

Emily thinks nothing of the handsome stranger's ungentlemanly behavior. Every man either stares or becomes shy when first meeting her stunningly beautiful daughter-in-law. Emily has unconsciously aimed for the chair in the middle and now turns to look fully at Graham's face. For several seconds, she stops breathing, then gulps in air and on the exhale, she almost utters her dead son's name aloud.

The man standing next to her is of the same height and build as her late son with square shoulders that taper to a V-shaped waist. Although his hair is a lighter shade of brown and has a natural curl, the similarity of the man's face to that of her son's is uncanny. Emily's eyes rest on his big brown ones, then on his square jaw and moves up to his chiselled nose and farther up to his forehead where the hairline begins low into a fullness that begs to be swept back. She is unnerved by the feeling of familiarity.

The lawyer makes introductions and polite expressions of "How do you do?" and, "Very well, thank you," are said all around.

Neither Graham nor Lilith reveal that they know each other. Lilith's cheeks flush as she recalls their first kiss the night of the play at the theater. She shakes that dreamy moment out of her head and scolds herself to pay attention to the lawyer's words.

Everyone sits as Mr. Trolley points to a woman at a small table in front of the window and mentions his secretary's name; Lilith's distraction with Graham's presence and her memories prevent her from hearing it.

"We will take breaks every hour or so until we are finished. Before I begin, are there any questions?"

Even though they all wonder why a full two days are required to read a Will, no one speaks up. So, Mr. Trolley begins, "As you know, a widow by the name of Mrs. Delilah Neustat, passed away of old age a few weeks ago. With the evidence unearthed by the private investigators from The Benson and Decker Agency, I have her three heirs sitting here with me in her home—Mrs. Emily Breat, Mrs. Lilith Breat, and Mr. Graham Lestor."

Unbeknownst to the ladies and to Mr. Lestor, there is a sixth person in the room—out of view, seated in a wing-back chair behind a tall cabinet. Only the lawyer knows of his presence. The man, who was the last of the guests to arrive the night before, is allowed to listen in, provided he remains unseen and silent until called upon by the lawyer.

"Mrs. Emily Breat, your maiden name is Thordeaux?" Mr. Trolley asks, pronouncing the surname as Thor-ducks.

"Yes. It is!" she exclaims, strangely pleased by the mention of her name and surprised to realize that its mispronunciation still bothers her after all this time. "But it is Thor-doe as the letters e-a-u make a hard o sound and the x is silent," she clarifies.

The sixth person shifts his weight in his seat with anticipation and relief upon hearing Emily say the name correctly. *Finally*, he thinks to himself.

"Very well." Mr. Trolley murmurs as he scribbles a note. He reads what is written under her occupation, lifts his eyebrows, "And up until recently you worked in a brothel? But as a bookkeeper, not a ... *tsk tsk*."

"No, I certainly was not one of the *tsk tsk*, as you refer to the women who work there, Mr. Trolley. I assure you that I only worked as Madam Deb's bookkeeper."

"Of course," he says, clearing his throat. "My apologies."

Emily nods her head once, smiles at the fact that he was too embarrassed to accurately mention the profession, and recovers her good manners, "I am sorry if I responded rudely."

"Not at all. Moving on then. Mrs. Lilith Breat, your maiden name is Green?"

"Yes, it is."

"And your late husband's first name was Daniel?" Lilith nods in agreement. "Were you also an employee of the late Madam Deb?"

Lilith turns her head slightly in Graham's general direction but does not focus on his face as she answers, "Yes. Part-time. She hired me to sew and repair garments for her working girls. I am otherwise employed full-time as a school teacher in the northern part of the City of Delton."

Having convinced himself otherwise, Graham now feels ashamed upon hearing Lilith's response.

"Thank you for that clarification. For simplicity, may I call you both by your first names?"

"Certainly," the women answer in unison.

"Thank you. Now, Mr. Graham Lestor, you are a permanent resident of England, is that correct?"

"That is correct."

"You were born in the city of London?"

"Yes."

"And were you ever employed by the Madam?"

"No. I have never properly met the woman and I have only seen her once. I work for my father. We are currently involved in the disbursement of land holdings, and specifically numerous properties in Delton."

"Where did you see her?"

"She was just standing with a group of—how is this relevant, Mr. Trolley?" asks Graham in disdain.

"It is not, Mr. Lestor. Kindly disregard. Before we get to the reading of the Will, Mrs. Neustat wished for me to read her letter to you."

He looks up to see that they understand. "I begin," says Mr. Trolley and takes a deep breath.

All three heirs look on in awe at the inch-thick file folder he retrieves from the desk drawer on his right.

Graham thinks, *A letter? That is more like a book!*

Emily is surprised as well and thinks, *So now we know why we will be here for two days.*

October 1867

My honored guests,

Thank you for accepting the invitation to be here today. I realize that we have never met and for that I apologize.

I was born and raised in Portland, Maine, which makes this even more of a mystery to you, I am sure.

You need to know my full story in order to understand how it is that we are all connected. I will commence with my oldest recollection; it was brought back to mind through a dream, or should I say a nightmare, that I had the other night. Shockingly, it has connections to Madam Deb's early life.

As the lawyer narrates Delilah's well written letter, the listeners often visualize the events unfolding before their eyes.

1
Delilah

Delilah Neustat tosses and turns in her bed. She mumbles, then tosses again, more frantic now. She kicks with her feet and punches out into empty space with her fists. Her mumbling suddenly increases in volume. "No! Mama." She is begging now.

With a jerk, she sits straight up in her bed, eyes wide open, heartbeat quickened. She sweeps away tangled, long, white hair from her face and wipes the fresh tears from her cheeks with the corner of the bed sheet. Extending her shaky, wrinkled hand to the night table, she feels the lantern and turns the knob to adjust the wick. The globe lights up with life.

I have never dreamt this nightmare two nights in a row, she thinks. At the foot of her bed is her portable, folding desk box. She opens the lid, takes out paper, ink, and a quill pen, and begins to write.

On August 1, 1790, the day of my seventh birthday ...

She stops writing as she allows herself to be surrounded by thoughts of the home of her youth.

Red spruce, maples, and eastern white pine stretch to the skies where patches of green fields fight to keep the trees from taking over. Ribbons of gravel road lead to grand estates and to beaches, both private and public. Portland, Maine will always be the most treasured scenery of her memories.

She can't help but replay every detail of the dream in her mind once more before writing it down:

"Would you like a cup of tea?" asks the little brown-haired girl, smartly dressed in a new blue and white tunic. Not waiting for a reply, nor anticipating one from her new doll sitting on the toddler's chair at the little table, she pretends to pour steaming liquid into the child-sized china teacup.

At that moment, the girl's mother, Beatrice, walks into the nursery and observes her daughter imitating the perfect hostess to her dolls and stuffed toys. Beatrice turns to sit on the bench underneath the window, ignoring the nanny knitting in the corner, rocking in her favorite chair.

The child is excited by the rare appearance of her mother in the nursery during playtime and in the hopes of pleasing her, says, "Look Mama, I am giving tea to my most special friend, Charlotte."

"What did you say?" asks the shocked woman, turning toward her only living offspring. "What did you call her?"

"Well Mama," replies the girl sheepishly, becoming frightened by the sudden dark look on her mother's face, "She is your special friend so I invited her to my party."

"How dare you!" exclaims Beatrice as she rises. In two strides she reaches the child and slaps her on the face with an opened hand.

The strength she put behind the assault makes Delilah fly out of her chair. While the girl is in the air, she wails and grabs onto her cheek. She no sooner hits the floor then her mother grabs her by the arms and starts shaking her, yelling, "SHE IS NOT A PLAYTHING!"

When released, the child falls back, landing on the rug in front of the fireplace. Only then does Delilah begin to weep, her hands reaching up to her face to soothe the ache. The nanny quickly and quietly kneels to comfort and protect the girl from her unstable mother.

Beatrice feels no remorse. She stands straight and says sternly, "Only I have the right to mention her name. Not you. Never you. Do you understand, Delilah? Do you?"

She leaves the room, just as unexpectedly as she arrived, not waiting to see her frightened daughter nod.

Beatrice rarely shows up in the nursery. When she does, Delilah cautiously watches the cold woman in silence. Any words spoken by this stranger of a mother always revolves around the mysterious child, Charlotte.

"Charlotte would have loved this," or "Charlotte would have done that," or "Charlotte would have looked pretty in pink. She would have had lovely curly hair, unlike yours Delilah. Your hair is plain as the fur on a brown mouse."

Delilah always makes sure to agree with whatever her mother says.

Two weeks after the tea party, Delilah's father, tall and lean, visits her. Sitting on the window seat, he summons, "Delilah, Papa has a story to tell you."

As she approaches him, she innocently brushes her right cheek with the back of her pudgy, little hand. He picks up his pretty daughter and places her on his lap. According to her short memory, he has never come to visit her in the nursery and she fears that fact. The dread shows on her face.

"There is nothing to be afraid of, pet. I am only going to tell you a story. It is about you! You see, when you were born, you had a twin sister. Do you know what a twin is?"

She shakes her head.

"Well, instead of having just one baby, the mother has two at the same time. That is known as twins." She nods that she understands. He continues, "Your mother and I were truly happy to have two baby girls. We named you Charlotte and Delilah."

The wide-eyed girl interrupts, "Charlotte, like Mama's special friend? The one I am not supposed to talk about?"

He inhales deeply and nods.

"Where is she?" asks Delilah.

"She is in heaven. You were only three months old when she left us so you would not remember. Why, three months is not even a year and you are seven times older than that already, so it was a very long time ago. You slept in the same crib and one morning your mother found you sleeping with your head resting on Charlotte's back. Your sister had died in her sleep. Do you know what dying is?"

"That is what you do to get into heaven," replies the girl.

"That is correct. Heaven is a nice place, especially for babies, but your mother wishes that Charlotte was here instead, playing with you. Mama did not want your sister to go to heaven so soon. Do you understand?"

She nods.

Beatrice stays away from Delilah for days at a time, leaving her care to Nanny Isabel. The distorted role of a substitute parent in the child's life is reinforced by the location of the nanny's bedroom with its adjoining door to the nursery. Isabel and Delilah are only seen by the other residents of the household when they venture downstairs to eat or go outside to walk in the gardens.

Although her days and nights are filled with her duty to the little Delilah, the wise and experienced nanny never rightfully gives herself entirely to her charge. She knows that one day her skills will be needed elsewhere and she cannot afford to fully love this girl, or any child for that matter, if she wants to do her job well and survive the loss.

Delilah grows older—and unloved.

2
Delilah

More than seven decades later, Delilah can remember the sting of her cheek. She grabs a hold of the bed sheet and dampens it with more tears.

The letter continues …

It took me years to understand that had I been the one to die instead of my twin sister, Mother would have wished Charlotte was me. Her anger towards me was a reaction to her loss, not a reflection of our relationship. However, I changed the day of my seventh birthday because the assault made me feel unwanted, even hated. I was also left with the impression that I was responsible for Charlotte's death, or I should say rather, that I sensed being blamed for it.

I needed my mother and I needed her affection. I became defiant in order to gain her notice, but I never received the discipline that I deserved nor the love that I craved. That made me feel like no one cared about me at all.

My father decided that I was a problem to solve. He released Nanny

Isabel of her duties. I suspect my father made those arrangements thinking that I would grow closer to my mother if I no longer had my devoted nanny. He was wrong.

Eventually, mother could no longer handle my attention-seeking outbursts and hired another nanny—one who was very strict. My parents must have hoped that I would be intimidated into listening and behaving. I lied about how a piece of my mother's jewelry ended up in the nanny's room, and she was sent packing.

I had countless nannies after that, but the only one I remember with fondness was Trudy. She was a buxom young lass, full of spit and fire. She was such a delight to have as a nanny. She was as affectionate and attentive as her position allowed.

Back in Portland, Maine and back in time, the soon to be ten-year-old Delilah wakes crying from a bad dream. She rises from her bed to search out her nanny but stops when she hears noises in the adjacent room. This is the first time she has heard giggling and conversation on the other side of the door. She shies away. Even after the noises stop, she doesn't seek Nanny Trudy, but cries herself back to sleep.

A few nights later, lively moaning wakes her up. She listens until she hears the noises coming from the nanny's room stop and the sound of a door close. Twice a week for months to come, she hears voices and moaning from next door.

Delilah had become a light sleeper and one night when she wakes to the sound of muffled voices, she approaches the adjoining door to hear better. Trudy is speaking clearly enough for Delilah to hear her say, " ... but I love you, Alfred."

Delilah recognizes her father's voice when he replies, "Do not be daft, I love my wife. And do not dare do something stupid or you will find yourself out of a job. Understood?"

Trudy must have nodded, because Delilah doesn't hear her say anything more before the door that leads out to the hallway clicks shut.

Years pass. Trudy is replaced by daily tutors the same day Delilah is moved out of the nursery. Her casual play is upgraded to formal lessons in society etiquette, drawing, and piano.

But regardless of her improved manners, at dinner each evening, Delilah is spiteful and rude—especially toward her mother. Her displays of anger and resentment change over time, becoming more destructive, expensive, and passive aggressive.

One day, she purposefully breaks an irreplaceable vase that her father had gifted her mother. Another time, she leads all the horses out of their stalls and sets them loose. It takes the rest of the day to fetch them all. A couple of the horses get sick as they indulged in an abundance of grain out in the field—food normally good for horses, but not when they engorge themselves.

Another day, Delilah steals her father's liquor that he keeps in his study, and then she leads him to the outhouse where the bottles of expensive liquids are resting on the most disgusting heap of refuse possible.

But acts like these are only child's play compared to what is yet to come.

3
Delilah

Delilah's pretty face lights with joy as she rides her favorite horse to the barn. It is her sixteenth year and her body has changed to that of a young woman over the winter months. Along with her developing body, her schemes to bedevil her parents have also matured and the new stable boy merits a second look.

She dismounts and approaches the young man to give him the reins to her horse. He looks up from his work and is surprised that she is standing there in front of him. He throws his head back to toss his long, auburn hair away from his blue eyes, the movement curiously making Delilah catch her breath. Her heart flutters and she blushes as a result of her attraction.

She asks, "Give him a good brushing, will you? I am afraid I worked him hard this morning." She pauses. "What is your name?"

He inquisitively looks her up and down and she blushes anew. Delilah's dark eyes capture his interest and her petite frame is to his liking. He is lured by the shapely woman and doesn't care if she sees him looking at her with lust.

Flattered, he replies, "Ray."

"I am Delilah."

"We all know who you are."

"Well, do you now?" she says, surprising herself by the mature and calm sound of her voice.

He snickers as he looks into her eyes and lets them wander down to her pink lips, then to her silky-white neck, and further downward to her chest; at which point she inhales deeply to make it look bigger. He enjoys the inexperienced tease and takes a step closer to her, his chin almost touching her nose.

Ray needs to test further, so he reaches around her to switch the reins from one hand to the other. His arms brush up against hers in the process and when she doesn't move, he says knowingly, "Do you need help removing your riding boots?"

It's her turn to snicker, "I will get a carrot for the horse first. You go ahead and start brushing him without me. Then we will see about my riding boots."

She saunters away, looking back momentarily to see him watching her until she turns the corner.

The letter continues …

As you may have guessed, I shamelessly lost my innocence to that young man that summer. I was alone once more, and bored. I looked for companionship and friendship from the servants in my home because I received none from my parents. I craved human contact, good or bad.

One day, just like that, Ray was no longer working for us. I couldn't go whining to my father about it, he likely was the one who had sent him away.

It didn't matter. I wasn't in love with Ray. Besides, I was ready to move my sights towards someone else. A man who was much more mature and forbidden.

Three dull weeks went by before the desolate Delilah devises a new adventure to help fill in the time. At half past four on a muggy Thursday afternoon, she's sitting with her father in the cool shade. When Alfred hears someone call out his name, he puts his paper down and rises from his seat on the terrace to go greet his visitor. She watches them shake hands and then come to sit in the refreshing shadows.

The man, Thomas Cowell, is a business associate of her father's as well as a neighbor. He is younger than Alfred by at least five years, so that makes him about thirty-eight years old. Alfred reclaims his chair and Thomas sits facing Delilah, nodding a polite greeting.

Alfred starts to talk excitedly about the battle the United States currently is fighting with France. When he realizes that his daughter is likely oblivious of this event, he explains briefly, "It is a naval conflict, Delilah, against French privateers who are seizing American ships in the Caribbean and on the East coast."

He sees her eyes become dull and lose expression—a sign that she's no longer listening. He refrains from explaining further and focuses on his visitor instead. But snippets of their conversation elaborate that more than three hundred American ships were captured and that Congress had reassembled the United States Navy and authorized the use of military force against France.

Delilah, who has ignored her father's voice for so many years, has no difficulty locking her sights on Thomas. She picks up her fan and starts to cool herself from the heat. She observes Thomas shift his gaze back and forth from her father's face to hers.

Out of her father's peripheral view, Delilah reaches for her skirt and Thomas's eyes follow her hand. She lifts the fabric above her ankles, continuing with the pretense of needing to cool herself. Delilah senses him longing to see more of her exposed limbs.

At this point, Thomas pulls on his tight collar. Alfred notices and says, "Loosen your tie, Thomas. It is too hot out here and besides, we are at my home. Please make yourself comfortable."

Alfred rings a bell and a servant appears. "Bring us more lemonade and a glass for Mr. Cowell," he instructs and then returns to the topic at hand.

Delilah smiles at Thomas and thinks, *He is a good-looking man for his age.* She tilts her head to the right. *He could use a better haircut.* She lets her eyes wander down to his chest and abdomen. He sucks in his tummy ever so slightly. She smiles again, thinking, *Oh good. He has noticed where I am looking. I wonder if he is a good lover?*

Alfred observes Thomas looking back and forth from him to Delilah and senses that Thomas might think that any news on Napoleon as too sensitive to be discussed in front of the girl, so he says, "Delilah, could you leave us to talk business?"

"Certainly Father, but do not make it all work. Will you join us for supper, Mr. Cowell?"

"I am sure Mr. Cowell is expected at home, Delilah," interjects her father.

"As a matter of fact, Alfred, Mrs. Cowell is visiting with her mother for a fortnight."

"Well then," Alfred responds, "join us if you have no other commitment, Thomas."

"I would be delighted," Thomas says, flashing Delilah a grateful smile.

Delilah gets up to leave them alone to continue their discussion and announces, "I will tell the butler to set another place." She puts her hand on Thomas's shoulder and says, "I hope you like roast beef, Mr. Cowell."

"Yes, I do. One of my favorite meals."

A few minutes later, Delilah leaves the kitchen with something in her hand that she quickly places in her pocket.

Without fear, the young woman walks down the hallway to her mother's dressing room and starts rummaging through the neglected gowns in the closets. For years, her mother has shied away from all social activities and Delilah is certain her father will not remember what his wife had once worn. Delilah wants to wear something that is not part of her own wardrobe, a dress that makes her appear grown up and worldly, but not too provocative that her father will notice.

She picks out a pink chiffon with a heart shaped bodice, suggesting a deeper, more mature body underneath. Sheer fabric covers the skirt, gathers at the waist, and extends up to collect at the neck to form a design to make a woman appear decently covered, yet slightly daring.

Delilah is a few inches shorter than her mother and wonders if the difference of those extra couple of inches will cause her to step on the sweep of the skirt and trip. She doesn't have time to hem it up and hopes the extra length will not be noticeable when she is standing. She can pick up the extra skirt material when she is required to walk.

Not quite ready to alarm her father with a full mature look, she wisely decides to leave her hair down—as is the fashion for girls her age—giving her a youthful and innocent appearance. Gathering her hair up would make her look at least eighteen and that is not what she wants her father to contemplate.

After walking through to her mother's bedroom, she opens a window, reaches into her pocket, and places a handful of walnuts on the sill. Then she leaves a trail of the favored snack across the carpet, before moving back through the dressing room and down the hall.

4
Delilah

Delilah knows that Beatrice won't be joining them for the evening meal as only two place settings had been set—that is, until she tells the kitchen staff that Mr. Cowell was staying for the evening meal.

Delilah's father neither notices nor comments on her attire when she enters the dining room; he is just pleased she is prompt and behaving appropriately. Their dinner guest, however, delivers the reaction she has been yearning for. Thomas ravages her with his eyes, takes her hand and brings it to his lips. He even follows her to her chair and helps her sit.

He leans forward and whispers, "You look delightful," as he stares down the front of her dress. She knows that from that angle, he can see more of her young breasts than he has counted on and she breathes in and out quickly so he can see the movement of her chest through the delicate material.

She gives a small nod in acknowledgement and he brushes his fingers on her shoulder as he moves to his seat across the table, facing her. He feels alive again, like he had during his first year of marriage, nineteen long years ago.

Alfred moves to the head of the table. As Delilah expected, he is so exhilarated with the anticipation of the diversity of topics that Thomas's presence will provide that he hardly notices his daughter. Meals are usually a quiet event as he barely speaks to Delilah at the supper table about anything other than the chaos she has created that day.

As the third course is being brought in, a servant approaches Alfred and whispers in his ear. Alfred quickly rises from his chair and blurts out, "If you will excuse me, Beatrice needs me. Thomas, please do not let this interruption prevent you from enjoying your meal."

Delilah waits until he's almost in the hallway and asks, "Do you want me to go in your stead, Father?" but her voice doesn't quite reach the door.

"I hope it is nothing too serious," says a concerned Thomas.

"Oh, knowing Mother, it could be a spider!" she replies, shaking her head and forcing a laugh. Then frowning, she whispers, "But it could be something serious. Mother's health has never been robust."

Inexperienced at this game, Delilah hopes her fake distress will make it easier for her to lead the conversation while pretending to be distracted. "I am unsure of my appetite at the moment," she exclaims.

Thomas assumes Delilah is quite bothered about her mother's situation. "Do you want to leave and go to her? I could go home."

"No. Of course not. How rude of me. Father can handle whatever it is. Does Mrs. Cowell go out of town often, Mr. Cowell?" and just like that, she changes the subject.

"You do not have to be so formal when we are alone together, Delilah. Please call me Tom."

She smiles. "All right."

"To answer your question, yes. My wife often takes our two children to visit with her mother who lives by the inlet, eight miles south of here. The cool air coming off the water there makes the summers bearable."

"I do not recall ever having met her. Is she as pretty as you are handsome?" Delilah's eyes pop wide open and she quickly brings a hand up to her lips and says, "Oh, I am sorry. Did I say that out loud? I, I never meant … " she stammers.

"That is perfectly fine, Delilah," he chuckles, pleased to be on the receiving end of an infatuation. He has always felt that he is an attractive man even though his wife never notices, or rather never mentions it. "Do not concern yourself. I am not offended in any way. If you must know, Mrs. Cowell is a plain woman. Respectable and proper, but certainly not as pleasant to look upon as yourself."

"Oh, Mr. Cowell, you make me blush." She is truly flattered. No one has ever really complimented her on her looks, or her intelligence, or even commented on her skills or knowledge in a positive way.

"On purpose. I am just paying you back the courtesy. Now please, call me Tom or Thomas. Let me hear you say my name," he demands.

"If you insist, Tom."

"Again."

"Tom," and she adds melody to it, "To-om." She giggles and he grins.

They soon finish their meal and go for a walk in the garden. Delilah, places one hand on his arm, gathers as much of her skirt as she dares with her other hand, lifts it and leads him to the back wall of plants. "Is this not the fullest rose bush you have ever seen, Tom? Who would know that the stem of such a beautiful flower could cause such harm?"

Then with her chest pressed up against his arm, she nudges him forward to the red carnations. He leans down and pinches off one stem, he turns to face her and places it in her hair, behind her ear. He has always dreamt of doing such an intimate thing for a woman.

She brings a hand up to her lips, slightly opens her mouth, and stands, blinking in awe. Of course, he is proud of himself for making a young woman swoon over his simple gesture.

She stutters, "Tom! How, how simply romantic. Do you do that to every girl you meet?"

"I daresay not! Even though you are the most beautiful young woman I have ever met, I merely wanted to show my appreciation for your hospitality this evening. That is all."

Just then, Alfred calls out from the house. "Coming Father," replies Delilah. Before they leave the seclusion of the tall, neatly trimmed bushes, she lifts herself up on her tip-toes and kisses Thomas on the mouth. She giggles, grabs her skirt with both hands and dashes toward her father's voice. Tom follows, grinning with pride.

Alfred apologizes when the younger man comes into view, "I am so sorry for the interruption, Thomas. A squirrel found its way into the house and Beatrice was in such a fright."

"Oh dear. I hope it did not give you too much trouble."

"No, it is all dealt with. Well, I am not hungry anymore, but I wonder if you would join me in the study for a brandy and a cigar."

"Certainly. I should warn you that I have a meeting tomorrow morning and I must not be too late this evening."

"Of course. You know, Thomas, I wonder if you would join us again tomorrow night. In fact, why not join us for every supper meal until Mrs. Cowell returns? I will provide you with company and you will provide me with conversation." He glances at his daughter, hoping she hasn't behaved like a spoiled child while he had been called away. "It appears Delilah has also enjoyed your company."

"Well, if you put it that way Alfred, I accept. It would be my pleasure to have my meals here. I would be so bored at home until Mrs. Cowell's return." He veers his head and winks at Delilah.

She licks her bottom lip and smiles back, sending her father a seemingly innocent look. But it is not innocent. Delilah knows exactly how she will allow Tom to seduce her. Having already taken liberties of one unsupervised walk, both Tom and Delilah interpret Alfred's nonchalance as permission to continue with unchaperoned strolls in the garden.

After each meal, the men withdraw to the study for brandy and Delilah waits patiently for them to finish and insists on a walk in the garden. Alfred has never really spent time in his garden and reaffirms that flowers do not interest him. Thomas wisely feigns interest and an oblivious Alfred bids them goodnight.

Parting soft kisses between the odd pair soon leads to passionate embraces among the fragrant plants. But the romance is not moving fast enough for Delilah; she fears that Mrs. Cowell may return from her trip before the younger woman can find out how manly Tom really is.

For more than a decade, Thomas has entertained the idea of an extra-marital affair, but did not know how to proceed with the act of infidelity. Up until now, he could only imagine holding a woman with passion in his heart and lust in his thoughts. He tries valiantly to restrain his desire of Delilah—making up excuses to go home early and regrettably leaving her panting for him in the garden. Confronted with the possibility of a betrayal by stepping out on his wife and breaking his vow to be faithful, he convinces himself that nothing more could occur between Delilah and himself and that he must inform her of his decision to stop seeing her.

Delilah leads him to the bench in the shadow of tall bushes where she directs him to sit. She lowers herself to his lap and he comfortably embraces her. She places her arms around his neck and kisses him. She pulls away and watches his eyes follow her free hand move to caress her own bosom. She gyrates on his lap and pulls his hand up to her chest to take over.

Delilah confidently flutters her eyelashes at him and hungrily says, "I want to be with you, Tom. We must figure out a way to be together."

In his vulnerable state, with his hardness pressing up against her, he finally caves and replies, "I agree. We must do something, but what? I cannot deceive your father in his own house."

"Of course not. How about your house? Is it possible for me to meet you there after your work day tomorrow? Father will not expect to see me, or you, until supper time."

"Yes! Yes, that is possible. We have a cottage that is not presently occupied. It is over a hill so is not visible from my house. Remember where I was standing last week when I called out to your father?" She nods and he continues, "Follow the path and it will lead straight to it. Meet me there tomorrow at four o'clock. Oh, my sweet Delilah, it has been such a short time since I have met you and yet here I am, falling for you. Alas, you are so young." *Maybe too young*, he thinks.

Deep in his embrace, he can't see that she has rolled her eyes when she replies, "Pshaw, I am sixteen. I want this, Tom. I want you. That must mean I am old enough for us to be together if my body wants you too. Does it not?"

She has no idea how much he has yearned to hear a woman speak to him of such desires. He thinks, *Surely, no man can or should pass up a hungry, eager lass.*

She only wants to have sex and since Ray's departure, no other employee has caught her eye. And now, she has moved up to higher prey—from her father's employee to her father's friend.

The letter continues …

We carried on our scandalous affair even after Mrs. Cowell returned home.

Curiously, it was also around this time that Mother began to regularly join Father and I for meals. Mother and Father were spending more time together and my mother had risen from her depression. Not surprisingly though, our relationship remained cold.

5
Delilah

A week later at the breakfast table, Delilah observes her mother spooning food onto her plate. Had Beatrice stood facing Delilah, she would not have been the wiser, but her mother's revealing silhouette causes her to ask astonishingly, "Mother! Are you pregnant?"

"Well, do not look so shocked, Delilah. I am a married woman!"

Beatrice is close to her third trimester but barely appears pregnant due to her high-waist clothing. Delilah wonders how old a woman must be before she can't have any more children—after all, her mother is shockingly forty-one-years old.

On November 22, Beatrice gives birth to a boy and they name him Frederick.

Delilah has few opportunities to bond with her brother as Beatrice spends all her days alone with the baby and the wet nurse cares for him at night. Delilah observes her mother's attentiveness to the newborn and wonders if Beatrice had ever been like that with her—kissing and cuddling. Delilah has never felt loved and the cruel effects of her mother's depression has cut deep into her young heart. But she is beyond yearning and beyond jealousy of her brother. She is unloved and therefore unloving.

Out of view of the nursery, Delilah leans up against the wall and sighs. Since the birth of his son, Alfred too, has ignored her, even when she has made mischief. She needs to do something for attention, to be noticed. Something that will bring on more than her father's angry words. But what?

Delilah's original goal with respect to her trysts with Tom was to cause her parents grief if the secret affair was revealed, but her adventures with the married man had backfired. No one asks her what she does during the day and no one has cared enough to even spy on her.

She compares Tom to Ray and finds him lacking. Her hope that his age and experience would reveal new things for her to learn does not materialize. His lust remains locked in his comfort zone, never venturing beyond it to attempt fun games to play or even experiment with different sexual positions in bed.

The next late afternoon of dalliance with Tom, Delilah pushes up hard and rudely says, "Get off me. Umf, I am so tired of you. I am tired of us. We do not do anything outside this bed. I want to go dancing and out to dinner and to the theater. I am not coming here anymore, Tom."

He begs for her to reconsider and agrees to spend time together on her terms—but out of town. He doesn't want a scandal.

But she does! Therefore, she ends the affair. Not only is she bored, but the dalliance is not leading to the desired results—misery for her parents. Tom knew from the beginning that she was free to walk away at any time. He can only cherish his memories of her now and return to his dull existence.

However, their interludes have had a result. One which Delilah's parents would not be able to ignore. Delilah enters her father's study and stands in front of his desk. Her presence makes him wonder what she wants now and how much it will cost him.

Without any fanfare or emotion, Delilah announces, "I am with child."

"What?" Alfred looks up from his papers abruptly. "How? When? Who?" he asks.

"You know how," she says almost seductively. "When and who does not matter. I am pregnant. Now what are you going to do about it?"

"He is going to marry you, that is what. Who is he?"

"I am not getting tied down in a loveless marriage, Father. Besides, he is not aware and I will not tell him."

"Tell me who he is!" demands her father sternly.

"Pff! No," she chuckles and shakes her head from side to side.

"Then I … I will disown you, Delilah!" Alfred threatens.

"Ha! I do not think so," she threatens back. "You disown me and I will tell Mother—and all of Maine—that I heard you fornicating with my nanny Trudy while you thought I slept in my room next door. And, that you also sleep with all the pretty young maids who work here!"

"That is not true, Delilah. There was only Trudy and that was five years ago. Your mother was sick. No one will believe you."

"Actually, it was seven years ago and it does not matter if people believe me or not. They will doubt. Your reputation will be tarnished and that is all that counts."

Alfred tries to stare her down but concedes when he thinks of what this news will do to Beatrice and their renewed bond. He can't believe his daughter would do this to him and her mother. But then, who is his daughter? Does he really know her? Obviously not.

She knows she has conquered when he asks, "What do you want?"

"I want to give it up for adoption. Buy me a ticket to England where I will give birth. I will be out of your lives. Give me ten thousand dollars.

You can live a new life here with your wife and baby and pretend I never existed."

A fair exchange, he thinks. Defeated, he agrees.

It takes the better part of a week to make all the arrangements. Delilah can no longer stand to look at her happy mother and Beatrice doesn't bid her only daughter goodbye when she learns that Delilah is going abroad and the scandalous reason why. Beatrice thinks, *She is finally leaving here.*

Bitch, thinks Delilah, when she walks down the steps to the front door for the last time.

On his daughter's last day in America, Alfred stays in his study, determined not to wish his troubled child farewell. When the carriage is halfway down the road, he rushes to stand by the window to glimpse the horse-drawn cab disappearing in the distance.

The letter continues …

I never saw my parents and brother again.

The misguided incidents of my youth shaped me to become a person unworthy of kindness. This, combined with blindness to my own responsibilities, ruined any chance of my having a normal relationship. One would think that my privileged upbringing would provide so many advantages, yet I cannot help but say that was not the case.

Although I didn't know anything about Madam Deb's youth until recently, I would dare say that she led a better life than I. Imagine that. After all, you see, she was loved.

Emily fondly remembers a long conversation she and Deborah had and says, "I think Mrs. Neustat may have misunderstood something in the investigators' reports. Madam Deb couldn't possibly have had a better beginning in life than she did."

The lawyer sits back in his chair and says gently, "Emily, if everyone is in agreement, would you share with us how you know that?" Graham and Lilith both nod.

Emily agrees and responds, "Well, six months ago, Deborah fell and hurt her head. In order to make sure that she was fine, I stayed with her in her room all that day. She reminisced about her past and now that she herself is deceased, I don't think she would mind if I shared her story with all of you."

6
Deborah

In the southwest territory of Michigan, in the summer of 1794, seven-year-old Deborah fights the urge to cry out. She inhales deeply while she touches the bloody wound on her forehead that was quickly staining her brown hair to a wet black. Her mother had just pushed her inside the two-room shack and she had fallen hard, hitting her head on a shelf on the way down.

A minute earlier, they were still standing outside for curious onlookers to see, so Maggie whispered, "Stop that. You scratch like a girl." She had become upset as she watched the girl squirming from the discomfort of the dirty, itchy shirt that covered the child's torso.

Maggie never hit her while they were on the move because she didn't want to attract unwanted attention from the accompanying group of travelers. Experience also taught Deborah to expect that the moment they were alone, the woman would release her frustration.

Now that they are out of sight from their new neighbors, Maggie shoves the heavy, tied-up blanket that holds all their possessions into Deborah's arms. With clenched teeth, she says harshly, "Unpack our things," and closes the door to the only exit.

Even before Deborah finishes putting away clothing and other articles, she senses Maggie standing behind her. She turns slightly and sees that Maggie's feet are planted squarely on the worn floor, one foot apart. The sound of Maggie's wooden spoon tapping the side of her own thigh signals Deborah to wrap her arms around her head and drop to the floor in the fetal position if she is to protect the softer parts of her body.

Whack! Whack! The sounds repeat countless times. Ten minutes later, an exhausted and contented Maggie is snoring on the unmade bed. Deborah rubs her left side and feels the heat from Maggie's angry spoon. She consoles herself with the fact that Maggie no longer ties her to the bedpost to apply the regular beatings. As long as she scrunches down on the floor and lets Maggie face her demons, things will be relatively quiet for the rest of the day.

Deborah's hair had been chopped off before they left the previous town. Whenever Maggie would cut her hair short like that, Deborah knew they would be relocating soon.

"This time around," Maggie had said to the girl while she cut her hair, "your name will be Bobby. You hear me? Nobody's business but our own on the reasons why."

Deb had nodded. For as far back as she could remember, every time she had asked why her name changed and why she was to pretend to be a boy, she'd never gotten an answer. She learned to be silent, to not cry, and by all means, to not show she cared about anything. Not even for a little rabbit that she found hiding under the tall blades of grass, as it would later become supper.

At least once a year, Maggie uproots the pair and relocates to another town, always moving westerly. Deborah has been given so many boys' names, it doesn't matter which one Maggie calls out, Deb answers just to avoid another beating.

The men from the town they just left called the woman Maggie. Deborah can't make herself call her Ma because the term is too kind a word for this monster. The woman is all she has and has known her only as a witch, a tyrant.

Due to her young age and dependency, Deborah never considers running away. She is too reliant on Maggie for her survival. To avoid extra beatings, she doesn't venture too far away from the shack the two call home.

It didn't matter to Deborah that they left their former home. She didn't have friends to say goodbye to as she had never been allowed to stay in school long enough to make any.

If someone of authority comes around and insists that Maggie send the *boy* to school, teachers soon assume that the child must be what they term as slow or retarded. Deborah has never been in one school long enough to learn anything of value.

Deborah hates school, especially recess, when the kids are mean to her. "How can you not know your last name?"

"Yeah!" the small gathering support in unison.

"Are you a bastard, Bobby?" "Bastard!" "Bastard!"

They bully the friendless child past her breaking point. She wins the fist fights, all of them. The boys, no matter their size, go home with black eyes and she goes home for her daily meeting with the spoon.

There are times she fearlessly asks Maggie what her last name is. Maggie feigns deafness, drunkenness, or ignorance at Deb's question. She will never provide Deborah with the answer.

7
Deborah

Years later, in another small and forgettable town in the southwest region of the Territory of Michigan, the soon to be thirteen-year-old Deborah turns onto her left side, facing the wood burning stove. The morning sun's brightness coming into the room from the small window above the stove wakes her. When she rises, she notices a darkened wet patch on the dirty wooden floor from where she has just laid and she is puzzled by the discovery.

Maggie is already up and about, and sees the red stain on the girl's clothing that covers her privates. With trepidation, Maggie knows that the safety she felt for the last ten years of treating the child as a boy will soon be over. She had feared questioning glances from onlookers or persons of authority when the girl's face lost its baby fat and began to appear more feminine, but nobody really paid any attention to the changes in the child and she realized she had worried needlessly. Now, with this new development in the girl's maturity, Maggie could only hope that the distance she has put between them and their beginnings is beyond trace.

Maggie, who has never shown the child any kindness, throws a rag at the girl and says, "Go find more like that. Place a clean one in between your legs before putting on your underpants when this happens."

Deborah is confused with the changes in her body. Maggie doesn't explain anything and Deborah thinks that there is something terribly wrong with her—until the girl notices the pattern is also afflicting Maggie.

Several weeks later, on a cold September morning, Maggie hurriedly opens her bedroom door and rushes to the only exit leading out of the shack to vomit the excessive drink from the night before. She almost bumps into Deborah and doesn't notice her struggling to bind her chest as per Maggie's latest command.

An unshaven old man by the name of Harvey Seevers sits up in Maggie's bed and observes the young woman in the other room trying to flatten her chest. His lust, still unsatisfied because of his own imbibing, motivates him to overpower the naked girl and he violates the only innocence she still possesses.

Minutes later, when he lifts himself off the stunned girl, he feels a knife at his side. He freezes.

Maggie accuses, "How often has he done that to you? Answer me, *Bobby*!"

A stunned Deborah replies, "Just this once. Why'd he do that?"

Maggie ignores the girl's question and turns her attention to the man while still holding the knife to his side, "Is that true? Is this the first time?"

"Yeah. I didn't know he was a she until I saw her get dressed, Maggie. Honest!"

"Well then, you owe me one dollar on account of her being a virgin, but now that she's been had, tell your friends. Starting tonight, they have to give me fifty cents if they want a piece of her."

Deborah doesn't know what people in other shacks do or don't do. She has seen many men come and go from Maggie's bed and initially thinks that what has happened to her is an everyday occurrence. But everything has changed, starting with the clothes Maggie threw at her with the instructions, "Now you need to look like a girl. Wash your face and comb your hair!"

After a couple of weeks of these sexual encounters, it dawns on Deborah that Maggie's daily beatings have ceased. She also notices that her body oddly reacts to the men's touches with tingling. Maggie has never touched her unless there was pain associated with it, nor has she ever laid a kind hand on her head, or face, or shoulder. These men's hands fondle her body and even caress with a tenderness that she has never known, a truly new experience.

Deborah's education of what her female body can do has begun and for the better part of the next year, she is more financially lucrative than Maggie. They can now afford to buy food and liquor on a regular basis. Deborah knows that Maggie relies on her young body to purchase these luxuries and she becomes bold in her attitude toward the older woman.

Maggie hates this feeling of losing control over the child and develops a jealousy that is soon spewing with rage. One day, knowing no one would be coming around until payday, Maggie clobbers the girl with all the might her fists can muster. She finds that beating with her fists, although personally painful, is more satisfying than if she uses the old spoon.

By the time Deborah recovers enough to move around with ease again, she has learned to keep her cockiness in check and watch for Maggie's unpredictable bursts of violence. Deborah has never fought back against Maggie, and even though she beat up boys who were slightly bigger than herself, she doesn't dare find out if she can overtake the older woman. However, she doesn't know how long she can tolerate such abuse before she does something drastic either.

A couple of weeks later, Maggie's two-room shack is overflowing with drunk men who are waiting for their turn with the new and inexpensive treasure. A fight breaks out and Maggie tries to settle them down. But, as she herself is intoxicated, she fails to have an impact on the group of inebriated men.

A now wiser Deborah takes this chance to climb out the bedroom window and bolt. She runs as far as her legs can take her as she heads northeast.

The next day, Deborah wanders into the kitchen of a saloon of a nameless town so small no one bothered to put a sign up to announce it upon one's arrival. She begs for food and a place to stay. Out of the kindness of her heart, the cook in charge of the kitchen takes her into her home. The older woman treats the girl's scalp until it is free of lice. She makes Deborah take a bath and gives her girl's clothing to wear.

Deborah works alongside the cook in the kitchen and, for the first time in her life, she feels safe and out of Maggie's reach. She feels cared for and is surprised when her heart beats with a desire to wake in the mornings. She even greets the old cook with a smile, something she has never given Maggie the privilege of seeing.

However, when abuse is all a girl knows, combined with an inadequate upbringing, she gravitates to familiar routines. Deborah soon reverts to known behavior and starts bringing customers to her room. Although she wants the freedom to choose what happens to her, she is unaware of the consequences of her wrong choices.

Deborah's immaturity helps her focus on her desires for material things like new clothes and a pair of shoes that fit properly. Prostituting herself is the only way she knows how to afford such things. Certainly, the meagre pay from kitchen work would never sufficiently provide for these luxury items.

When the cook notices what is going on, she evicts the ungrateful child. She points toward a house down the road that is known for sinful debauchery and yells, "Go where you belong, whore!"

Madam Violet stands in her doorway in answer to the girl's knocking. Her face, painted with an exaggeration of rouge on the apples of her cheeks, assesses the value of the girl in front of her and says, "I don't know if you'll fit in."

"Please, I've no where else to go," begs Deborah, who is unsure of what she did wrong at the cook's house.

The Madam sighs and says, "Very well. You'll start with cleaning and cooking. If I like your work, I'll think about taking you on as a working girl. Now go around the house, the door at the back leads to the kitchen."

Deborah soon feels at home in the brothel with her routine of cooking and cleaning. She often watches the men follow the girls to different bedrooms; she knows all too well what goes on in those rooms. She can't imagine doing anything but her household tasks, and if she's lucky, working as one of the girls one day.

It was always Madam Violet's intention to promote Deborah from cleaner to servicing men. She took her time as she wanted Deborah to think she had earned it somehow.

Although Deborah spends very little money on clothing, as she usually walks around in her underwear all day and most nights, she spends almost every penny she earns on things she never had before, like a new scarf or hat—and sweets. She doesn't think to try to save or hoard her money. With no locks on the doors, her funds would quickly disappear anyway as the other girls help themselves to whatever they find. Even the customers are known to steal!

Deborah is truly intelligent and quite capable of learning, but she has just never been given the opportunity. Such a chance arises when a new girl moves in and is willing to teach her reading, writing and simple math. She doesn't know why she couldn't seem to learn when she was younger, but is grateful for the knowledge now. With that little bit of education, a desire to absorb knowledge is unleashed. There are few books in the brothel, but soon Deborah has read them all several times. Soon, she is spending money on books instead of sweets.

Before anyone realizes, Deb has taken on more responsibility with respect to the running of the business. However, the raise in pay that came with the responsibility causes trouble and loud arguments at that hen house. After a couple of years, she decides to leave and join a wagon train heading southeast.

Deborah follows at a distance because the respectable women in the group get upset with her presence. When the wagon train reaches the booming town of Delton, Michigan, she parts ways with the travelers and plants her roots in the brothel known as Clarice's. She's now seventeen years old.

Emily focuses on the shocked and disgusted faces looking at her. She adds, "I asked her why she took on the last name of Seevers as he obviously wasn't her father or her husband. Of all the last names to choose from, why take his? Deborah replied that she needed to have a last name once she went into the business and adopted the name of the man she first had sex with—as it seemed fitting. I think I might be the only person who knew that it was not her real last name."

Mr. Trolley thanks Emily for the summation of Deborah's young life. "You are correct. Mrs. Neustat most certainly did not have all the pieces of Madam Deb's story."

8
Delilah

Mr. Trolley turns the next page and continues, "Now, if you will recall, in March of 1800, a seventeen-year-old, pregnant Delilah is en route to London. Her letter continues."

The letter continues …

The ship's movements on the sea magnified my morning sickness.

The woman in cabin number 23 never comes out for meals and no one but crew members even know that she's on board the vessel.

On the last morning of the third week into the six-week voyage, the cabin maid finds the occupant lying on the floor, unconscious. Thankfully there is a doctor on board and he is summoned. He quickly determines that Delilah is severely dehydrated and undernourished and water is immediately administered in small quantities.

"Where am I?" Delilah asks the doctor when she regains enough energy to speak.

"Safely back in your bed, dear. You will be all right. You just needed to drink more fluids. I must say, you have a bad case of sea sickness so I suggest you drink this laudanum. You should be strong enough to eat soon."

After he measures out the medicine, he puts the bottle back in his bag. "I will just go over to that chair to read and watch you for an hour."

The young mother-to-be rests better knowing that a doctor is present to monitor her progress. However, as the passing of the hour nears, she suddenly doubles over in agony in her bed.

The doctor rushes to her side and thinks that something else must be causing her pain. His suspicions are confirmed when he pulls the sheet back and sees the fresh blood stain on the bed. He rushes to the cabin door and finds a floor attendant, "Get me a nurse right away." He goes back inside to help the poor girl.

"Why did you not tell me you are with child? You stupid girl." Yet he knows he is solely responsible as he should always ask a female patient this question, no matter how young and innocent a girl appears.

The letter continues …

The rest of the trip is obliterated from my memory. I know I lost the baby, which was a relief to me at the time, but there was a complication. The doctor gave me more laudanum so he could try to fix the problem, but I was still aware enough and the pain made me thrash about.

When I woke up, he told me he had accidentally cut me and there was significant blood loss. He was afraid he may have rendered me infertile. He strongly suggested I go see a doctor when we docked in England, just to confirm.

When we reached England, I did not seek out a doctor as he advised. At the time, I didn't care if I had been rendered infertile or not. I didn't want children. I feared I may not love them just like my mother didn't love me. How could I think otherwise?

9
Delilah

Three weeks later, a weak and wobbly Delilah steps off the ship. Free of the pregnancy and still ten thousand dollars rich, she decides that she will visit the sights of London and experience all the excitement the city promises. But first she needs to get stronger.

Delilah has no difficulty finding a place that provides Board and Room for Women Only. She registers as Delilah Fowler—a last name she borrows from a sign she saw advertising a lawyer's office up the road.

As she doesn't want to be disturbed, she pays for one month in advance and borrows several books from the landlady about London and its history to help pass the time while she convalesces. Except for the scheduled meals and use of the shared bathtub, she stays inside her room to fully recover from her mishap.

By the third week, she feels well enough to walk outside daily and visit some of the places she has just read about. By the fourth week, she feels better than she ever has, especially with the knowledge that she likely cannot get pregnant again.

On one of her walks, Delilah comes upon a neighborhood that

promises more society amusements. The three city blocks contain several places to enjoy meals with friends, an opera house, both a music and concert hall, two museums, shops and even a lending library. This is the place for her. In a few short days, she finds a stylishly furnished house to lease and moves her few possessions to her new rooms.

She doesn't know how to make friends as she has been sheltered from other people her own age her whole life. As a small child, she had nannies, and as a young woman, private tutors. As well, her mother's illness prevented her from holding or attending a coming-out ball which would have introduced her to young women of similar ages and interests with whom she could have developed friendships. But Delilah doesn't easily get discouraged, so she makes a plan to watch others until an opportunity presents itself to meet a stranger.

She observes people as she sits in various restaurants in the area. One day she overhears a conversation from an adjacent table. "Welcome to London Mr. Dentz. This is my partner, Mr. Stewart." She looks over with a quick glance. The youngest man is shaking the hands of the other men so obviously is the visiting Mr. Dentz.

Did I hear correctly? Dentz? I wonder if it is the same Dentz family from Philadelphia, thinks Delilah. She had heard her father mention the wealthy family.

She searches her purse for her book. When the waiter comes to her table, she puts a coin in his hand and asks, "Would it be possible for another cup of tea? I have about an hour to wait until my next appointment."

"Certainly Madam."

The conversation she is listening in on is truly boring, especially when they go into details of new fabrics from China and the process of turning them into sellable garments. Once the two older gentlemen leave, Mr. Dentz, a handsome man in his early twenties, puts papers away in his satchel and also gets ready to leave.

"Oh, excuse me, sir," says Delilah, waving. "I believe you dropped this." She knows he hasn't as it is a receipt for a garment she purchased the day before.

"No." He hands it back to her after a brief look. "I am afraid this is not mine." He flashes the young beauty a smile and tips the hat he has just placed on his head. "Good afternoon."

She nods and watches him depart. She quickly leaves money on the table for her meal and follows. She sees him climb a set of stairs up to a popular hotel in the area, the Staunton. She doesn't follow him inside, but decides to return to the area the following day.

The next afternoon, Delilah is window shopping near the Staunton to keep an eye on the departures from the busy hotel. She spies him leaving the front steps and shadows him to a nearby restaurant. She stops at a women's dress shop and pretends to admire an array of day hats while keeping an eye on the restaurant entrance. *If he is not meeting anyone, he should be done with his meal in thirty minutes or so*, she thinks.

Delilah finds an empty bench a couple of buildings past the restaurant where she sits and waits. After half an hour, and afraid that she may have underestimated the time required for his meal, she quickly makes her way back to the dress shop. Twice she approaches the restaurant when she sees the door open, but is disappointed to find other people leaving the establishment. Both times, she turns away from entering in the pretense that she forgot something.

But her third attempt at entering the restaurant and purposefully bumping into the patron pays off. It's him. They smile at each other and exchange a polite greeting.

After studying his habits for two more days, they meet once more when she suddenly rises from a bench in a garden as he is walking by. She feigns surprise when she comes face to face with the Philadelphian. This time they express more than their begged pardons.

"We have to stop doing this," she smiles at him, trying to sound more sensual than just friendly.

"Perhaps we could head in the same direction?" he asks, smiling back.

"Perhaps. Where are you headed to?"

"I was going for an early supper. I thought I might go see what is playing at the theater afterwards. You? Where are you off to?"

"The opera house, but it is a repeat of last week's show. Hmm, where is this theater?"

"Why not join me for supper?" He shakes his head and quickly adds, "Oh, pardon me, you appear to be without chaperone. Is there someone's permission I should seek first before asking for your company?"

"I am without chaperone because I am here on my own. I assure you though, I am quite capable of looking after myself."

"No doubt." He extends an arm and she takes it. "My name is Martin Dentz. I am from Philadelphia, a large city in the State of Pennsylvania in America. Have you heard of the place?"

"A little, but please tell me all about it, Mr. Dentz," she responds, secretly glad she was correct about his identity and wealth.

"No please, that is my father's name. Call me Martin."

"I will gladly do that Martin if you call me Delilah."

After describing his hometown, Martin asks her last name.

"Fowler." Delilah's perfected New England accent can easily be mistaken for a British one, especially to an unwary Philadelphian pair of ears. Adding that she hasn't lived in London easily explains away any differences in her accent and dialect. "I was born in London, grew up in Derbyshire, but after … " she adds with drama, and then hesitates.

"What is it? No, do not mind me. It is none of my business if you do not want to talk about it," he says reassuringly.

He is so easy to fool.

In the weeks recovering her strength, she had read about a tragic accident involving the collapse of a bridge that killed all the people who had the misfortune of being on it at the time. "It is all right. I do have a need to talk about it. Have you heard about the catastrophic collapse of the Derbyshire bridge a few months ago?" she asks sadly.

He shakes his head no.

"My parents were on their way home and never made it. I am an orphan. Someone else lives in my old home now, which is fine because I did not want to stay there after … well, you know."

He nods.

"So, I sold almost everything we had and moved here to London just to see if this is where I should start a new life. All I have left are a few thousand pounds and my memories."

"I am so sorry to hear that. What a shocking story. You poor thing, Delilah. Do you not have family to go to?"

"No. My parents came from much farther north and there may have been other relatives at some time but they never spoke of them. I think there was a falling out on both sides. I am afraid I am all alone." She bends her head down for emphasis, searches for a kerchief in her purse and dabs at her eyes.

"Well, I do not know what to say, but I do know that I want to be your friend."

"I would like that. I do not know anyone here in London, except for the owner of the rooms I am leasing," she says warmly, and captures a piece of his heart—even if it is from pity.

"That is settled then. We, friends, will see London together. We will share meals and for now, we have a play to go see."

She exhales loud enough for him to notice. She frowns, "I am afraid I will not be able to share all meals with you, Martin. That will be too expensive for me."

"My dear lady. I would never let you pay for anything while you are in my company."

"Oh! I—I do not know if that is proper."

"It will not be forever. I am going back to America in three months and I would be delighted if you could spend some of that time with me when I am not working on my father's business affairs."

"Well, if you put it that way, I accept. I will be on my best behavior. What does your father do?"

Martin talks about his father's garment business right up until the moment the wicks in the lamps are extinguished in the theater.

The letter continues …

That was the beginning of our courtship. Martin was a sweet man. He was four years older than me, handsome and rich. I daresay, I married him for his last name and money. Now that I wasn't waiting for a baby to be born, I badly wanted to go back to America and prove to myself, and everyone else, that I could be deserving of a new and better life.

Graham thinks, *Martin Dentz was married to Delilah? Is this my connection?*

10
Delilah

"My dear Martin," Delilah says at lunch in the corner restaurant, "if I was already your wife, we could share a cabin and save money on the voyage. I think your mother would understand if we married now. We can always have a wedding reception in Philadelphia later on." As much as Martin wants to become a husband in every way to his new wife, he knows that his mother would not be pleased to be excluded from planning the wedding; he reminds Delilah that it will only be another couple of months before their expressed vows, and surely if he can wait, she can.

Delilah's reasons for a quick London wedding involve more than saving travel expenses. Not only does she want to firmly and quickly attach herself to Martin through wedding oaths, she is afraid her father might discover her scheme if the announcement includes a photograph of the couple. Vengeful or not, her father would expose her lies and her plans would be foiled.

She perseveres with her argument. Martin is tempted. Her plan makes sense and the more she talks, the less merit his arguments have. She sees him faltering and easily persuades him to concede. She convinces him she doesn't feel the need to announce their upcoming nuptials in society newspapers, or to find half a dozen ushers and bridesmaids to stand up for them, or to spend a fortune on a tailored gown or all the other fanfare involved in a wedding of such an upstanding member of one of the most prestigious families in Philadelphia.

They are quickly married in London and honeymoon on the ship in a first-class cabin that suits Delilah very well. Her attentive and sweet husband assures her she deserves such luxuries.

Upon their arrival home on September 22nd, the newlyweds are told that Martin's father is in conference in his study and his mother is having afternoon tea at a neighbor's. They decide to drag their tired feet into Martin's bedroom for a short rest.

After an hour, Delilah still doesn't feel refreshed and tells Martin that she won't join him downstairs until the supper meal. Martin happily leaves to greet his parents in the drawing room.

When he enters, his mother, Irene, scolds him, "How could you do this to me, Martin?"

"I did not do anything to you, Mother," replies Martin perplexed.

"I do not get the pleasure to host my only son's wedding! Instead, you have a secret service in another country! And to a woman we do not even know! A common woman without any living family or social connections to speak of! What about Valerie? She will be crushed!"

He sighs. His mother can be so dramatic and aristocratic.

"Valerie will be fine. We were not betrothed and I am sure she fully expected me to meet new and exciting people. Could you at least wait until you meet Delilah before deciding who she is or is not and whether or not my marriage is a disaster?"

"Where is your new bride anyway? Hiding? Is she afraid of us?"

"Certainly not. It was a long trip, Mother. She is just resting. She will be downstairs for supper, I assure you."

Martin's father has not interfered until now, "How was business?"

"Really, Edward! That is all you have to say on the matter? How was business?" asks Irene, incredulously.

"What is there to say, dear? The matter is done. It is closed. I, for one, am looking forward to meeting the woman who turned our son's head. Now seriously, how did you get along with our parent company, Martin?" The men head toward the study in conversation.

Irene throws her hands up in defeat and then motions for the butler to follow her to the kitchen.

The evening meal unfolds like an award-winning play with Delilah as the star. Edward is quick to love his new daughter-in-law and Irene has to admit that she likes the girl.

Delilah has spun a web of lies about her past and answers their questions with perfectly made-up fairy tales mixed in with some truths—a background that consists of loving parents, nannies, tutors, dancing lessons, ponies and what not. Delilah finds herself chagrined to realize that she is grateful for parts of her upbringing after all.

Martin sits with pride, listening to Delilah talk about her past. Irene is impressed with the girl who is well versed in music, literature and even needlepoint.

Irene engages Delilah with planning a nuptial reception that will last an entire weekend. There will be breakfasts for family and guests, lawn games to play, a dance, a soiree, and afternoon boat rides—all where wealthy business associates, friends and neighbors can gather to meet and congratulate the young couple.

Delilah, as the main attraction, goes from one glittering display to the next. But by early October, all the planning and festivities have ended. There are no more fireworks or admirers to compliment the blushing bride. She is now expected to take on the role of society matron like all the other well-to-do married women.

Martin settles into his own routine of going to work with his father every day and spending a small fraction of his time with his wife. It is practical for any newly wed couple to live in the groom's house until they start their own family, which Delilah knows means indefinitely, thanks to her inability to bear children.

Irene holds afternoon teas to introduce her daughter-in-law to the appropriate women's committees and the two then attend the reciprocating parties. They hold meetings for society's ladies to discuss pressing issues of their city such as loose dogs in the neighborhood and the construction of more wooden sidewalks around the shopping areas.

Delilah's idleness turns to boredom. She is weary of society's proper ladies and their monotonous causes. She wants to attend parties and dance—with or without Martin. She hasn't bargained on the dreads of a loveless marriage. Even shopping without spending limits doesn't placate her.

Delilah thinks up fun things to do while she waits for her husband to return from work. Sometimes she stages their bedroom with discarded shoes on the floor, a dropped kerchief, a misplaced hat and even a tossed pillow or two. Martin then enters their bedroom to find his bride crying on their bed, disheveled.

"What is the matter my love?" he asks as he gently removes strands of hair from her pouting face. At the beginning of these harmless games, as he tries to console her, their shared embrace ends up in love-making and a delay in being prompt for supper.

But Delilah soon decides that her pretend ennui is real, and it is Martin's fault. Where is the adventure? The teasing, amusing man she married?

Her fake tears have also become real. When he asks why she was crying, now Delilah replies, "Oh, women need to cry on occasion, darling. I guess it is just my turn." When he talks to his mother about it, she confirms that it is so but doesn't elaborate on the mystery of it.

Grasping at anything that might keep her interest, one day Delilah says, "I think we should buy our own house. Can we get our own home, Martin?"

Stumped, Martin replies, "No one I know of would set up their own household before starting a family. Are you telling me you are expecting, Delilah?"

"No, I am not in the family way. I would just love to decorate our place and feel like I am contributing something to our life together. That is all."

"Hmm, give me time to think about this."

"Sure, darling. But promise to not take too long," she pleads.

Martin discusses it with his father.

Edward says, "I think you should put your foot down on this, son. Husbands get to decide on these big decisions. She must know that you would know best when it is the right time to buy a house. She cannot be forcing you to do this, otherwise she will start thinking that she will have a say in other important matters. No, I say you should think long and hard about what you are prepared to lose control off."

Relieved to hear his father's opinion, Martin determines that Delilah is just testing the water and she will soon occupy herself with other matters more suitable to her delicate nature.

Delilah's disappointment, inactivity, and lack of motivation eventually shows an ugly adult version of itself. She's tired of Martin and has no qualms telling him that he and their life together bores her. Their socially acceptable outings to the theater or opera or a yawn-inducing ball at a neighbor's home, are void of many people their age and aren't exciting enough for her. There's no challenge, no adventure. Every chance she has, in the privacy of their room, Delilah verbally attacks Martin, blaming him for her unhappiness, and emasculating him in the process.

Of course, she doesn't misbehave like that outside the bedroom. Delilah is her sweet, likeable self in front of his family—as she knows where the financial comforts originate.

It soon becomes unbearable for Martin to spend time with her and he eventually moves his pillow to an adjoining, unoccupied room. Only the servants know of the newlywed's disturbing sleeping arrangements.

Martin becomes quiet at meal times in order to avoid more criticism from his wife. This change in her usually jovial, outspoken son, causes his mother concern. Irene looks for counsel about it from the strangest person—Valerie—who at one time was considered Martin's most likely betrothed.

Valerie becomes alarmed listening to Irene tell the story and asks, "Do you think he is ill?"

"No. He has a normal appetite and good color in his face. He just does not appear to be his old self. Delilah has not said a word about it, she does not seem to notice. Well, maybe that is because she does not know him well enough. So, I thought I would come to you. You have not seen him in a while but you have known him since you were children. Could you ask to meet him in the park—just to talk—and let me know what you think? I would really appreciate you doing this for him, as his friend."

Irene doesn't know what she's asking of the younger woman. Valerie is still in love with Martin and couldn't believe that he had chosen another to wed. Nevertheless, she convinces herself that she can put her feelings aside in order to help the man who can, at the very least, still be her dear friend.

She sends a note by messenger to his workplace. Martin replies that he will be delighted to meet with her in the park the following afternoon.

He might have acted reserved at the start of their meeting, but he soon falls into his old pattern of enjoying her company. Valerie reports to Irene that she finds Martin to very much be like his old self and can't detect an attitude that is out of the ordinary. Irene, although still puzzled, is relieved.

Martin feels such joy after his meeting with Valerie that he writes her a note requesting they meet again in a few days, and again later the following week.

Valerie also soon returns to her less reserved and informal method of communication with Martin. She too regresses to old habits and innocently compliments him on how he looks, how he dresses, how well he reportedly did on a business deal she heard about, and so on.

Martin laps it up and his resulting cheerfulness due to her praise lasts for days. He isn't receiving the validation and attention that he feels he should from his own wife and he forgets about Delilah's drama while in Valerie's presence.

In his bed alone at night, he often thinks, *Delilah no longer asks me about my day or my work. Does she even care? Valerie cares. Maybe that is just friendship, but I would hope that a wife would want to know what goes on in her husband's life. What is wrong with our marriage?*

He lies there dreaming of the next rendezvous with Valerie and during the day, his thoughts return often to Valerie. Now, two years into his marriage, he comes to the conclusion that he has made a terrible mistake.

Martin confesses to Valerie, "I love you. I will forever regret not realizing that before leaving for England. I would never have married Delilah had I known how I feel about you. I am sorry if telling you this causes you pain."

She touches his arm, looks him in the eyes and says most sincerely, "On the contrary. You have caused me no pain by telling me this. I love you too, Martin. I want to spend the rest of my life with you. Is there any way we can do that?"

He tilts his head back; his eyes water and the tears spill over. What a mess he's created. Maybe that's why Delilah is so cold. Maybe she can tell he never really loved her!

Valerie and Martin don't know how, but they vow they will spend the rest of their lives together.

Martin lets a week pass before entering his former bedroom where his wife is trying on another new dress.

"What do you want?" she asks, coldly.

"I want a divorce, Delilah. You need to know that I do not love you and even though I have not told you as much, you have probably sensed it, and that is why you have pushed me away. I am sorry if I hurt you. Can we talk about this?"

Delilah thinks fast. She is delighted to hear he thinks he caused the rift between them as it will be easier to make demands this way. His family will be happy to be rid of her and, if she plays her cards right, she will benefit monetarily.

The letter continues …

I'm not proud of myself. I was deceitful. I realized Martin's weaknesses and took advantage of him. He was a fool. I know he did love me once, and had I been capable of love, we would have lived a full life—childless, but certainly loving.

So, we divorced. I happily agreed to not discuss any of the sordid affair of a broken-down marriage, especially with newspapers. After all, the Dentz clan had a reputation to uphold. Only their family members and close friends knew about the distasteful divorce. Their only condition was that I take back my last name of Fowler, which of course I did, as it pleased me to know that my past would continue to remain a secret.

They need not worry about gossip as I didn't have any friends to discuss my failed marriage with. I went on my way to a new home, across town on Chestnut Street, richer than I could have imagined with an ill-deserved monthly alimony payment and most of my father's initial amount of money.

Martin and Valerie moved to England where I believe they married and had children. I never heard from him again.

"Oh dear," the lawyer exclaims, looking at his watch. "Lunch is waiting for us precisely at noon. I will see you all back here at one-thirty."

Graham leaves in a hurry. He knows Lilith doesn't want him to join them for lunch, nor would she want to pretend to be civil to him. He heads for his room where he pulls the cord for his lunch to be brought up.

11
Deborah

All too soon, the six occupants are back in the study, seating arrangements unchanged.

The letter continues …

Years later, I learned that Madam Deb had enjoyed a long-term liaison with a special man. He was your father, Emily. I was surprised, to say the least. Madam Deb and he seemed to have a very odd relationship—one that had to live under the eyes of society. They could not have been more different in class and position.

Mr. Trolley senses an addendum to the morning's story and asks, "Emily, do you care to elaborate on the details missing from Mrs. Neustat's letter and the agents' reports?"

"I most certainly do. It's a long re-telling," Emily is sorry that the deceased widow will never hear the truth, but is relieved that she has an opportunity to enlighten the others. Emily thinks back on that same day when Deborah had fallen and hurt her head.

Deborah's narration of her first seventeen years aside, Emily says, "Tell me the rest, Deborah. You know you want to." Emily moves the chair closer to the bed.

As has become her habit of late, eighty-year-old Deborah scans her room and looks at her treasures and belongings. It took many years to acquire the possessions and display them just the way she likes. She sadly thinks, *Why did I bother? No one comes to my room anymore to see all my nice things.*

These days, in the year of 1867, she spends more time in her room than elsewhere and often reflects on her longevity. Even though she is a madam, she considers she's had a good, decent life over all. She worked hard to overcome her early life and she succeeded. Not only is she financially well off, she is surrounded by affection—especially the sisterly love from the women she works with.

She looks to her right and in the corner stands her desk and chair made of red oak, a set she proudly could afford to purchase in the early 1840s. She loves sitting there, writing letters and in her daily journals. The double-door armoire on the left side of the desk is made of cedar and is still aromatic. Dismally, it no longer holds elegant dresses and alluring peignoirs, but only comfortable and plain everyday attire. The armoire is followed by Queen Ann armchairs, upholstered in regal purple velvet, and finally, a maple wood curio cabinet.

Through the cabinet's rounded panes of glass, her eyes pause on a porcelain doll she received as a gift from a man who turned out to be her last regular caller. Her misty eyes glance over the stylish perfume decanters with frayed tassels on the second shelf, stiff with lack of use. On the next shelf sit a pair of dusty opera glasses, dulled paste-jewelry, well read books, dainty clutches, and a treasured music box. Several of the curio items she purchased herself, but most were gifts from men—

clients—whose names and faces are long forgotten.

Neither woman really wants to say anything about time running out. Deborah worries about Emily's lonely future and Emily wonders about it too.

"Deborah!" Emily encourages, "I have all day. I can tell there's something you want me to know."

The Madam thinks, *Huh, when did she become the big sister?*

She replies dismissively, "Emily, you know most of it, I'm a prostitute. Have been all my life. Did you know that I've always insisted that people call me Deb or Madam Deb when it comes to business? Only my dearest friends call me Deborah. Decades ago, I chose May 31, 1787 as my birth date. Truth be told, I don't know the day, month, and I'm not exactly sure of the year of my birth!"

Deborah watches Emily straighten the part of her skirt that covers her lap and notes that Emily's face has remained unchanged from when they first met, with only three small wrinkles at the sides of each eye to give away the marching years.

Emily's room down the hall is smaller than Deborah's and lacks the elaborate furniture and personal treasures evident in Madam Deb's. From the beginning of her employment at Madam Deb's, almost four decades ago, Emily saved almost every penny she earned, spending only small amounts on sewing materials or an occasional new book. Deborah knows that Emily considers herself plain and boring, and dresses to match her beliefs about herself.

With a nod towards Emily's dress, Deborah diverts the conversation, "Today is Thursday because you're wearing your tan dress. Yesterday was a pale green, the day before was a drab yellow. Tomorrow will be a light grey."

"I know all about my habits. I wear the same dress on the same days of the week because it helps to organize them and me. What's wrong with that?"

"I remember the elegant outfit you wore when you arrived on my doorstep. You looked like you had just left a society luncheon. Why don't you ever buy clothing like that?" Deborah asks, remembering the flawless young lady who looked like a debutante on their first meeting.

"Because it would be pointless. No one ever comes to see me and I have nowhere to go. You know that."

"But that's the point! I feel responsible for your boring and drab life."

Emily just looks at her. *Yes, I have a quiet life*, she thinks, *but do I not choose that life?*

Deborah continues, "Other than our friendship, I've given you nothing more than food and shelter for the past decades, Emily. You've never courted, you've never been to the theater or to a ball. You've never had any fun. Working for me has done more harm than if you had met and married a farm hand. I should have encouraged you to follow your heart."

Gently and no longer scolding, Emily says, "Stop that. You know I did what I had to do for my sister and for Daniel. You've certainly given me more than basic necessities. You're more than a friend to me and I'll always treasure my years with you. As for my heart, no one ever came near it and I'm sure that was of my own doing. Please don't feel sorry for me. Now, go on. Tell me what you want me to know."

Deborah's baggy eyelids lift almost as if she's looking above the rims of a pair of glasses. "Fine." She surrenders and lowers her voice when she repeats, "Fine."

She props herself up on her goose-down bed pillows and says, "Get me a glass of water, will you, pet? This is going to be a long one. Now, before I start, reach into the curio for the book *Sense and Sensibility* by Jane Austen, please."

Emily does and hands it over to her. Deborah touches the book reverently and then passes it back to Emily. "That's yours. Samuel gave it to me, now I'm giving it to you."

12
Deborah

On a lazy Friday afternoon in the fall of 1810, twenty-two-year-old Deb exclaims for the second time, turning her mousy-brown haired head to avoid him, "I said no kissing on the mouth, Samuel!"

"Why? Why will you not let me kiss you? We have done everything but that! I want to kiss you! After all, I need to know how to do that, too," whines Samuel.

"No, you don't. When you meet your wife to be, you can practice and hone the art of kissing on her. Now leave me alone," says a determined Deb.

She is very fond of Samuel and always believed that kissing a man would lead to falling in love with him. She can't let herself fall in love with Samuel. Sex is just her job, but kissing is personal. She can't trust herself to push away any confusing sentiments that might arise if she kisses Samuel.

He leaves her bed, combs his disheveled light-brown hair back and gets dressed. The soon to be twenty-year old, hazel-eyed Samuel can never win against Deb. He knows she means it. She is more knowledgeable in some aspects of life that he ever will be.

She rolls her brown eyes, but as she doesn't want him—her one true friend—to leave her room upset, she gently explains, "Kissing is for lovers, Samuel. What we have together is terrific sex. You know as well as I do that we're not in love. We like each other—yes—but not love. When you meet your betrothed, you'll see the difference, I promise. You'll understand then what I'm talking about."

Common sense makes her realize that she isn't destined for real love and even though she likes most of her regular male visitors she knows that Samuel is more special than the others. After all, he is the only one who has ever asked for her company outside the brothel.

Samuel talks to her about everything that is going on in his life and he tells her she is the only one he confides in. He treats her with respect and no one has ever done that before, so he is easy to like. She does love him, oh, not love like a husband, as he can never be that, nor like a brother either because of the sex they have, but as a friend with a bonus—the combination.

This rare gift of a relationship started to blossom shortly after their first encounter, eight months earlier. They met on a night when Samuel and his colleagues from college decided to spend their monthly allowance on something daring and forbidden.

The young scholars started their evening in a saloon and had their initial taste of hard spirits. Too soon, they felt the effects of the alcohol and the owner of the tavern sent the boisterous lads home to sleep it off. The chaste men still had coins in their pockets and decided instead to leave the establishment in search of another sinful adventure. In Delton, it had been easy to find drink, and at eleven o'clock at night, just as easy to find a brothel.

Deb watched the young men arrive and let a *'tsk'* noise escape her mouth—she was not in the mood for virginal quests. She let the other girls choose first from the drunken lot, ending up with Samuel, the quiet one.

The other young men were all annoyingly whooping and hollering all the way up the stairs to the bedrooms of pleasure. Deb, on the other hand, decided she would take her time and have a bit of fun. She filled up a couple of glasses with cheap liquor and handed one to him. Samuel polished his off in seconds with anticipation of what his paid fee promised. He was quickly aroused when the lightly freckled young woman seductively sat on his lap and tilted her head back to guzzle off her glass of whisky and provide him with his first up-close view of cleavage.

As he had yet to yell out one whoop with glee, she decided that he had earned a slow and thorough seduction. For every step up the staircase, she undid a row of ribbon holding up her corset. By the time they reached her room, Deb was half naked. Samuel was a happy drunk, alert and still very willing.

"Let me help you take your clothes off," Deb said. She easily manipulated the sleeves of his coat jacket to tie his hands behind his back. She then pushed herself away from him and took the rest of her clothing off to prance in the nude in front of him. He thought her body to be perfectly beautiful; he didn't know that she was the most sought after by the male visitors to the establishment.

Only when Samuel showed great maturity in not advertising to the whole house by yelling out his desire, did Deb proceed to ease him into the fun of adult games. She helped him get passed his clumsiness and innocence by encouraging him, making it a memorable night—one that ensured repeat visits.

The owner of the establishment, Madam Clarice, had taught her girls that when handling young, inexperienced men, it's best to not be condescending or contemptuous, especially as it may deter future business.

"But what if I am not a good kisser and no woman ever wants to marry me?" Samuel asks with pouting lips.

"Oh, stop. Nobody's ever any good at kissing at first. I'm not. That's why I don't want you to practice on me. Save it for the future Mrs. Samuel Thordeaux," emphasizing the 'oh' sound. *Why not just change the spelling of his name to Thor-doe and be done with it?* Deb often thinks.

He shrugs. He knows she won't change her mind but he leans into her bed and kisses her on the cheek anyway and says, "See you next week then."

"Sure thing," she says as she watches him leave. "See you Monday."

At the very beginning of their odd relationship, he asked her to meet with him on her day off, which was usually Mondays. These weekly outings always included a meal and another activity. They either shop at the local market, go for a stroll in the park, view an exhibition at the museum, or even observe the afternoon rehearsals at the theater hall. Deborah may never have had the privilege of experiencing such events without her sophisticated friend. She feels special on Mondays, never worthless.

Additionally, after his last study session on Fridays, Samuel's generous allowance permits him to afford weekly business visits with Deb. It most often occurs an hour before her shift really picks up.

Samuel leaves through the back door. As usual, after a visit with Deb, he's in a good mood and their parting dispute about kissing is quickly forgotten.

13
Deborah

"Your father became one of my regular clients when he was nineteen, Emily. I didn't like him at the beginning, but he did grow on me. Samuel insisted we share more than sex. I'd never had that kind of relationship with any man before, and I was curious to know how normal people lived, so I agreed."

Emily asks, "So like what? You dated? Courted? Held hands? Kissed?"

"No. Not quite. There was no courting. He took me out on the days when he had free time away from school, mostly on Mondays and sometimes Tuesdays when the city was very quiet. I felt more like his escort than a debutante being courted. And, there was never any kissing!"

"So, you never kissed my father?" Emily has difficulty imagining having sex without kissing.

"No, Emily. It's too intimate," Deborah replies.

"Have you ever been kissed passionately?" Emily asks, curious now.

"Yes," she whispers. She's never forgotten James, her first love. Deborah remembers a memory, unable to decide if it's a good or bad one. Good because of what she learned, or bad for—the same reason!

In the fall of 1802, fifteen-year-old Deb has worked at Madam Violet's for over a year. One day, she's summoned into the private room. The use of this room costs a man ten dollars for one hour, so she knows she's in for something out of the ordinary.

Deb's given a special assignment. Even though she's had her share of sexual experience, she's naive on other levels. James, a young and wealthy man in his late twenties, is always on the lookout for this specific type of girl.

James has a standing reservation for Thursday afternoons at precisely three thirty, as that's the time that the maid finishes cleaning the private room and stocking it with his personal preference of bourbon and cigars.

Deb enters the room and her presence interrupts a conversation James is having with Violet. The Madam then stands by in silence and watches him examine the girl.

"Does she have anything to wear other than these baggy knickers?" he asks.

Violet lies and says, "It's her first day. She hasn't made any money to buy something decent yet."

"Fine. She will do for now," he exhales and Violet leaves the room.

Deb wonders if he'll ever talk to her directly or not so she asks, "Do you want to go to my room?"

He replies, "I do not go to other men's beds. Take your ugly knickers off."

She does, and he feels her legs and buttocks as he speaks, "Ah, you have shapely legs and a nice ass. Now stand up straight," he pushes her shoulders back and places a hand in the middle of her back which extends her chest out further, all the while making comments indicating his approval.

Her shoulders back, Deb is having difficulty breathing in her tight corset. He compliments the color of her dark hair and the contrast to her fair skin. He even notes her faint freckles and her delicate jaw-line.

"If I decide to come back for you next week, you will be required to bathe, including washing your hair before I arrive. You are to come to this room ten minutes early and to put on what you will find in a package on the bed and you are to change back into your own clothing before you leave this room. Under no circumstances are you to have any customers before me on Thursdays. Madam Violet is fully aware of my specific requests, so do not worry about her schedules."

He has never taken his eyes or hands off her partially nude body and now asks, "Have you been with anyone today or since your last bath?"

Deb assumes he has forgotten what Madam Violet has just told him and replies, "No."

He grabs her and in one swift motion, he undoes his pants and has sex while standing up. When he is done, he sets Deb down and walks over to the basin and washes himself before getting dressed.

Still breathing heavily, he puts his lips next to her ear and says, "Be here next Thursday." He places two dollars into the brassiere of Deb's corset and says, "This is for you. Never tell Violet about this extra money." He leaves.

Just as promised, on Thursday afternoons, after Deb bathes and goes to the private room, she finds a package waiting for her. She changes into whatever is inside. For the first time in her life, she touches silk, satin and lace and the delicate clothing up against her skin, mixed in with the expectancy of his presence, excites her.

This being his second visit, he asks, "Do you want to play a game?"

"Of course," Deb replies softly, hoping that he can't hear her heart beating loudly with anticipation. She has never spent so much time in conversation with a man who is with her for the sole purpose of sex.

She didn't know the game and he made up all the rules. He'd breathe in her ear and tell her how he wanted her but mostly, he wanted her to pretend that she didn't know what she was doing. She protested and said she really didn't know what he expected from her. But then he would shush her up and say, "The fun has begun."

His game was to master the art of seduction. He did things to Deb that no other man had ever done before or since—like the time he stood behind her, smelled her hair, licked her ear, caressed her bare skin and slowly ran his hands all over her body. He did that until she couldn't stand by herself anymore and needed to lean into his body to support her own. Everything he did awakened goosebumps and waves of excitement. No one had ever taken his time, nor ensured that she enjoyed his efforts.

When her excitement reached a climax, he threw her on the bed. Regardless of the position she landed, he mounted and was done. Then he would wash up and depart—never leaving a chance for further conversation.

Each time with him is different. She inhales deeply when he inspects her, all the while pulling her shoulders back with her chest sticking out. He always compliments how lovely the garment he chose looks on her and he plays with the material resting on her upper thighs.

On one of the earlier Thursdays, Deb wears a see-through black lace peignoir and excitedly waits. He approaches her and notes a stubborn tress of hair that keeps falling over her eyes. She tries to pin it down.

He says, "Let it be."

James then feels her cheek bones and traces the length of the stray tress of hair. He caresses her face and he kisses her on the mouth. He smiles knowingly when he asks, "Is this your first kiss?"

How did he know? She sighs and nods.

Deb wasn't playing a game when she answered in all honesty. He didn't care if it was the truth or not because how well she replied is what pleased him. He said she was a good student and kissed her again, and again, passionately.

For the following eight months, the Thursday afternoon trysts continued. Deb never fully understood what the game was, and didn't want it to stop. For her, life began on Thursdays with the clothing, the kissing, his attentiveness, the seduction, and mostly the sexual enjoyment that she experienced. All of which led her to believe that she was falling in love with him but more importantly, he with her.

The game came to an abrupt halt on a Tuesday. Deb was wearing the only decent dress she owned and was out shopping at the market when she spotted James and innocently approached him. "Good afternoon, James."

He looked her up and down with confusion, and then with disdain in his voice said, "You have obviously mistaken me for someone else."

A young woman approached him, took his arm, and asked him who he was talking to. He replied, "No one, dear." James then asked his companion if she had purchased what she wanted while he led her away in a different direction.

There was no package waiting for Deb that Thursday so she remained dressed in her unflattering underwear. He arrived precisely at three-thirty.

He told her how disappointed he was with her for ruining the game that—up until Tuesday—she had played so well. The rule she broke was acknowledging him outside the brothel and for that small ignorant infraction, he slapped her in the face with a powerful backhand. She fell to the floor and tried to explain that she didn't know it was a rule, but he leaned forward and silenced her with those long fingers of his covering her lips.

"How could I have known?" she cried when his fingers released the hold.

Then he showed her his true colors when he murmured, "Do you really think that I would say hello back? You are a whore!" He spat in her face and added, "You are dirty and not worthy of acknowledgement. You have made choices to be used and that is what I was doing. It is just as well, I am bored with you. You will never be anything but a dirty whore for the rest of your life. Besides, I have met my future wife and I am more than ready to seduce her. Do not expect gratitude for doing your job—slut."

The roughness he displayed excited him and this was new to him. He saw no reason why he couldn't take her one last time so he ripped her clothing, raped her and slapped her in the face once more. Satisfied with how well he played his own game, he left grinning.

Deborah sighs and takes a drink of water. She hadn't gone into great details of her encounters with James but said enough for Emily to understand how she was deeply hurt. "I never saw that disturbed bastard after that day.

"I never wanted to be fooled again either. Afterwards, if another man wanted to play games in the bedroom, I made sure I knew all the rules before we started. I couldn't understand how James could kiss me the way he did and not feel anything. If I was so dirty, how could he stand to place his lips on mine? It was a very hard lesson for me to learn," she said quietly, her voice choking. Her shoulders suddenly drop, she bows her head and weeps tears of longing and relief—relief from having shared her greatest and most disastrous love story, at last.

"I'm so sorry that happened to you, Deborah. He strung you along and then discarded you like trash," Emily sums up.

"Well, let me tell you, it certainly toughened me up. I learned the hard way that love can never be just one sided. I also learned that hurt is more than the physical pain someone like Maggie put me through. The emotional hurt is much worse. I watched my many bruises fade and disappear but I didn't know how to heal my feelings inside and lift my self-worth."

"Is that why you wouldn't kiss my father?"

"Absolutely. I knew Samuel wasn't in love with me the way I interpreted the word love and I didn't want my heart broken again. Worse of all, I didn't want to risk losing your father over an emotion if I could help it."

"Can you tell me more about you and my father?" Emily asks.

"Of course, pet." She calms down and says, "I just got started."

14
Deborah

For a tempting sum of money, the brothel opens for business at any hour, even on holidays. Usually, it is closed daily from one in the morning to two-thirty each afternoon. Most girls choose to work seven days a week with an occasional day off monthly or bi-monthly to run personal errands. As all shops and businesses are closed on Sundays, there's no point being off work on that day as it usually proves to be a busy one indeed.

Deb loves her life—especially when she compares it to her abusive upbringing. At least here she is fed, clothed, clean, and doing what she thinks is the only thing she can do well—and only occasionally find herself on the receiving end of angry fists. She has very little responsibilities and quite enjoys the friendship she shares with the Madam and many of the other girls.

In her eighteenth year, she had wisely opened a bank account to safeguard her money. Now, in her twenty-second year of life, she's proud to have accumulated a total sum of $1,745.82 from her lucrative employment as a prostitute.

Madam Clarice recognizes Deb's mature and trustworthy attributes and lures her into accepting more responsibilities with the promise of an increase in pay. Deb needs very little training and soon takes over the Madam's duties several nights a week. This includes making sure the money for services and liquor is secure, assigning the girls, and locking up; but mostly importantly, having the first choice of men to service.

But when it comes to money, Madam Clarice is paranoid and thinks that everyone will cheat her out of her profits every chance they have. Deb is wrongly accused of short changing the till and finds that taking on more responsibilities dips into her extra earnings. But clever Deb soon puts aside a tenth of the house's own money for such false discrepancies and in essence the Madam ends up stealing from herself.

Samuel's two visits per week with Deb continue—even after he graduates from college. The amount of time they spend together outside the bedroom is important to Deborah—she has never been treated so normally. This time is equally important to Samuel as it builds his confidence, especially around women. He doesn't hold back any thoughts from her and his confiding in her helps Deborah open up about things in her own past.

Whenever he invites her to go anywhere with him, she wears one of her new dresses with a matching hat and gloves. Her dresses clearly do not reflect what she does for a living as the soft materials are subtle, very chic and stylish. When he picks her up, Samuel gives her a nod of approval on her attire and, for a short period of time, she feels like she belongs in his world. He treats her with appreciation, often presenting her gifts—a flower, a ribbon for her hair, a new bottle of perfume, a book they might have discussed, a small piece of jewelry, or some other thoughtful trinket.

"You were how old when you learned to read and write?" he asks incredulously, as they shared a meal.

"I think I was fourteen or fifteen. The girl who taught me used to be a school teacher. She ended up getting a job at Violet's brothel after refusing the advances of her boss—who had fired her for reasons of—let me see," and she looks up toward the ceiling on the right, "insubordination. Yes, that's the word. Well, the irony was, she became what the man wanted from her, except this was on her own terms and for money.

"She also taught me to count, subtract and multiply. I have great difficulty dividing large numbers, but I find I don't need to do that as often as I need to count. So, I don't care if I never get any better at it."

He is surprised by her intelligence with so little schooling. He thinks, *She could have been so much more.*

Samuel had an affluent upbringing and cannot understand why anyone would not have been taught to read and write as a child. Deborah does not dislike many things about Samuel, but his ignorance on their social differences truly annoys her.

There might have been a time when Deb entertained the idea that she and Samuel could be more than friends and lovers, but his fierce disapproval of her choice of employment over marriage quickly squashes any such notion. He doesn't mind taking her out in public, as long as it is to a quiet coffee house in an unfashionable district, or to an afternoon theatre dress rehearsal, but he makes it perfectly clear that he can never be seen in society with a woman of such a scandalous profession.

Samuel is developing a keen sense of entrepreneurship and helps many school friends and acquaintances accomplish their business goals. As his experience increases, so do his fees for his advice. Word of his astute business sense gets around quickly and his portfolio of lucrative clientele grows. His business success does not go unnoticed by the mothers of single daughters coming of age and he begins receiving invitations to the parties held in honor of these young women.

He seeks Deborah's opinion on his wardrobe. Looking over the scarce and bleak selection, Deborah is afraid she might not be able to help him in time for one of the important debutante dances coming up on Thursday, the following week.

"Is that all you've got?" Deborah asks him.

"Yes, that is it. My entire collection. You have seen it all," explains Samuel.

"Well, you usually wore your college uniform when you came over on Fridays and, I must say, the rest looks all the same. Drab! So, it's decided then. You must get new clothes. Start with a new suit if you're going to attend these parties. You need to make the right impression, Samuel. After all, these mothers' approval will ensure your future and your proper place in society."

Although Samuel decides that he will listen to what Deb tells him to do, he counters with, "But, I do not have time for a new suit, Deb."

"Only if you go to the busiest tailor in town! But you do have time if you go see my friend, Ralph!"

"An unknown?" gasps Samuel.

"What's wrong with that? It doesn't mean he's not good, you know! Listen, there are two reasons why you should go see him. One, he's a new tailor, so he isn't too busy and can make you a suit just in time for the party. Two, and I think this is the most important reason, is that I believe you'll break away from the ordinary and outdated style when you wear what Ralph creates."

Deb sees Samuel shaking his head, so she urges on, "Think Samuel! If you succeed at making Ralph's new suits—and other menswear—a desired product because of how *you* look in them," she says poking his shoulder, "you'll not only help Ralph make a name for himself, but you'll prove that you're not afraid to be different."

Within the hour, Samuel heads over to Ralph's establishment with Deb's written recommendation. Ralph knows that the newest fashion has yet to reach Delton so he tailors a double-breasted dress coat of fine wool along with a light-colored waistcoat over a white linen shirt.

Samuel, in his trendy new suit, succeeds in receiving many compliments. He becomes the envy of his colleagues, fellow businessmen and clients. Word about the tailor's new and different clothing style quickly spreads throughout the city.

The same success is then experienced by Samuel's unknown barber, Ernest—another one of Deb's friends. Samuel is brave to go along with Ernest's suggestion of a mustache instead of a beard, and medium length cut hair instead of wearing a wig for the event of a debutante's ball. If Samuel is going to be sporting a new style of suits, he decides that his face can be daring as well.

Emily examines the eighty-year-old's eyes, finds them to be clear and comments on all that Deborah has just told her, "Well, indeed. That's definitely more like a brother and sister relationship."

Deborah clarifies, "Don't get me wrong. The weekly visits that were part of my business with your father didn't stop just because he was searching for a wife."

"Oh, I see." Even though in her heart Emily knew of her father's indiscretions, she had briefly hoped it had ended long before he met her mother.

15
Deborah

Lilith feels empathy for her friend and mother-in-law Emily, and asks, "Is that how your father met your mother then? At a ball?"

Emily looks at the lawyer who nods, encouraging her to elaborate on a story as told to her, first by her mother and partly by Deborah.

The debutante ball season begins in mid May and ends in August. Samuel doesn't accept every invitation he receives, but the address for the ball to be held on June 13, 1811 piques his curiosity; he has always wanted to see the inside of the vast mansion.

Samuel walks passed the reception room to the ballroom and marvels at the brilliantly lit pillars supporting the balcony floor above. Thirty, long, thin candles adorn each pillar in a circular descending order as if placed on a miniature spiral staircase. Young men and women are dancing in the center space framed by the series of columns, other couples sit on settees near the walls, or stand about as they enjoy a refreshment while taking a break from dancing. The pillars hold up the floor above where parents and chaperones can unobtrusively observe their charges below.

As can be expected, upon Samuel's entrance, a mother is overheard asking the hostess, "What can you tell me about him?" The hostess, and all women standing next to her, turn their gaze slowly in the direction signaled by the mother. Like every mother, they all want the best suitor for their daughter.

"Who? Oh, yes. That young man is Mr. Samuel Thordeaux. He will be very successful—you mark my words. He handled a contract for my husband's business and in no time at all, my husband was opening a branch office. However, he never puts himself forward in conversation. You must begin the conversation yourself. Perhaps he is shy?"

"Or maybe he lacks social graces," the woman nearest the hostess replies with the hopes of discouraging further interest in this young man from the other mothers until she scrutinizes him herself over the side of the balcony. She lists in her mind what she already knows. He is of average height at five feet nine inches tall and stands up straight, indicating good breeding and good manners. However, he rarely joins the other fellows, which could be indicative of some social disconnection. She decides to approach him later in the evening in the hopes that she can discover more about him—and if he measures up to her standards, possibly interest him in her own daughter.

While the mothers have their selection criteria, their daughters note that Samuel Thordeaux is handsome, is a sharp and stylish dresser, and wears a hairstyle that makes his otherwise ordinary hair beg to be tousled.

It is true that Samuel doesn't put himself forward, but not for the reasons the mothers believe. He is usually found behind the scenes—observing and rarely participating in the required rituals beyond the obligatory dance with the hostess's daughter. He observes, scrutinizes the young women who are attending, dances as necessary, and leaves. Except for the pleasure of visiting the splendid building, tonight is just one more such ordinary evening. Until …

As he looks at the entrance to the ballroom, Samuel observes a late arrival. Like all the other young ladies, she has neatly coiffed hair—hers is blond. Her eyes are blue, she has a tiny button nose, and one crooked tooth that happens to make her smile very alluring, and her frock is a pinkish color. But there is something about her that is different. She looks around to see if any of her friends are in attendance and soon realizes that the other young women are already enjoying the dance.

From the moment his sight rests on the young lady, Samuel knows she will become Mrs. Samuel Thordeaux. He thinks, *That's it. It's her smile. It gives her the appearance of having a brilliant personality. It is intriguing, genuine and attractive—unlike many of the other young women, trying too hard to be appealing.*

One of the mothers he knows somewhat approaches him. He nods acknowledgement that he has seen her and meets her halfway. Before she can speak, he motions toward the latecomer and says, "Mrs. Peters, how delightful. I was just wondering if I could impose upon you to introduce me to the last of the arrivals." He bows as he reaches to kiss the older woman's hand.

Mrs. Peters isn't expecting his polite request but responds, "Gladly." She is flattered that a young man of such high regard among all the mothers would seek her assistance. She leads the twenty-one-year-old bachelor to the seventeen-year-old Elizabeth and her mother, Mrs. Henry Breat.

After a quick introduction, Samuel says to the young lady, "And now, the party has truly just begun. Would you do me the honor of dancing your first waltz of the evening with me, Miss Breat?"

He can't tell if she's interested or just being polite when she does a half curtsy and replies, "Certainly, Mr. Thordeaux."

"May I get you a refreshment while we wait for this piece to finish?" he asks. His smile is hopeful.

"Yes, please. Could you escort me to where the other women are sitting?" she asks.

"My pleasure," he says and places a steady hand on her elbow to show her the way.

Elizabeth almost jumps at his touch as a small electrical spark flashes between the two of them. Its occurrence is unexpected and feels more powerful than it actually is. After the spark, he wraps his fingers around her arm and she halts her step. She looks down at his hand near her elbow and lets her eyes wander up to his shoulder and finally rest on his eyes. Samuel observes her every blink *en route* to his face.

He smiles again and breathes out in a whisper, "Is everything all right?"

"Why yes. Forgive me. I was just, ah, startled. Please, proceed."

"This way," he says with a knowing grin. He had felt her attraction as she had leaned into him when she paused, and again when she fluttered her long eyelashes at him.

He drops her off at a circle of settees in a far corner. Before he releases the hold on her arm, he sees her eyes focusing on his lips, so he quickly looks down at hers and then up again as her eyes see where his have landed. Without using words, they've shown their mutual attraction to each other.

He leaves the circle and soon comes back with a glass of punch which he hands to her before moving to the space behind the sofas where most young men wait for indication that their dance partner is finally ready to fulfill the promise.

Elizabeth can't explain why she fears he may leave the building if she waits for the music to end before signaling her readiness to dance, so she rises immediately on its last note.

"This is the first time I've seen you at these soirees," Samuel points out as he leads her to the dance floor.

She blushes when she realizes that he's noticed her absence. "I have not attended many since my own coming out party last year. We spent a month in Philadelphia for my brother's wedding. Thankfully, there's nothing to keep me from attending all the balls I want now. It is time for me to get reacquainted with everyone," she says.

She turns, curtsies in beat with all the other young women and steps into the dance.

He knows she means that she needs to show she's still available and in the market for a husband. These soirees are the most popular way for a respectable young lady of good standing to find one.

The evening progresses without incident. Samuel dances two other waltzes, one with the daughter of the hostess and the other with Mrs. Peters' daughter. As he does not want to invite gossip, he does not ask Elizabeth for a second dance. His decision to court Miss Breat is most certainly no one's business but his own.

16

Samuel

Two long weeks _____ _____ help in penning an invitation for Eliza____

Miss Elizabeth Breat,

If it pleases you, I will hire _ __rriage for two o'clock this coming Thursday afternoon and we will take a short ride on the shady side of the road to the park.

Permit me to escort you on a half-hour walk and locate a bench to observe the ducks at the pond. I promise to return you safely to your home by three-thirty.

The messenger boy awaits your reply.

Mr. S. Thordeaux

All the while they are writing it, Deborah counsels Samuel in courting matters.

"Don't scare her away by moving too fast," she says.

"How quickly I walk could scare her away?" asks a dumbfounded Samuel.

"No, silly. I mean, if she accepts this invitation, don't ask her out again too soon. Oh, and don't put your arm around her until a couple of months have passed. And for heaven's sake, don't try to kiss her until she appears to be begging for it."

"Two months?"

"Maybe three!"

"Ugh! I could not wait that long if I was not already having sex with you," exclaims Samuel.

Maybe he didn't mean it, but his comment makes Deb feel like she's just an object to him. She doesn't appreciate his blunt and hurtful words but is too afraid to start a disagreement and risk losing him by mentioning it. She hasn't cried emotional tears since the incident with James and is surprised by the waterfall that is threatening to break through. *Maybe it's more than his comment?* She wonders. *Is this the beginning of the end of us? Of everything we are to each other? Friends? Lovers?*

Samuel sends the note by courier the next morning and receives a prompt reply. He smells the lavender scented paper before opening it.

Mr. Samuel Thordeaux,

It would please me to accompany you on a walk in the park. My mother and our neighbor will chaperone. ~Miss E. Breat

Elizabeth is not only attractive but she is well-read and her ability to remember details of books she read as a child awes him. She has a delicate innocence about her that makes him want to protect her. He is also impressed with her immediate desire to help a child who had fallen and scraped a knee at the park that first afternoon.

Samuel, handsome and owner of a promising future, easily makes the right impression when he first meets Elizabeth's parents, Henry and Gertrude. As the courtship advances, he never objects if a chaperone is offered and he praises Elizabeth's parents for all the good he sees in the young woman. When Samuel meets with Elizabeth's father alone, he is clear on his desire to go beyond mere courting the young lady.

"I am very fond of your daughter sir, and my intentions are to determine if Elizabeth and I can build a future for ourselves together."

Henry discusses the matter with his wife, Gertrude. Elizabeth's mother already knows how her daughter feels about Samuel—her suitor has been at the core of all the young woman's conversations lately. The couple receive permission from her parents to court and even unsupervised excursions of short duration are granted.

Weeks later, Samuel finds out that Deborah's advice is correct— kissing is definitely special, even more special than the act of sexual intercourse. Samuel makes a move to woo Elizabeth further. He parks the buggy in a secluded spot, and looks into her eyes while he moves closer to her. She leans into him, lifts her sweet face to meet his lips and closes her eyes. He adores her innocence and lets a smile escape briefly. He places his right thumb on her soft cheek and his fingers at the back of her neck, gently pulling her face closer to his. She opens her eyes and her lips part slightly. She watches him lean in and she closes her eyes again. He teases and caresses her now blushing cheek with his thumb again and she opens her eyes once more. She understands that he wishes for her to keep her eyes open while he lowers his head and brushes her lips with his.

He is surprised at the softness which leads him to dreamily close his eyes, and she follows suit. He applies more pressure with his lips and takes her bottom lip and holds it in between his. With both lips on her parted ones, he then inserts his tongue in her mouth and tickles hers with it. She sways and feels faint at the slow seduction. Finally, he pulls away while taking his hands off her face. She is left speechless and weak.

He now understands what Deborah tried to explain before—*kissing is between two people who care for each other. Your mind has to be present while kissing as it is a shared motion. Unlike sex, you have to be entirely aware of what your lips, and hers, are doing. You feel them touching, your senses are awakened and participating. Your lips lead or follow in the actions taken because it's an act of give and take.*

Elizabeth felt his kiss ripple over her, awakening every inch of her body. He's her first kiss and she is his.

On Saturday, June 13, 1812, exactly one year after the day they met, Samuel and Elizabeth shared a last name. Emily was born on May 9, 1813 and a second daughter, Adeline, was born on March 10, 1816.

Samuel has always hoped for a son; one to join him in his growing business. However, an announcement of a pregnancy that will bear him a son never comes. Elizabeth's health becomes poor and she's advised to have no further children.

Samuel hides his disappointment as he doesn't want to say anything to upset Elizabeth. Instead, he decides to make a drastic change in his life—their lives. Shortly after Adeline's third birthday, he uproots his family and moves to Philadelphia in the hope of finding medical care to improve Elizabeth's health.

He purchases ten acres of land on North Sedgwick Street and has a mansion built. Samuel provides all the material things Elizabeth could ever want and fulfills her personal needs with his love and affection. The couple grows closer together while cultivating a tight group of the members of high society. Soon everyone of any note knows of the couple. They are in high demand for social events and, for Samuel, for business connections.

Samuel masters the art of coaxing new clients into trusting him with their money and management of their business affairs. He relishes entertaining on weekends at home with potential clients, who are soon seduced by his wealthy lifestyle. Just as Deborah groomed him for a more sophisticated look, his clients all clamor to mimic him and his way of living.

Weekly, Samuel's activities involve three or four days of work in Philadelphia and one or two overnight stays for meetings with long standing clients back in Delton. Samuel doesn't really need any out-of-town contracts to build his business, but he doesn't want to cut ties with Delton, or with Deborah.

When away from home on these trips, Samuel pays Deb a handsome sum of money to spend time with him in his hotel room. He never asks if she wants to spend the night as an unpaid lover. She never forgets that she is being paid to be with him, but she can, at least, console herself with the fact that she doesn't have to share any of the money he pays her with Clarice—as these are her days off.

Samuel lavishes Deb with elaborate gifts. She grows to dislike this habit as it only seems to re-enforce the confusing line of their relationship as both a business deal and a convenient affair. However, she is very fond of him, loves him even, and can't or rather won't, put a stop to his lover-like overtures of gift giving.

These visits are the reason for which Deborah continues to purchase conservative clothing to wear out in public. Every few months, she shops for new attire to surprise Samuel with, and he constantly approves of her choices.

Samuel feels safe in Delton while out in public with Deborah, especially since Elizabeth's parents moved to Duluth more than fives years earlier. Delton is far enough away from Philadelphia and a small enough city that his activities would never reach the society pages of Philadelphia newspapers.

Back home, an oblivious Elizabeth masters the balancing act of managing a large mansion with a compliment of nine staff. She relishes organizing social soirees, Samuel's business events, and dinners with politicians and wealthy clients.

Growing up, both Samuel and Elizabeth thought they were privileged. However, when Samuel's endeavors provide riches beyond their imaginations, they know they are a couple to be envied. The wealth of their youth is nothing compared to their current opulence and they relish flaunting it.

Both had attended the best schools their parents' money could afford and benefited from private tutors over the summer months. Both had been raised by nannies, so when they were away from home in a boarding school, they never experienced pangs of homesickness as they never fully bonded with their family members while growing up. They never yearned for the reassurance and comforting arms of a parent.

Their blooming new wealth, the move to Philadelphia, and the pace of their busy lives, create an invisible barrier between them and Elizabeth's family in Duluth, estranging them further from their roots. Neither Samuel nor Elizabeth care about the lost family ties; they are too busy to accept invitations to family events like weddings, anniversaries or birthdays. Even funerals of close family members are ignored. Anything that is not announced or reported about in the pages of the society section is not considered sufficiently eventful to merit their presence.

In contrast to her own upbringing, Elizabeth hires tutors year-round and does not enlist nannies after the wet-nurses leave. She becomes the best mother possible and ingrains the importance of family in her daughters. For the girls, no one else in the world matters more than their close-knit family of four.

Silence fills the room when Emily stops speaking. Mr. Trolley calls for a break.

17
Delilah

The letter continues …

Philadelphia was big enough for both the Dentz family and me. Their circle was a dull, sober, business one and mine certainly was not. I was delighted to be single again, in America, and nowhere near my parents in Maine. I attended all kinds of balls and soirees and worked my way into a cluster of friends.

I became popular with the men in the group when they learned that I was a divorcee, but mostly because they could socialize with a woman without a mother's overseeing stare. Their curiosity earned me endless invitations to the opera, to the theater and all kinds of fun activities.

Then it happened. I met someone and fell in love. Yes, me! His name was Victor. The first time I saw him …

The heat on this day in late June of 1809, and the active sport of boxing outdoors makes Victor wipe his brow on his sleeve. He laughs as he pats his competition on his back. "Do not worry, Charlie. You will win one against me some day."

The two friends have an ongoing battle of strength and strategy in the ring. Charlie is rarely defeated by another opponent—except Victor—and it bothers him, but not to the point that it affects their friendship. The usual crowd of onlookers applaud the pair as the men leave the area to wash and change.

Delilah walks up to the terrace table and sets her clutch down on it. "Who is that?" she asks, glad to see new blood in the mix.

The woman seated next to her waves to friends who have just arrived. She rises, but before she leaves to go greet them, she replies, "Victor? He is my brother's best friend. Oh, yes! You were not here last summer. Victor was in Europe and he just got back. He and Charlie are such good friends, they usually just pick up where they leave off."

The twenty-seven-year-old Delilah is interested. She's had enough time to analyze all the available men in this circle of single friends and has come to the conclusion that she will have to change circles. But something about Victor makes her catch her breath and no one has done that since that handsome stable boy, Ray.

When Victor comes out of the house after washing off the sweat from the intense match, she is more than intrigued to find out more about this man who seems so certain of himself. For a man who is only three years older than her, he looks like he knows what he wants, and makes double sure of it before going after it. She finds herself observing his every move and admiring his confidence.

The wind picks up his blond hair and teases it. His nose is long and thin, his mouth houses a mischievous smile. He approaches her table and asks, "Why have I not seen you before? Where have you been?"

Delilah is mesmerized by his beautiful grey-blue eyes and stammers, "Hello. I am … "

"I know who you are. Delilah Fowler, once known as—Dentz?" he had leaned over and whispered the last four words.

She grins. Nods. "How did you … ?"

"Mysterious, intriguing, no—beguiling. Correct again?" he interrupts.

She laughs. He made her laugh, that is rare.

"It is my business to know things, but do not concern yourself. I will not tell anyone about the Dentz connection."

So, he knows. Everyone else thinks my former husband's last name is Fowler, she thinks.

Victor has a genuine interest in getting to know her. The feeling is mutual.

"Come on," he invites.

"Where to?" she asks.

"Does it matter? I just want to spend time with you, get to know you."

"All right. If you are sure you want to be seen with a divorcee."

"I like a little scandal. Now, let us see what else we can conjure up."

She giggles. He flashes her one of his inviting smiles and she is breathless.

They become inseparable right from the start. Delilah eagerly clears her calendar to accommodate all of Victor's invitations. She is surprised to feel skipped heartbeats when he touches her hand, or sees his quick smile when he notices that she's looking at him.

At the beginning of their courtship, Victor mentions that what he wants most in life is to become a father. He uses all of his good manners and best behavior to show her he is serious and has nothing but the purest of intentions toward her and their future together. Delilah convinces herself that he said those things about parenthood because he thinks she wants or needs to hear them; she cannot believe that a man's priority would be to become a parent.

Victor is suave and debonair; but what makes her fall in love with him is his undivided attention, his admiration, his nods of understanding when she is speaking, and his full support of her ideas.

As their courtship advances, she finds herself increasingly frustrated that Victor hasn't pressured her into his bed. Her method of roping in a man with sexual activity to do her bidding is challenged. She is unsure what to do to keep him interested in her.

Since Martin, she hasn't had a relationship with someone who wants to get to know her first; and until Victor, Delilah has never wanted to really know a man before sleeping with him. She has, up until now, always just desired a man for the benefits he brought to her life.

This unfamiliar territory confuses her—especially when her heart flutters when she lays eyes on him as he enters a room. Even their first kiss was beyond anything she had ever experienced before.

She replays in her mind the lovely dinner they enjoyed before the recital at the concert hall. This was followed by a short visit with his parents. The older couple retired after a brief conversation inquiring about their evening. The hour was approaching eleven when Victor rose from the sofa and extended both hands to help Delilah stand.

"Shall we go? It is late and I have a mid-morning meeting I cannot miss," Victor says.

"Then just walk me to the carriage. The driver can wait until I am safely inside my house. You do not have to escort me," offers Delilah.

Victor lifts her hand and kisses the back of it. He places it over his forearm and leads her to the hallway entrance.

Waiting together in the foyer for her ride, he nudges her closer to him and admires every inch of her sweet face. "I love your little nose, your playful eyes and the way your cheeks hide dimples until you smile. So pretty. And yet, I would say your best feature is your lips, they … " and he bends to kiss first her nose, her eyes, then her cheeks and finally her lips.

Delilah Fowler is smitten! She falls hard and is afraid of her feelings. She has never loved another human being before and doesn't know how to deal with all her emotions and doubts. She just knows that she wants to spend the rest of her life with Victor. The best thing about being in love is the discovery that Victor falls just as hard. During the peak of fully bloomed flowers in the summer of 1810, they are married. Life is suddenly full of happiness, mutual respect, and love.

Delilah is often surprised to learn that she is interested to know how he spends his days away from her. She is also astonished to learn that he always rushes back home to share the details of his day, and then to inquire about her own.

Six months into their marriage and following a comment of Victor's disappointment at the discovery of the presence of her monthly courses, Delilah seeks the medical opinion with respect to her inability to conceive. After the miscarriage and surgery on the ship, she was fairly certain that she was not able to conceive, but now she is anxious to give Victor what he wants so desperately.

The doctor confirms what she suspected. She is barren. But how will she tell Victor? Disappointing him causes her great anxiety. When should she approach him about this truth? How should she divulge the sad news without revealing her scandalous past?

Victor is oblivious of her barrenness. His delight in his joyful marriage and happy wife often overshadows his looking forward to fathering a child.

On their first wedding anniversary, Victor asks playfully, "Are you not gifting me with an announcement that you are expecting a baby?"

A knot forms in Delilah's stomach at his question. She anticipated this moment would one day come—just not today. Her immediate discomfort by the question is exposed by a flush of red that rises from her chest to her cheeks. With dread, she recalls that Victor believes she has only been in Martin's bed before him, thus the blush. Misunderstanding the change of color to her face, he beams a wide grin at the good news only to be crushed when she shakes her head.

Trusting his love for her as endless and unconditional, especially with the blissful first year of marriage behind them, Delilah decides to disclose the sins of her youth. Unfortunately, her inexperienced confessing self mistakenly starts her story with the miscarriage on the ship. Too late, she realizes that she should have begun by telling Victor of her mother's illness and how terribly lonely her childhood was, so he would understand how unhappy she had been.

"Hear me out, Victor," she starts talking faster when she sees his shock and grave disappointment. "When I discovered I could not have any children, I was relieved, but that was then. You have to understand, I did not want any children because I thought I could not love them. I know that sounds ridiculous, but I was not loved by my own parents. And I am sorry … I am terribly sorry."

Flustered as to what to say next, she breaks down in tears by her lack of clarity. Victor is more than disappointed to learn of her deceit. He has always felt self-assured in knowing the truth about both personal and business matters prior to closing any deals. Delilah's secrecy about her past infidelity puts him on the defensive, tuned to watch for other trickery. He immediately rejects any notion to believe another word she says. His pride makes him blame his blind love for her, the first and only love he will ever cherish—but he will be fooled no more.

"You could have told me before we wed," he yells. "So, you are not British? You were not a virgin when you married the first time, and you have always known that you could not have children? How could you not tell me any of that?"

"You told me you knew." She stands all alone in the middle of the room while he paces.

He reels to face her, shakes his finger and yells, "What makes you think I knew that? I knew about your marriage to Martin and that is all! You used him to get back home to America, did you not? You are a regular little liar, are you not? You practically ruined his life, Delilah. Is that the real reason he moved to England? To get away from you and any potential scandal? What else have you not told me? What surprises wait for me around the corner, Delilah?"

The memory of making love with his best friend Charlie flashes before her. She is ashamed to admit to herself how deceitful and untrustworthy she truly is. She will never divulge the details to Victor of promiscuity with the men in their circle of friends; especially about the time she shared a bed with his best friend. She has been true to Victor since they met, but she knows he would not understand and, more importantly, forgive her previous liaisons. "Nothing. I have said it all. You know I love you very much, Victor. While I knew that you did not know the whole truth about my past, I was afraid that if you knew you would not want to be with me, and that I would lose you."

With no sign that he will approach and console her, she is oddly reminded, at a time like this, of the happiest day of her life. "Would you have married me anyway?" she asks. "Please tell me, I need to know."

Victor responds, "We will never know now." He is hurting and wants to hurt back, so with an elevated voice, he says, "On second thought, yes, I do know. I would not have married you. More than anything, Delilah, I want to be a father. You knew that from the very beginning and you had so many occasions to tell me about … " and he points to her belly. Close to tears he adds, "Why did you not? Now there is all this pain that you have caused. I am so angry with you, I cannot stand to look at you. You say you love me, but your lies tell me otherwise." He silences himself by slamming the door behind him.

She wails and throws herself onto the bed. Victor hears her crying but his wounded heart drives him to the men's club to drown his sorrows. He returns late and spends the night in the guest bedroom.

Delilah has never felt hurt like this. She cries herself to sleep and when she wakes, she begins crying all over again. Can't he understand that she has never been loved? At what point in their relationship should she have trusted her love for him and his for her, to brave the moment and tell him of her tainted history? She can't answer that.

It takes her five days to stop crying and it takes him twice as long to talk to her again. And when he does, he says, "I have not decided what I am going to do about us and until I do, I will continue sleeping in the room across the hall. Please do not try to fix this, because you cannot. I am the one who must come to terms with it all, Delilah."

An unwanted pattern keeps repeating itself in her life. Once again, she's all alone. This loss is a new kind of wound. She feels ashamed when the truth forces her to grow up and realize just how selfish and self-centered she's always been. She blames her parents for all her troubles, but knows deep down that at some point, she could have changed herself. She doesn't know how to stop this pain and prays that Victor can and will.

They eventually become civil to each other again and, in front of company, Victor and Delilah act as if there are no issues between them. He even puts an arm around her shoulder or waist when others are watching. She cherishes these instances and leans her body against his, touching his arm or shoulder. She bravely looks him in the eyes with all her love spilling out, in the hopes that it will reach his heart.

But the second they are alone again, he becomes aloof and unforgiving. His eyes are masked by a fog and he re-erects the walls that protect his heart.

With the hurt always fresh, many tears fall from her cheeks. She never stops loving him and never loses hope. She never looks for solace in another man's arms because she doesn't want to destroy any chance of being with Victor again.

Many months later, three weeks before their second wedding anniversary, Victor comes home from work and announces, "Father's business is moving. He is opening a store in Duluth and one in London, England. He asked me to choose where we want to live—Duluth or London. I told him I would tell him my answer tomorrow morning."

Delilah is just about to speak when he holds a hand up and says, "You do not understand. I have already decided and you do not have a say in the matter, Delilah. I am going to England and you are staying here. My parents will be moving to Duluth for father to focus on the new store so they will not find out for months that you have stayed behind."

Although his eyes are cold as they look at his distraught wife, his face clearly depicts his own shattered heart. How he wishes his heart and mind could feel the love and forget the rest, but they can't.

She mumbles, "We could adopt a baby, Victor. We would be wonderful parents together."

"You really do not understand, do you? Yes, we could adopt, but it will never change the fact that you lied to me. I cannot trust you, Delilah. It is over. We are over."

Victor's news is more sorrow, a final blow and causes endless tears that feel like sand scratching her exhausted eyes as the clear liquid flows over the rims onto salty cheeks.

Tear drops freely drip down his face as he himself looks on at his inconsolable wife, "That is my final decision. I will leave you with this house and enough money for the upkeep. My lawyer will be in touch with divorce papers."

He turns to leave and stops at the door. He still wants her to hurt as much as he does, so he says, "You know I could have loved you forever."

She is brave enough to show her own sorrow and before he leaves, he hears her say, "I *will* love you forever, Victor." Then she whispers and hiccups, "I love you my darling, always."

Alone, they both lament and mourn, one broken and one who cannot forgive what is unforgivable.

18
Delilah

The letter continues …

There are so many hard lessons to learn in life. Victor never came back from England—not even to visit. While too young, he died abroad in 1828, unwed and childless.

I still cry when I think of what I did that cost me everything beautiful that life has to offer. It took me years after my divorce from Victor to come out of the house and begin to live again.

In May 1822, Mrs. Clarkson, one of my neighbors, extended an invitation to me to attend her annual lawn party and I accepted. The party lasted all afternoon and late into the night. I met countless other neighbors and friends, and that is where I was introduced to Edgar Neustat.

He was ten years older than me, yet he had the attitude of a younger man to go along with his youthful appearance. He was no more than three inches taller than me, had a protruding stomach, a nose that reminded me of an eagle's beak and dull-grey eyes. But he had a lovely smile. He was fun and generous with his money. His spontaneity to do things like get up and dance, or go for an unplanned ride to the countryside, or to attend a party *after having declined the invitation, stimulated and teased my senses like no one else had for so long.*

But his boyish looks and good manners were deceiving. On the night we were married, on that very night, he turned into a red-headed bully. Just like that.

I was already 40 years old when we married in 1823, yet he fully expected me to be able to produce an heir. What is it about men wanting children? Is there no other way for them to leave a legacy?

Unfortunately, when safely married, Edgar showed me his true colors. He was what is called today a "con man." The money he so frequently flashed about during our courtship was gone. Our marriage ended up consisting of two liars who could not tolerate each other. He received an allowance from me which enabled him to attend men's clubs where he could drink and gamble. Otherwise, he would be underfoot and annoying.

The doctor blamed his death on heavy drinking when his heart gave out in 1829. I vowed never to marry again. To what purpose would it have served to have wed again? Being childless ended up being my only true accomplishment in life. I mean, can you imagine another unloved child in the world?

For the next thirty years, I traveled extensively. I was never alone, and never with the same companion. After inheriting from my late parents— which I will tell you more about later on in my letter—and after Edgar's passing, I afforded myself, and that of my current male friend (if he did not have the funds), first class treatment everywhere we went.

Mr. Trolley adds, "It is certainly something to ponder—the difference between living a privileged, loveless life residing in a mansion and the seemingly unfortunate life of becoming a madam of a brothel with people considered to be loving."

Mr. Trolley called for a break, and Emily rises. In silence, she walks to the window and gazes at the blowing snow pelting the glass. Her thoughts form easily—she wouldn't have liked Delilah as the unruly, self-centered child, or as the young woman with her reprehensible promiscuity. Emily has no regard for her own father's indiscretions either. He, being a married man, had more than a sexual relationship with a prostitute—they were lovers and friends. She wonders if those two women were that way because they hadn't been taught to respect themselves. Her thoughts end with gratitude for her mother's influence.

Lilith hasn't changed her mind with respect to her feelings for Delilah—so far, she wouldn't have liked the woman. She was fond of Deborah, not only because she was close to her, but of the two women, Deborah seemed more considerate—even humble.

Graham leaves the room and walks the hallways. He thinks that Mr. Trolley's comments are unworthy of a rhetoric, and yet he surmises that these two women led sad and lonely lives. His upbringing is perfect compared to theirs, but he knows better than to boast about his fortunate past to others who are less blessed.

19
Deborah

In keeping with the late widow's request, Mr. Trolley continues to encourage the benefactors to share their stories. He doesn't pick up from where he left off in the letter. Instead, he asks, "Emily, do you know how Madam Deb became the Madam?"

"As a matter of fact, yes, I do. Believe it or not, on that same day that she had fallen and hurt her head, she told me exactly how."

Deborah reflects back to the spring of 1827, "When I turned forty, Madam Clarice ran off with one of her rich fellows. I remember it was on a Sunday. She left a short note, telling us to fend for ourselves.

"I must admit that by then I had been taking on more of her work; but I never did much else than assign the girls to the customers, pour drinks, collect money, and lock up the doors. I was disappointed that she left without selecting the next madam and I feared I was out of both a job and a home.

"Lucky for me, your father arrived on Monday for one of his usual meetings. I met him in the park that afternoon and told him that I, too, would be moving to live and work somewhere else—I just didn't know where yet. He wouldn't hear of such nonsense. Samuel was convinced that with his help, I could take over the brothel. He assured me he could teach me how to handle the business end and make it better than Clarice's.

"Of course, with my limited education, I had no idea how to do any of it, but this was your father's strength—helping a business get started or back on its feet. It didn't matter what kind of work the business was involved in. So, he wired your mother that he had pressing business problems to tend to and stayed here the rest of the week.

"He'd give me instructions and repeat them in different ways until they made sense to me. The first thing he did was to help me move my possessions into Clarice's bedroom. I didn't know it then, but he suggested all kinds of things like that, to get the message across to the other girls that I was now madam.

"On Tuesday, he observed me for the full day as I took Clarice's place in the boudoir. The next morning, he went into action. During the hours that the clients weren't keeping me busy, he taught me what I needed to know behind the scenes.

"He was a good teacher. I learned how much food and liquor to order and how often to do it. I learned how to do paperwork, pay bills, keep records, and surprisingly, my limited education didn't slow me down much. We then organized the women into shifts. On the third day we hired Josie as the cook, and on the fourth, we hired our first watchman, Jim. On the fifth day, I took in my first new girl. Everything was soon ready for me to run the business all by myself.

"Samuel put up the money for the addition to the brothel that today is the residential side of the building. From the outside, you can't even tell that it wasn't always the size it is now. He planned it all out in a matter of days. He was very clever.

"We never did find Clarice's private records, but we did find the deed.

He paid a fair sum to change the name of ownership to mine. Because Clarice was gone and I didn't know about her past agreements with the law, I more than once, over the following months, thought I would be arrested. However, as Samuel predicted, eventually officers came around and expected personal favors of a sexual nature in exchange for protection from arrest or a challenge to my ownership.

"I don't know how Clarice acquired the land, but I know that I worked hard to pay for my acquiring it legally. I repaid my loan to your father within five years, but I never forgot that he was solely responsible in making me a successful businesswoman. When he sent you to work for me, I could not refuse to take you in. I owed him so much.

"I've never told anyone that it was your father who persuaded me to dress the girls the same way I dressed when we went out on our weekly dates. I remember arguing with him that the dresses would be a waste of money, considering what we do and how long the girls would be wearing the dresses before they were removed for the task at hand. He assured me that most of the customers had boring lives or overworked wives who never went to any trouble or fuss for their husbands. He also pointed out that most of the married customers couldn't afford fancy dresses for their own wives and for a little while, they could pretend to be someone or something they weren't—rich.

"Samuel told me about his own reaction at seeing me dressed up like a debutante when he knew full well what I could do once naked, and he was sure most men would feel that way too. He assured me that if my girls could spruce up their appearance, the men would come back to see what else they would do.

"I reluctantly took his advice. The change was slow, but I'd say even the girls enjoyed dressing up instead of down. In the 1820s, the waistlines on our dresses were closer to the waist and tightly cinched. The skirts would expand out wide and looked like a bell. The sleeves were so huge that our arms looked twice the size of our waists. Thank goodness the clothes were smartly decorated with colorful stripes or flower patterns. I wasn't enamored with that fashion, but I wore it nonetheless to encourage the girls to do the same.

"The girls worked harder at seducing the men because they weren't showing off their shoulders, bosoms, and legs. I'd say most men have visited more than once because of a simple change to the girls' wardrobe."

With watering, disheartened eyes now, Deborah says, "After the first week, Samuel would always stay with me Monday nights in my room here in the brothel. He still paid me as I'm sure that made him feel better. Tuesday mornings, before he took off, he'd check up on my progress and make adjustments where necessary. Although your father had not visited me for several months before you arrived, I knew your coming was the end of our long affair."

Emily can't help herself and says softly, "You still love him, don't you?"

"Yes, Emily. Your father is the only man I truly ever loved."

Emily puts a hand up to her chest and even though she knows of her father's infidelity, with all sincerity, she says, "I'm so sorry about you losing your dear friend, Deborah."

Tears finally fall onto Deborah's cheeks and she whispers, "No one has ever said those words to me. Thank you, Emily." They give each other a sad smile of understanding.

Following the revelation of these memories, Deborah closes her eyes and in no time her breathing becomes rhythmic. Her thoughts go to a difficult time when Samuel was absent for months. She was lonely, frantic for his business savvy, afraid of what might have happened to him, and frustrated that she had no means of communicating with him.

Emily is just about ready to get up off the chair and leave her old friend to rest when Deborah asks, "Can you tell me about your mother's passing and how it changed Samuel? He had stopped coming around about eight months before she died and I always wondered."

"Oh, it was awful, Deborah," Emily begins. "Mama was beyond frail after she became sick in the spring of 1830. She had always been thin, and yet we could all see her additional weight loss. She was so weak and there was nothing the doctors could do. Papa sent for specialists from New York and even from as far away as Europe. He kept up his spirits to encourage her to brave on, but she died alone in her room, in the quiet of the night.

"He was visibly upset that he wasn't in the room with her when she died. His face became distorted and—the best word I can think of to describe it is—tortured. His eyes remained puffed up from all his weeping. He never even bothered to take hold of his emotions when visitors would come by to pay their respects. He would sit for hours in her favorite chair, staring at the fireplace or out a window. He put his feet up on the settee just as Mama had. He wandered from room to room, crying—and sometimes his whole body convulsed with his loud sobs. He was—pathetic," she finishes, whispering the last word.

"Ahem," Emily clears her throat as she forces herself to move beyond the pity she had felt back then. "Weeks later, his associates and clients came by to seek his counsel on their business matters, but he turned them all away. Days on end would become weeks of the same routine. Papa wouldn't get dressed for work in the mornings and he would not always shave. He started drinking and kept a bottle as a constant companion."

Emily continues, "One day, I approached him as he was in his study and I hoped he was lucid enough to understand what I had to say."

"What did you need to tell him, Emily?" asks Deborah, all wrapped up in any news of her old friend, even as sad as it was.

"I had to tell him that he needed to replenish the household budget as the mercantile bill was due to be paid. There weren't enough funds to cover the staffs' salaries either, but I wanted to start with our basic necessities being covered.

"Papa heard me all right. He looked at the binder I was holding, rose from his chair and reached for it. I was so encouraged that I handed it over as I hoped he was going to take charge. He opened the first page even though I marked the book half way through to the present day. He brushed his fingers on one page after another. You see, the earlier entries were in Mama's handwriting." She shakes her head.

"As sombre and as calmly as he could, he said to me that he would look after this." She imitates her father, "'Come see me tomorrow, my dear. About this time?' 'Of course,' I replied. I was so relieved that it appeared that he was finally going to start functioning normally again."

Emily needs to stretch her legs, rises from her chair and walks to the window to look out onto Chester Street. She says, "The next day, back in his study, he had a glass of whisky on the desk but thankfully, no visible full bottle nearby. He motioned for me to sit, so I did.

"'Emily,' he began, 'you appear to be very good with numbers.' 'I am Papa,' I said. He then took a long swig from the glass, opened a bottom drawer and disappointingly replenished the liquid from a bottle stored there. Then he said, 'You need to work, my sweet. I am thrilled that you are good with numbers. I know someone who needs a bookkeeper and I will send you to work for her. You leave next week.' I don't remember much of what else he said after that. I was dumbfounded."

Deborah nods and having learned something about Samuel, shares her thoughts, "I'm afraid my friend felt deserving of the punishment of losing the love of his life for his mortal sin of adultery. His actions you described, Emily, prove his guilt. He sent you here in the hopes that he could redeem himself. I'm sorry he did that to you."

Emily's mouth gapes open. She comes back to the chair by Deborah's bed and replies, "And, I'm sorry he decided to never see you again, Deborah."

Deborah smiles. She knows that Emily would never have thought that when they first met more than three decades ago, but they had become the very best of friends, always relying on each other.

Deborah sees Emily's lower lip quivering and asks, "There's more? What is it, Emily? Please tell me."

"Well, it was something I realized only after Adeline died."

Mr. Trolley clears his throat to cover a gasp coming from the corner where the mystery person is sitting. "Pardon me. Please, go on."

20
Emily

Two young women stand in front of their twelve-room house. The older of the two is wearing the only travel ensemble that fits her—an overly warm wool dress and matching navy-blue jacket. Their mother's illness had negated their need for new traveling clothes and now their financial struggles deter any such extravagant purchases. The hired driver of the one-horse carriage waits patiently.

"Do not leave me, Emily," sobs her fourteen-year-old sister, Adeline, her otherwise beautiful face swollen from her tears.

"I must. You know I cannot stay. Neither of us will have what Mama wanted for us, but we must go on living. We have said all this before, Adeline. Now, let go of me. Go on." She gently removes Adeline's trembling arms from around her waist.

Seventeen-year-old Emily places her thumbs on her sister's soft cheeks and wipes away the tears. "Look at me." Adeline's eyes move upwards, and Emily puts on a brave smile and says, "We will write each other every week. I promise that one day I will send for you. We will live together again, of that you can be sure."

The blond-haired, blue-eyed sisters give each other one last look before Adeline nods and lets her sister go.

Two minutes into the ride, Emily gives in to her own pressing sorrow. *How could Papa send me away? Does he not love me anymore? What will happen to Adeline? Oh, Mama, I miss you so.*

The train ride from Pennsylvania to Delton takes only one hour and fifteen minutes. It is followed by a hired cab ride to the place indicated on the envelope addressed to Deborah but instructive for Emily's sake: Madam Deborah Seevers, 10 Malloy Avenue, access through the employees' entrance on the side of the building on Chester Street.

The cab driver hastily leaves the young woman the moment he drops her bags at her feet. Emily knocks on the side door of the brothel and Josie, the cook, answers momentarily.

"Good afternoon. I am looking for Madam Seevers," Emily inquires.

"Please, come this way." Josie leads Emily to Deborah's private parlor, first door on the right.

Five minutes later, Josie carries in a tray holding tea and biscuits. "Madam Deb will be here shortly." Emily sits, looking at the appealing biscuits on the tray. Her stomach had been jumping since sun-up and so she had denied herself breakfast rather than risk a stomach upset.

As it is a Monday, when Deborah hears of a visitor, she hopes it is Samuel; his absence in the past several months is a mystery. The presence of a well-dressed and pretty young lady in his stead puzzles her.

"Good day," Emily says, rising when Deborah enters. "Madam Seevers, I have brought you this letter that I am sure will explain my being here today." She hands it over to Deborah and adds, "It is from … "

Deborah interrupts, "I know who it's from. I recognize the handwriting." She holds her head high as she struggles to keep her emotions in check. A letter from Samuel cannot bear good news.

Emily averts her eyes and wonders about her father's business relationship with this beautiful and—yes, dare she even say—sensual woman. Emily watches her reach for the letter opener on the side table and sit down before perusing it.

"Please help yourself to tea while I read."

Emily pours herself a cup of tea and then sits, observing Deborah's reaction to her father's message. She hadn't dared open the message, and is hoping to discover more about her father's relationship with this Madam Seevers, but the expression on the older woman's face discloses nothing.

My dearest Deborah,

I am experiencing difficulties at the present, but they are temporary I assure you.

In the meantime, I have sent my oldest daughter to work as your bookkeeper. I was surprised and pleased to learn of her ability with numbers. I am sure you will find her skills a benefit to your business.

I remain, your friend forever, Samuel.

The message is void of information. Deborah is disappointed with his note—he had always shared his feelings and thoughts with her in the past. *Maybe he is afraid his daughter would have read the letter?* She wonders.

"So, you're here to work. Do you know what my business entails?"

"Ah, no. Why? Will it matter? I can keep books on whatever it is you do."

"Well, I don't run a fabric shop."

"I am sure I can do the numbers for whatever it is, Madam Deb, otherwise, my father would not have sent me."

"Don't be too sure about that. What's your name?"

"Emily, Madam Deb. Emily Thordeaux."

"I will call you Emily if you call me Deborah. Now, how old are you, child?"

"I will be eighteen next May. Old enough to not be referred to as a child anymore," says Emily defensively.

"I'm sure. That's just a habit of mine. Pay no heed, pet."

Emily notes that she has not apologized. As if reading her mind, Deborah says, "I don't apologize unnecessarily. What I said is not an insult. I don't often say I'm sorry because I always think before I speak and when I do say I am sorry, you'll know that I mean it most sincerely."

Deborah stands, which makes Emily get up too, and instructs, "Now, I'm a fair boss. You listen to me and we'll get along quite nicely. Pick up your things and follow me."

Emily does as she is told.

Once outside the parlor, they walk down the hallway toward a set of French doors, but when they reach them, they turn left, to another hallway that reveals a short set of stairs leading to the second floor. On the way to the stairs, the women walk past two doors on their right. "We have a watchman and a full-time cook. Those are their bedrooms," Deborah informs Emily, noting her glances at the closed doors.

At the top of the stairs, Deborah points to the door immediately in front of them and says, "This is my room." She then leads Emily down to the right, pointing first right and then left, "This is the water closet that we will share. Across from it here, is the office where you'll spend your working days."

A little further, she points left once more, "This is a storage room. It's probably big enough for another bedroom but I only use it for storage at the moment." Deborah points to the last door on the right, "This will be your room. Josie will tell you where to find sheets and towels. For now, just drop your bags here and come back with me to your office."

Before turning to leave the bedroom, Deb knocks on the farthest bedroom wall. "We have walked through the private side of the house, the residence. But it is the business that is on the other side of this wall that will require your accounting attention. Those of us who live on this side access the business through those French doors downstairs."

In the little office, Deb smiles as she will soon escape the dreaded doldrums of office work. "Now, this will be your desk. Please, have a seat."

Emily looks at the large wooden desk facing the entrance. A wall of shelves behind the desk displays record books and office supplies. Two guest chairs face the desk. Two pictures, one of a waterfall and the other of a field of bent-over wheat seemingly accosted by a strong wind, hang on the walls. They look out of place in the dimly lit room; not unlike how Emily feels.

Deborah wishes Samuel had told Emily about the nature of her business. It would have made this conversation much easier. How do you delicately introduce the subject of a business based on sex? She decides to just blurt out, "Do you know what a brothel is?"

Emily knows what the word means—but she is unsure whether she should say that she does know. Doesn't knowing the answer to such a question suggest that she is less of a proper lady? She decides to take the more innocent route and replies, "No."

"Do you know what sex is?"

"Madam Deb, Miss Seevers! That, that is a disturbing question!"

"Ah, so you do know what it means then."

"Yes, but I do not know why you are asking me such things."

"Because I'm a madam of a brothel. It's a place where men come and pay women to have sex with them."

Emily blushes and feels faint at the declaration.

"Don't worry. You won't need to do anything outside this room."

"Outside this room? Do you expect me to, to … What exactly do you expect me to do in here?"

"You clearly misunderstand. You're not here to work as a prostitute. That is what's on the other side of your bedroom wall."

Emily's look of relief doesn't quite overshadow the disgust. Deborah thinks, *Just like her father. She didn't even try to hide that look of disdain on her face at the mention of the word "prostitute."*

"I'll rely on you to do all the paperwork of my business. I come in here most days from ten in the morning until two in the afternoon. The more you learn, the less I'll need to be here. You'll know the routine by the end of the week. It's really very simple. You see … "

Deborah spends the next hour talking about the flow of the paperwork and the two sets of books that Emily is expected to keep and why. It takes almost all that time for Emily's blushed cheeks to return to their normal color.

"I must get ready to go to work now. Why don't you unpack and make a list of the things you need from Josie. She's in charge of the laundry and such. I won't be joining you for supper, but that'll give you more time to get familiar with your surroundings. The kitchen is just past Josie's bedroom. She will make you an evening meal."

Deborah pauses. "Emily, I'm glad you're here," she lies. "I hope you'll be too, one day." She turns to leave the small office.

"Wait, Madam Deb. What did my father's letter say?"

"Nothing other than him having full confidence that you have the skills to do this job well. Now, please call me Deborah."

Deborah heads to her room, thinking about Samuel's well being. She is relieved to know he's still alive, however she isn't any wiser about anything else. Now, more than ever, she despises the fact that she's never had any ability to contact him directly. At his request, she had agreed to never write or wire. She always had to wait for a Monday before asking his help with anything or for telling him something important. Now what? She knows Emily's presence means a permanent stop to his visits. He certainly isn't going to visit with his daughter under her roof.

Several minutes later, Emily hears Deborah dash down the stairs and through the set of French doors to the other side. The silence tells her it is safe to cry and she runs out of the office to her bedroom and throws herself onto the bare mattress. She is so unhappy with her predicament. What kind of a life is she going to live now? What can she do about it?

Deborah is proven correct. After just one week, Emily knows almost all there is to know about the paperwork required for the business. Much like her father, she can clearly see where small changes would improve record keeping and business strategy. Deborah is keen to listen and adopts many of Emily's suggestions. When Emily makes necessary corrections and starts suggesting slight changes to schedules and accounts, Deborah pays attention.

For the rest of their lives, these two women will consult and listen to each other. Deborah soon relies on Emily for all the administrative needs of both the household and the business.

21

Emily and Adeline

The first week of letters from Adeline contain the rantings of a child who isn't getting her way:

Papa has me doing household chores. I do not know how to cook! Emily, I do not even know how to dust. I want to please him in the hopes that he will be kind enough to bring you back home. When I work all day and he does not even notice, I wonder why I bother.

Most days, I am all alone in the house.

Why, even the gardener resigned his post. He complained that there was too much work for so little pay. He had a great deal of work already, but then Papa wanted him to drive his carriage at all hours, too. So, he packed his things and left.

Oh, Emily, you would come back if I convinced Papa to send for you, would you not?

Emily's letters are vague and superficial. Adeline is not old enough to be able to read a deeper message in their contents, otherwise she would have sensed that Emily feels abandoned and is most unhappy.

Deborah is kind to me. She is willing to teach me what I have not already learned by myself regarding keeping business records. She has offered me Sunday and Monday as days off, but I find I have nothing to do nor anywhere special to go. I try to get out for a walk in the park every day. The park is across the street from the building where I work and live. I always exit the house from the door that opens onto Chester Street (that is the door for the residential part of the building). It opens onto a pretty space with a bench where I sometimes sit and think.

I have no friends here. Oh, the people are all friendly enough, but I have no one special—well, no one my age. I miss you.

There is a market on the other side of the park which is interesting to wander about. I rarely go shopping as I need nothing. I have no need for material for a new dress as I attend no tea parties, no coming-out soirees, no piano lessons, no—anything. I do indulge in a new book once a month.

I do not mind that I have nothing special to buy as I am saving all my pennies to send for you one day. I hope to be doing that soon. Be brave and patient.

Both girls often weep themselves to sleep at night. Circumstances beyond their control shape new and unwanted lives for them to live. Unfortunate incidences have made them paupers.

Samuel has died with Elizabeth. His is not a physical death—that would have been too beneficial for everyone concerned, especially his daughters. No—he died a much slower death; his emotional heart dying along with the physical death of his most precious wife. His guilt of infidelity filters into his every thought and turns him into a sad, self-abused and broken man, living in flesh only.

Months go by slowly. Emily understands from Adeline's letters of complaints that their father has yet to appropriately look after the financial needs of the household. This leads Emily to include money in her post for Adeline to buy food and other essential items.

I know it is not much but it is all I can spare. I will send more if it is not enough. Just let me know. I will take it from the savings that I put aside to send for you one day. It will delay our seeing each other once more, but you need to eat. Love, Emily

Gradually, Adeline's letters of the past three years change from those of a child's complaints to a more mature young woman's news. She ceases to focus on her life's unfortunate occurrences. She tells Emily about her separation from their father and how she obtains a new address.

Nevertheless, there is so much more she could have shared than what she wrote in her letters to her sister.

22
Emily and Adeline

A year later, in the late afternoon of a cold and windy March day, eighteen-year-old Adeline Thordeaux struggles to take another step as she heads toward the southeast side of Delton. She is in the middle of her ninth month of pregnancy and chides herself for not seeking out her sister Emily earlier.

A blizzard on the north side of Lake Michigan in early spring is not uncommon, but the winds from this one had unexpectedly traveled farther southeasterly. Gusting snow obliterates Adeline's view but the wind is conveniently at her back and helps her to push forward. As she has never been to her sister's home, she isn't sure she will find it in the fast-fading daylight.

With relief, Adeline is surrounded by buildings now and she can see their outlines well. She knows she's on the correct street when she sees a sign on the side of a building naming it. She is distraught as she has yet to see any house that resembles the description from one of Emily's letters.

After crossing an intersection, she notices a line of trees on her right. She is encouraged and thinks, *That must be the park Emily spoke of in her letters.* Adeline desperately searches for any light shining from a candle or lamp through a window or even faintly through shutters. If she finds anyone at home, even at a wrong address, she will beg to stay the night and resume her search in the morning. She is exhausted and doesn't think she can go on much further.

Her swift prayers are answered when she spots a dim light coming from a building fifteen feet ahead of her. She prods forward with renewed strength. Out of breath, she shifts the weight of the worn-out valise that holds all her worldly possessions to her left shoulder and with all her might, knocks loudly on the door.

Within seconds, a man's deep voice can be heard from behind the door. "Are you dumb, man? We're not open in this God-forsaken weather—you should have stayed home!" Regardless of his words, he releases the latches to let in whatever poor freezing creature is standing there on the other side.

A calmness encompasses Adeline as she drops into the big man's arms. He easily lifts her up off her feet and kicks the door shut on the gusting, stinging sleet. Jim carries her to the parlor of the residential side of the house, and as he passes the French doors, he calls out in his loud boisterous voice, "Deborah, Emily, Josie, come quickly."

By the time Deborah and Emily come down the stairs, Josie is stoking the fire and Jim is standing, looking down at the person he has placed on the sofa. Both women quickly assess the situation, push Jim aside, and take charge to remove the winter garments and layers of scarves from their mysterious guest. As soon as the heaviest garments have been pulled away, they can easily tell their guest is far along in her pregnancy.

In spite of the cold, sweat covers Adeline's brow. The snow that clings to her eyes and nose, melts and dampens her down to her neck. Her exhaustion reveals itself as dark circles under her eyes.

A shocked Emily recognizes her to be her sister as soon as the removal of the last scarf exposes her face. She gently taps the young woman on both cheeks and says, "Adeline, what are you doing here? Where did you come from? Why are you not at home, safe? *And* somewhere near a midwife?"

The forty-seven-year-old Deborah, recognizing Adeline's name and becoming hopeful to hear news of her dear friend Samuel, realizes that Adeline cannot answer Emily's questions. Deborah says gently, "Give her time, Emily. She has to catch her breath. Josie, please prepare tea and bread with jam."

After fifteen minutes of rest Adeline hears Deborah say, "Jim, can you go find Adeline's horse and put him in the barn?"

Adeline mumbles, "No horse." She inhales and gasps, "Left him in a shack about a mile back." Adeline doesn't see their eyes popping wide open and eyebrows lifting with surprise at her comment.

By the time Josie brings in the tea and bread, everyone is surrounding Adeline in the curious hopes that she will tell them what brings her here, at this hour, and in her condition. Deborah can sense that Adeline doesn't want to divulge anything to anyone but Emily. No matter how curious they all are, Deborah shoos Jim and Josie out of the front room and shuts the door behind her, leaving the two sisters to talk.

Adeline summons her remaining energy to tell Emily what has happened since she left their home. She has not told Emily everything in her weekly correspondence and hopes she will be forgiven for the omissions.

Holding on to each others hands, Adeline begins, "After Papa sent you away to Delton, his moods and behavior became even more unreasonable and I am afraid to say, somewhat violent. It was all gradual, of course, as small things just got more problematic—like his drinking and staying out late."

Emily's own memory flashes back to the month she had celebrated her seventeenth birthday, although it was not much of a commemoration. Her mother's illness had delayed her debutante's ball the year before. After her mother's death, her debut would only be possible if she could find a neighboring mother who would agree to double up and share the cost. She knew that every year that passed, she was less likely to find a proper husband and her place in society. To her dismay, instead of her father assisting her in finding a woman to help her enter into society, he sent her away.

Adeline continues with the telling of her story.

Samuel's drunkenness intertwines with his constant grief. His thoughts become garbled and Adeline overhears his delusional conversations. In his mind, Deborah and Elizabeth have met. He also imagines visiting Emily in Deborah's home and openly compliments them both on a job well learned and well done. He had never met a more independent woman than Deborah, so who better to teach his daughter how to support herself and possibly even her sister in the future?

As Samuel's drink became his constant companion, he no longer could tell night from day. He often found his youngest daughter in her room, eating bread with jam or raw vegetables. It didn't register with him that servants were no longer in his house and that Adeline was struggling to do the necessary tasks like cooking.

The remaining staff had left their posts once they realized that their late wages would not be forthcoming. Understandably, many left with expensive collectibles, stolen as form of payment.

One day, when Samuel found Adeline sitting in Elizabeth's closet with several of her frocks spread out, he lost his senses. "How dare you be in here with your mother's things!" he roared.

"But Papa … " she began, trying to explain why she wanted to be surrounded by her mother's belongings.

He wasn't paying attention and didn't notice the innocent purity of the scene. He was vibrating with anger, barely holding himself back from hitting her. He shouted for her to go to her room. Adeline rose and hastily hung up one of her mother's dresses before escaping more of his wrath.

Samuel locked the door and wept himself into a drunkard's nightmarish sleep. He never realized that his daughter also needed to grieve.

It could have been possible for him to survive on his vast savings but he had taken up gambling. To add to his troubles, on a particularly warm evening, he thought he had seen Deborah outside the opera house. In the hopes that she had moved to his city, he started to frequent the brothels of Philadelphia in search of her. Yet he never reasoned that it couldn't be her as she was burdened with caring for his eldest daughter.

Samuel felt the heavy loss of family and the companionship of the old, trustworthy friends that he and Elizabeth had alienated from their lives. The guilt and shame kept him from seeking anyone's council.

His youngest daughter was ill equipped to deal with his depression and grief. She certainly did not have the influence over him to insist he cease his costly vices. Even Emily, who was slightly less naive, couldn't have helped him had she been home to witness such a downfall.

Unfortunately, no other responsible adult, not even Samuel's barrister, was aware of what was happening. Samuel's finances were no one's business but his own. No one was in authority to put a stop to Samuel's out-of-control gambling and eventually he gambled away his estate, his daughters' futures, and the family's place in society. He was destitute and now desperate to find a reasonably safe home for his youngest daughter. He at the very least cared that much before sinking further.

Adeline almost felt shame when she described the time when her father's financial losses were discovered, and how scandal and shunning attached themselves to the Thordeaux name.

Emily could imagine all those tongues wagging and, in her naivety, resolved to one day change society's opinion of her last name. After she arrived at Deborah's home and fully understood the nature of Deb's business, she was furious. But instead of running away, she overcame her contempt of her father by attacking her work with vim and vigor, determined to earn and save every penny she could to reunite with her sister and set themselves up in a proper establishment.

Over several months in Madam Deb's employ, it dawned on Emily that her living arrangements would impede her meeting a decent man who could understand her dire situation. Even if she did meet such a gentleman, surely her family history would make her an undesirable mate. So, she vowed to never get close enough to a decent man or fall in love. She would never risk having the misfortune of losing a potential husband or humiliating herself further due to her father's unfortunate decisions. No decent man would invite distasteful baggage like Emily's past into his life.

Eventually, Emily grew to like and respect Deborah. She decided that prostitution was not a profession Deb would have chosen, but that events must have led her to take such a path. In the remaining entitled haughtiness of her youth, Emily *forgave* Deborah for her unfortunate choice of employment. As if Emily had a right to do so!

23
Emily and Adeline

Emily's side-tracked thoughts are snapped back by Adeline's faltering voice. "As you know from my letters, Papa would start drinking whenever he would wake and would not stop until he dropped on his bed, or fell asleep in his study.

"If you recall, I wrote shortly before my seventeenth birthday that Papa visited a business acquaintance and his wife at their home—the Gateway Estate. Do you remember we visited that place when we were small?"

Emily recalls the summer parties at the Gateway Estate. All the children laughing and the adults sitting in the shade, women drinking lemonade discussing the latest courtship scandals and the men drinking something stronger, talking about politics.

"Father apparently begged them to take me on as an employee. Although they did not owe Papa anything, they graciously accepted to hire me. You see, they were expecting their nieces to stay with them for the month of May and they hoped that I could tend to the needs of these twin girls. I really did not know what to do with the girls until I discovered their love of dresses. I taught them the simple art of sewing and matching materials and whatnot." Adeline's voice fades away.

Emily knows they are approaching the events that had been missing from Adeline's letters—the romance resulting in this pregnancy! A nine-month pregnancy is most certainly a significant piece of information to withhold!

Emily immediately regrets not borrowing the money from Deborah to pay the transportation for Adeline to join her in Delton. Emily has not been able to put aside enough money for the travel as she had forwarded Adeline a monthly stipend up until the time her sister was living at the Gateway Estate.

From Adeline's letters, Emily had not fully understood how desperate Adeline's circumstances had become at home with her father. Adeline would have asked Emily to think of a solution had their father not found a suitable place for her to live. But once she was settled at the Gateway Estate, she also wanted to give her new situation a chance before leaving Philadelphia for good and becoming a burden to her older sister.

The welfare of his daughters no longer a concern, Samuel vanishes into the most neglected streets of Philadelphia. No one knew where he could be found or cared to know his whereabouts and he was quickly forgotten by the elite circles of society. His gambling debt was paid off by the proceeds from the sale of the empty mansion, as he sold everything left that had value.

The carefree, worry-free life the girls once lived is only a fond and distant memory. Their correspondence revealed a commonality, they both considered themselves orphans and declared their father dead—just like their mother—to anyone who asked, not that many did. It's so much easier to go on pretending that they're destitute as a result of their parents' death than to explain all the unfortunate sadness and loss of wealth and reputation.

Adeline continues to tell Emily what her letters haven't. "I met David on my first day taking care of the girls. You remember him, do you not?"

"Yes. He is the youngest son. Quite handsome, if I recall. Go on."

Adeline is pleased that Emily remembers him. "Actually, he is their only child. He was everything Mama would have wanted for me in a husband, I am sure of it, Emily! He treated me like a lady and not like a servant, or someone hired to act as a nanny to his cousins. He was courteous and gentle in his manner of speaking. He was always so thoughtful and considerate of my feelings and well-being.

"I did not know how to be the keeper of his very active cousins. David made things easier for me with suggestions of walks in the park, swimming in the pond, and even going to the fair. He accompanied us on every excursion. A month after I arrived, the twins left and my role was redefined. I was assigned duties of a maid. I would have been better off with duties involving sewing, however they already had someone in that post.

"Happily, and unfortunately too, in just those few weeks, David and I had fallen in love. He assured me he would love me forever and that he would do right by me. I believed him. Especially when he said we would send for you to come live with us. How could he be anything but genuine with a promise like that?

"But life is cruel, Emily. I would be punished for Papa's weaknesses. David's parents would never risk inviting scandal into their home and especially not into their only child's otherwise promising future. When they found out about our friendship, they sent David away to Europe. I am sure he will forget me. He probably already has." She hiccups a sob.

"The night before he was to leave, we were both so sad with the knowledge that we might never see each other again that we got carried away. My gift of myself was all I had left to give. I hoped to become a fleeting smile in his later years when he would remember what little time we shared together.

"My most misguided choice to give myself in that way would become an adverse decision. I am with child. By the time I started showing, his parents badly wanted me gone from their home."

"So, David does not know?" asks Emily, wide-eyed.

"No. I was basically pawned off to the Clarksons who owed the family a small favor of sorts. I took that change of residence as an opportunity to also change my last name to Breat, mother's maiden name."

"I noticed that on the last half dozen letters, Adeline. I thought it was a clever idea to avoid connection to our father, but you had not really mentioned the full reason why you did it. Now I know," says Emily.

"I had other things on my mind."

"I wish you would have told me, Adeline. I would have borrowed money from Deborah and would have fetched you myself."

"Yes, well, I thought I should take care of myself, Emily—now that I was going to become a mother. Besides, I so hoped that I might see David again that I stayed in the area as long as I could. I was wrong, Emily, so wrong. He has forgotten me," she sobs.

"Stop that. Please know that I love you and I am excited that you are here. I cannot wait to meet your child. We will manage. Nothing will ever separate us again. Do you hear me?"

Emily isn't sure how she feels about becoming an aunt, but she would never turn away from her sister. Living here in a brothel is scandalous, however no one who is anyone knows she abides there. Adding an unwed mother to her life can be kept a secret in a house like this. But would Adeline be able to stay? And with her baby?

Adeline gives her a weak smile. She adds, "Yes, I hear you. You know, I never realized how far away Delton was from Philadelphia. When the weather turned bad and my hired coachman refused to go any further, I released the horse from its reins and rode it, bare back, for at least four miles. But I guess I had pushed that poor animal too far. He just stopped in his tracks and refused to go one step further. So, I dismounted in the most lady-like fashion I could manage and left him in an abandoned barn about a mile northwest of here—or maybe it was a shack.

"Anyway, I went too far north and realized that I would have to backtrack. Lucky for me I had the wind at my back because if I had to face it, by myself, in my condition, I am pretty sure I would have had to spend the night with the horse in that empty building," she almost chuckles but it isn't worth the effort.

Emily says, "I will give Jim the vague directions so he can go look for the horse in the morning."

Adeline nods and continues, "Emily? I am not feeling very well. Do you mind if I just go to sleep now and we can resume our chat in the morning?"

Emily gives her sister a warm hug and replies, "Of course, I do not mind. We can talk later when you wake up, Adeline. You can stay right here too. Are you comfortable enough?"

Adeline nods, closes her eyes and drifts off before Emily finishes puffing up the cushions surrounding her. Emily reaches for the comforter situated on the back of the couch and covers up her only sibling. Then she sits in the chair next to the sofa to keep an eye on her sister who is barely eighteen-years-old and soon to be a mother.

Emily mulls over everything Adeline has just told her and becomes angrier with each passing minute. She thinks, *I have to give David's parents a piece of my mind!* But knows she is bound to her sister, here in Delton, at least until she gives birth to this baby.

She only gives her father a fleeting thought. She had been very angry with him at the beginning. Then when she believed she had come to the end of her grieving for her mother, she denied any feelings she may have had left over for her male parent. That man who never acted like a father after his wife's death, made destructive choices, and ruined everything for everybody.

It was so easy to dismiss him from her heart as long as she didn't think about how he was during the years when Elizabeth was still alive. A little sob escapes her lungs. That had been a time when he was the best of fathers.

24
Emily and Daniel

Emily must have fallen asleep because moaning coming from the sofa wakes her up. She sits up straight, feeling the kink in her neck from the slumped position she has been in for the past three hours.

Adeline is feverish and thrashing about on the couch. Emily dashes into the hallway and wakes up the household when she calls out, "Deborah! Josie! Come quickly." She doesn't have to explain what's happening.

Deborah beckons Josie to go find a midwife. She knows it is pointless as Josie will exhaust herself fighting snow banks and winds but she begs Josie to try nonetheless. When she turns to go back into the parlor, she notices that Emily is motionless.

Deborah grabs the older sister by the arms and says soothingly but firmly, "Emily, she's not the first woman to be having a baby. She'll be alright. We'll place her on the floor, get some cushions and get things ready for the midwife. Now, shall we get started?"

A relieved Emily nods. Someone is taking charge and giving out orders.

Meanwhile and as expected, Josie can't find a midwife in the nearby vicinity. She treks further and further away until she runs out of streets to search. No one of any profession knowledgeable in Adeline's condition will be present in her hour of need.

Emily and Deborah do the best they can. Luckily, because of the storm, the house will not open for business early today or maybe not even open at all. When the working girls awaken and enter the residential side for breakfast, they happen upon this commotion and most ask if they can be of any assistance. Deborah sends one to fetch more blankets, one to get hot water, and one to get breakfast food cooked for everybody in Josie's absence.

Somehow in all that excitement, Emily remembers to tell the watchman about the approximate location of the building where Adeline has abandoned the horse. He doesn't have to be asked twice to go look for it—especially with a pregnant woman in the house who is about to give birth. He welcomes the excuse to get away.

Adeline's fever is worrisome. She is delirious, frantically screaming out, even cursing. After about an hour with no sign of Josie and a midwife, Deborah and Emily convince each other that they can help deliver this baby. Emily is reassured by Deborah that after the baby is born, her sister will be more coherent. For now, the two women are almost relieved that Adeline isn't aware that an expert is not in the room with them.

They can't tell if Adeline can hear them when they ask her to push and to breathe, when to relax and when to bear down. Adeline continues to flail about until the baby's head appears from the birth canal. Emily and Deborah can sense each other's panic. When Adeline's body goes totally still, they know that if either or both mother and child has a chance, now is the time to act.

Deborah instructs Emily to slip behind and partly under her sister's upper body. Emily pushes Adeline forward when Deborah tells her to. Deborah pulls the baby out and delivers him safely onto the blanket where she cuts the umbilical cord. Then she picks him up and slaps his little bottom. He wails from the assault but his cries fall on his mother's deafened ears.

Emily is numb and motionless, disbelieving. How could her young and strong sister just die like that? It's not possible! Then she explodes, "Deborah, do something! Adeline is not breathing. And where did all this blood come from? What is happening?"

Emily swallows hard. She is still sitting behind her sister in the position to help her push. She howls and starts rocking back and forth, her sister in her arms. "How could this happen? What am I going to do? I am all alone. Adeline, do not leave me. Do not … " she screams at the top of her lungs.

The scattered women around the room are glued to witnessing this scene of despair. The second last day of March 1834 is full of overwhelming sadness instead of hope and awe.

Ten minutes later, Josie returns, alone. By the time she arrives, Deborah and the other women have cleaned the baby and helped Emily wash her hands. In silence, Deborah gently removes the soiled apron from Emily's waist and sits her down on the corner chair. Then she motions for one of the girls to come help her clean up Adeline and to cover up her still body.

Exhaustion moves Emily from the room where her sister died and where her nephew was born, to her bedroom up the flight of stairs. Her face is ashen when she drops onto her bed and cries herself to sleep. Emily sleeps the rest of the day and all of the night.

By evening of that dreadful day, Deborah has enlisted the life-giving nourishment that the boy so readily needs. A young unwed woman was easy to find in this area, especially after Deborah promises to pay the wet-nurse for her trouble. It is easier for the young mother to move in with her own child and she soon occupies the storage room along with the two babes, across the hall from Emily's bedroom. Deborah writes up a contract that states that the nursing mother will leave the premises as soon as the boy is weaned. As the woman is only looking for money, she quickly agrees to the terms.

The watchman later reports to Deborah that he had located the horse. As there would be no way to know the true owner of the animal, the watchman sold the steed to the local livery stable for forty dollars. Deborah applies the money toward payment for the wet-nurse.

Emily wakes to find that her sister's body has been moved to the undertaker's. Not many people can afford such luxuries. Emily feels indebted to Deborah as she is grateful that Adeline's body is not kept in the house until arrangements can be made for burial.

Deborah attends the funeral with Emily and asks Josie to join them. It is a very quiet and quick affair that occurs before the baby boy is three days old.

Emily is given all the time she needs to grieve. Everyone does so differently, so Deborah doesn't question Emily when she finds her working hard with the books in the afternoons or even with the light from an oil lamp late into the night.

One week passes before Deborah gently asks Emily at breakfast, "What are you going to name the boy?"

Stunned by the question, a grieving and confused Emily wonders out loud, "I am not sure I should name him. I might give him up for adoption."

Deborah knows that Emily will have a long boring life ahead of her, especially seeing as she rarely steps out of the house. After her first month in Delton, Emily had even quit going to Sunday services when she heard that the minister and some of the members of the ladies' auxiliary group would pay new members a home visit—which, of course, she couldn't allow. The isolated Emily had ventured out even less so after that incident.

Deborah doesn't think it wise for the near twenty-one-year-old Emily to become all alone this early in her life, and possibly regret that decision later on. She convinces Emily to hold off until she has had more time to think clearly, she knows full well that if Emily spends more time with the boy, she will fall in love and never be able to let him go.

"Why should I name him? I can not keep him here!"

"What makes you say that, Emily?"

"Well, there has not been a baby here ever, as far as I know."

"We've had mothers with their babies, just none that decided to stay. But … "

Emily interrupts, "This is a brothel! What kind of a home is that to raise a child in. You have never had a baby, have you?"

"Why no. I've never even been pregnant."

"Did you ever want children?"

"Personally, no. I don't think I can have any. You see, a couple of years after I became a woman, I noticed that all the women in the brothel had a monthly cycle. I never did. My cycle occurred only once every six months and that is likely why I never got pregnant."

"Did you talk to a doctor about that?"

"No. Why tempt fate, right?"

"So, why would you allow one now?"

"Because, it's you, Emily. You're my closest friend. I would be devastated if you moved out because of the boy when it's of no bother to have the both of you stay. Besides, you wouldn't be alone in raising him. I would help and I suspect that everybody else in this place would pitch in. We're all very fond of you and having a baby around would be a welcomed change."

Deborah watches Emily struggle with her doubts and counsels her further, "Maybe name the boy for now. If you decide to put him up for adoption later, he may be able to keep the name. At least he would have something of his own that way."

That afternoon Emily is sitting at her desk, deep in thought and scribbling her sister's name on a scrap piece of paper. She fixates on the mixture of the letters and sees his written there—Daniel. She tells Deborah at supper time that the boy will be named Daniel and that his last name will be Breat.

Emily also changes her last name to Breat, as Adeline did when she was released of her duties at the Gateway Estate. The residents of Philadelphia had long ago forgotten about Emily and Adeline Thordeaux, and less than five people here in Delton would ever remember Thordeaux as Emily's original last name.

There is never another mention of putting Daniel up for adoption. Emily and Daniel will stay where they are welcomed and loved.

It took a while for Deborah to hear about the last conversation Emily had with her sister but when she did, she tried to imagine the man she once knew and loved—as a drunkard—but couldn't picture it. Samuel had been her silent partner and even after she had paid her debt to him in full, she knew she could rely on him for absolutely anything. Deborah didn't know until it was too late, that his income and accumulated wealth diminished to nothing, otherwise she would have tried to contact him and offer to help.

With the passing of time, when Deborah tried to envision him, his face would be overshadowed by Emily's. She would then eerily sense Emily's superior attitude toward her and just as quickly dismiss it to the younger woman's upbringing. Deborah overlooked that characteristic flaw in the girl just as she did with the father.

Both Deborah and Emily put their tea cup aside. It is late afternoon and luckily Deborah still shows no signs of repercussions from her fall. On the contrary, she is enjoying this precious time in conversation with Emily and urges her on with a question, "What did you learn after your sister's death, Emily?"

"Well, it was when I saw Adeline struggling during childbirth and not being able to communicate any of her thoughts and hopes, that I realized that Mama had also been so weak for so long that she could not even write down words or speak. I knew then in my heart, that if she had been able to tell Papa what she had planned for our futures, he would have made it happen. Papa was not himself. He was sick with grief. I believe that he forgot that Mama would have taught us the importance of becoming a proper lady and an upstanding woman that any man would be proud to have as a wife.

"She taught us that being graced with sure fingers to play a piano or blessed with nimble fingers to sew or draw would only add to our quality of life. If only he had known, he would have realized that arrangements should have been made to find us husbands—or at the very least send us to live with a relative."

"You realized all that the night Adeline died?"

"No. Not right away. It took me years to figure it all out, but it started with her inability to speak when it was crucial for me to know her dying wishes, especially with respect to her child."

"You mean like telling the father?" Deborah asks.

She nods. "Yes. I have been guilt-ridden with that. I think that Adeline would have wanted David to know, especially if he still loved her," Emily replies sadly.

"Stop berating yourself, pet. Guilt killed the man you once called Papa. Don't let it control you. Forgive your father and forgive yourself for not knowing Adeline's wishes."

Deborah's words reach Emily's ears and heart. Feeling the freedom of forgiving herself, Emily convulses into new tears for all her losses.

25
Emily

Mr. Trolley stands to refresh his coffee and asks, "That was a most treasured conversation you had with Madam Deb, was it not?"

"Yes. Indeed," replies Emily with fondness.

"I apologize for asking my next question, but I am curious now. How was life in a brothel with a newborn?"

Emily takes a sip of water, musing how different her life would have been without Daniel. Had he not been born, had there not been an infant for her to look after ... She shudders, then begins with her most precious and pleasant of memories and doesn't stop talking until she has shared her favorite stories about Daniel's childhood.

Emily had no doubt that she would have loved this child had he just been her nephew, but because of her sister's death, she loves the infant on a level that she didn't know existed. She is grateful for the opportunity of knowing how blissfully different and joy-filled her life has become.

But life with two infants in a house is challenging—in a brothel it's arduous. Some of the customers would complain if one of the babies cried

since one of the reasons many of the men had left their own homes for
a few hours was to get away from children and noise. Eventually, Emily
and the wet-nurse adapted to the babies' needs and rarely let them cry for
more than one minute. Except for breast feeding, the two mothers stick
to a regime of four hours on and four hours off. It is during one of those
four hours on Emily's shift, that brings her great trepidation, because
some things can occur in a brothel that wouldn't happen anywhere else.

Downstairs that evening, Deb overseas the brothel's customers as
usual. She recognizes a man she hasn't seen in a while and asks, "Where
have you been, Johnny? It's been months!" She hands the big beast of
a man a drink and walks with him to his favorite chair near the corner
where he can observe all the girls before making his selection.

"You mean before coming here? Drinking at Harley's saloon. Ha-
ha. Actually, my dear Deb, I've been digging up coal north of here. It's
been too long and I'm as ready as a bear out of hibernation tonight,
if you know what I mean. Maybe you have a special for me?" Johnny
slurs and winks.

Deb knows his specialty. "Do you really think one of the girls
working for me would be much of a virgin?" She laughs out loud. "No,
the best I can do is send you up to my room." They have played this
pretend game before.

"Oh yeah? When can I go up for my surprise then?"

She looks around, "Now's a good time. I'll be just a few minutes. Go
ahead. You know the way."

Johnny polishes off the liquor in his glass, grabs another one and
heads for the second floor. But instead of using the stairs leading to the
girls' rooms, he accesses the residential side of the building through the
French doors and uses the adjacent staircase there on his left.

He finishes the second drink before reaching the top step and places the empty glass on the floor by the wall. From this bent over position, out of the corner of his eye, he observes a young, slim woman shut a door on the far-left side and turn to enter a lit room on the right side of the hallway.

A surprise, hey? Oh, I knew she could deliver. I like blonds, he thinks, standing up and heading toward the light.

Emily settles down on the only chair in her room for a few hours of reading to pass time until it is the wet-nurse's turn to tend to the babies' needs. Even though she can hear the chatter from downstairs and smell the overwhelming smoke from cigars, she keeps her door open to better hear the two babies if one of them cries.

The hair on the back of her head raises up when she hears her bedroom door click shut and she feels the blood drain from her face to her chest.

She has halfway turned to see who is there when he is upon her already. Emily yells and jumps out of her chair. He catches her easily. How can she escape this grotesquely muscled man? He holds her right hand behind her back, presses against her body with his and grabs her by the jaw with his massive hand before she can scream a second time.

He squeezes her tender cheeks and her lips can't help but part. "There, there. No need to fuss, darlin'. I'm here to open my surprise. Ha-ha—open. That's funny." He exhales an alcohol filled breath into Emily's unwilling mouth.

"Don't fight me, deary. Unless you like it rough. Big Johnny will give you what you need. Just tell me how you want it, okay? No more screaming?"

She is surprised she can hear him speak as her heartbeat is pounding loudly in her ears. Emily makes a motion to nod even though he hasn't let go of her jaw, which is hurting worse than a toothache.

He covers her mouth with his and moves his free hand down her chest as she desperately tries to squirm away. She is shocked at his assault and fears what he may do next. As soon as her mouth is free of his disgusting face, she releases an adrenaline-filled scream and he quickly covers her mouth with his hand once more.

Being drunk, he easily becomes agitated and bellows, "Now you're just pissing me off. Oh, I'm going to enjoy this. I'll remember to thank Deb for a feisty one, later on. Wherever did she find you?"

He places his lips over hers so she can't scream and with the newly freed hand, takes turns tearing at her dress and undoing his pants. He will completely undress and do it all over again afterwards, but for now, he can't withhold his eagerness and need. In his drunken stupor, he falls on the bed, trapping her underneath him.

She panics but is helpless against this ape.

He leans in to kiss her bared chest and suddenly feels a knock on his head from something very hard. He turns his head up to the right, "What's … " he doesn't finish his question because he's looking into the barrel of a gun.

"You don't listen very well, do you Johnny? I said for you to go to my room. This woman's not for you. Do you understand? Get off her." Deb doesn't take the aim of her gun off him.

The guard standing at the bedroom door escorts Johnny out of the room, down the stairs and off the property.

Sheepishly, Deborah turns to look at Emily, "I'm so sorry, Emily. I don't know what possessed him. He misunderstood what I meant. He's drunk." She tries to apologize further but knows she's to blame for the grave mistake.

Emily rises and covers up her body with remnants of her dress. "Leave me alone, Deb. I need to calm down from all of this. Can you ask the wet-nurse to watch Daniel a little earlier tonight? I need to bathe his filthy paws off me and change clothes and ah … "

When Deb backs away passed the door, Emily closes it without finishing her sentence. Deb has no choice but to wake up the nursing mother to take over for Emily earlier than scheduled, then go back to her job downstairs.

It takes Emily a couple of weeks to remember, however, that Deborah said she was sorry. Emily found comfort in knowing that the other woman took responsibility for the attack. However, there is never a mention of the episode from either woman. Emily is shaken up from the obscenity and Deb, although remorseful, is all too agreeable to forget all about it. Three days pass before Emily can talk to Deb again and, when she does, it's about an entry in the books.

Deborah hires a carpenter to build a false wall at the top of the staircase with a hidden door. This way, if anyone who doesn't live there, ever happens to venture past the stairs, they will not be able to immediately see that more rooms are located down the hallway. They will assume the visible door to Deb's bedroom is all they will find.

To herself, she vows that she will always accompany whoever she invites upstairs again, no matter how well she knows him.

Having witnessed Emily's vulnerability after her sister's death, the working girls warm up to Emily. They are also curious about her baby boy. Emily soon feels a kinship to these young women and begins to enjoy their company. She shakes her head with disbelief, *There was a time I thought that acknowledging them would inevitably make me one of them! How silly of me.*

Emily never regrets keeping Daniel. She's in love with the boy and her heart swells when he wraps her finger with five of his, or smiles when he sees her enter a room. He reminds her of Adeline and brings her so much joy. She hates that she will lie to the boy one day about his unwed birth-mother and his absent father, but tries to balance the future deceit with her love. He grows up happy being on the receiving end of so much love from his mother, Deb as his grandmother, and the working girls as his older sisters.

Everyone in the house treats Daniel like gold. He is brought up in an environment full of love and the child provides the women with a semblance of a normal family life. The working girls make a fuss whenever he's around, even playing hide-and-seek with him and allowing the boy to tease them or win at some silly game.

Over the years, Emily is very careful to keep the growing boy away from the west side of the house. She insists he use the side door on Chester Street for all comings and goings. Emily also hopes that no one from Daniel's school will ever find out where he lives. She hopes he can lead as normal a childhood as possible without feeling ashamed of his roots. She knows how gossip can destroy a person, even an innocent one, but especially a defenceless, illegitimate child.

"Mama? Tell me about my father," Daniel demands as he finishes eating his breakfast on a summer day in his ninth year.

The question causes a cherished memory to flash through Emily's mind. It was a day when he had a high fever and although he was five years old, he couldn't sleep until she held and rocked him. While wrapping her exhausted arms around the burning child, she prayed that he would survive whatever he was fighting. The revelation was that she might never have to lie to him if he didn't survive the illness. She cried tears of joy when the fever broke, knowing that she would become the best liar she could be—instead of childless.

The request from the boy makes the fifty-six-year-old Deborah look up from her plate and over to where Emily, a youthful thirty-year-old, is sitting. Emily cautiously avoids looking back at Deborah. She doesn't want to mislead Daniel into thinking that there is anything underhanded in what she will say, and he is definitely astute enough to notice if she gives Deborah one of her I-can-handle-this looks.

"Certainly. I can't right now as I have to go to work shortly. So, how about you join me for tea this afternoon at two o'clock? We'll have it in the parlor, just you and me. I'll tell you everything you want to know."

"Okay. May I go play with Robbie now?"

"Of course. Be careful."

"I will Mama. I'll be careful," he yells back as he runs down the hallway toward the side door.

"That's a funny word—okay—isn't it?" asks Deborah.

"Yes. All the children are using it. It won't be long before we all use it one day," Emily says in return.

"Okay then," Deborah responds and they both smile. "So, what are you going to tell him about his absent father?"

"Well, I've been preparing for this day since he was born. I hate to admit it, but I've created quite a believable story for this boy. You don't mind not joining us for tea, do you?" asks Emily.

"No, I don't mind. I'll find something else to do. But you'd better fill me in so we have the same story."

Emily nods in agreement and begins her imaginary tale.

Later that afternoon, the young man is very anxious to hear about his father. He wonders why his mother hasn't talked about him. He doesn't understand why his mother wants to make the conversation so formal by having tea, so he surmises that what she has to tell him is difficult for her.

Emily settles in and begins, "Your father, David Breat, and I met at a picnic while I was still living in Philadelphia. He asked me, above all the other girls there, to join him for a walk in the gardens. It was a lovely afternoon, no, actually I think it was too hot, but I was so happy to accompany him that I didn't really notice the heat." She blinks and focuses on her son's eyes. He can clearly see that his mother was smitten with his father right from the start.

She sighs, "We courted and married before winter. We moved here so he could manage part of his father's business. We lived here for three wonderful years when his father told him about an exciting new creation in Europe … "

Daniel interrupts, "What kind of creation? Do you mean a new invention?"

"Yes! That's what I mean. So, who's telling this story?" she smiles and he smiles back. She continues, "It was a new invention that had to do with, oh dear, it has been so long, I've forgotten what it was. No matter. It's not that important."

She takes a sip of tea, reaches for a biscuit and continues with her web of lies, "He promised to write as soon as he arrived, but I never received a letter. So, I wrote his mother and that letter was mysteriously returned to me, unclaimed! I thought I must have the wrong address, but I knew that wasn't possible."

She hoped Daniel would not notice that her next lie was weak. "So, I then wrote to a neighbor of theirs and soon learned that David's mother was ill and in a home for people who suffered from consumption. The poor dear. That wasn't the worse thing though. What the neighbor wrote next was that they had received news that there was an explosion involving this invention and both your father and grandfather perished in that accident. You were two years old when he left for Europe, so you don't remember him. Nor do you miss him, am I right?"

"Right. I don't miss him, Mama. I was just curious. So, do we still have family in Philadelphia?"

"No. I'm afraid that we are the last of the Breats."

"None at all? How about your family?"

Emily was grateful he had not asked about her maiden name and thankful for the one truth she can tell him. "No. I'm an orphan. Not even a cousin or an aunt. Everyone I once knew is long dead."

Emily has no idea if he will ever go to Philadelphia and try to find roots there. Regardless, there won't be any. To her recollection, there are no more Breats, but by killing off everyone in her story, she hopes that he will be satisfied with this made up past and put an end to his questions.

"What did my father look like?" Daniel asks with chin supported by hands and elbows resting on the table. For once, she decides to just love him and doesn't correct his posture.

She thinks of David and what she remembered of him, which wasn't much. Then she thinks of a young Adeline in love, how would she have described David?

She extends a hand to brush the boy's hair back out of his eyes and replies, "He was a very good-looking man. He was so kind and considerate. He was also well educated and a gentleman. You might have your, ah, my eyes and my father's dark brown and straight hair—but everything else, your chin, your nose, and your smile, they're all from your father. You will probably grow up to be just like him. Choose to be a kind man, Daniel."

The boy nods and remembers his other questions, "Why did you have to work, Mama? Didn't my father leave you money?"

Oh dear. What will this curious boy ask next?

"Well, as I said, his father died with him. His parents had yet to meet you, otherwise I'm sure they would've included you in their Will. We never received any money from David's investments because his death—and more importantly—his father's death, caused their business to fail. I quickly became destitute. I didn't know what to do. I knew I had to find work, but I worried about what to do with you during the day while I worked. You were only two!

"I searched and searched. Then one of the businessmen I had made inquiries about for a job, who wasn't hiring at the time, told me that Madam Deb was looking for a bookkeeper. Deborah had a couple of spare rooms to rent and just like that, we made an arrangement for me to come work and for the both of us to live here.

"I believe you know the rest of the story. We've been here ever since." In the hopes that he ran out of questions—so she could stop lying to the boy—she asks, "Are you happy, Daniel? Do you like it here?"

"Well, there are too many girls, but at least they're likeable, not like the annoying girls at school. I really like living this close to the park across the street though. I can always find someone to play with there."

26
Deborah and Daniel

Deborah observes the auburn-haired fifteen-year-old boy. Daniel is growing up into a handsome young man and is now almost the same height as the watchman, the tallest person in the house. Her godson still called her "Deb-Deb" as he did when he first began to talk, but his voice had already deepened into a soft rolling growl.

Several of the girls have gathered in the kitchen on this lazy Sunday morning. Deborah notices that even though Daniel is being teased mercilessly by the more experienced and older women, he's lingering because of the newest addition—young and pretty Vera.

For now, it's all innocent, but everybody knows that it will eventually evolve. Deborah also knows better than to talk to Emily about it. Emily would keep Daniel in the infant stage if she could. Deb doesn't want Emily to put an end to him spending any time on either side of the huge, fifteen-bedroom house—after all, this is his home.

Deborah is very fond of the young man who she considers to be her grandson and determines that she has a responsibility of making sure the boy doesn't grow up to be shy and clumsy around girls. She isn't going to set him up with one of her working girls but she will let nature take its course. For now, she'll observe.

"Daniel," Deborah says the following Saturday after breakfast, "I need your help this morning moving a few things in the storage room next to the boudoir."

"Who, me? Sure!" He's eager to please. The obedient boy had never crossed his mother and ventured into those rooms before. He had only glimpsed into the boudoir that one time when Vera had fetched him through the hidden door and led him to a place at the top of the stairs where he could see but not be easily detected. Then, in a fit of giggles, they had quickly left the area when they saw the watchman look up the staircase right at them.

Although the brothel and the residential side are separated by a wall, a secret door at the top of the adjacent staircases allows access for the residents to freely move from one side to the other. Otherwise, Daniel would have had to go down the stairs from the residential side, through the French doors that Deb uses to enter the boudoir, and up the other set of stairs to Vera's room.

Deb says, "Yes, you. I need your muscle. I need things that are stored in a small space and I don't think that Jim will appreciate trying to get at them for me."

Daniel tries to follow Deb's fast pace through the boudoir towards the storage room but finds himself in the middle of the titillating room, going around in a circle admiring—everything! The closest things he has ever seen similar to the rich fabrics on the walls and furniture is the parlor on the residential side. But it failed in comparison to this one with its numerous chairs in various velvety colors, the designs of flowers in the carpet, the elaborate ashtrays, the mirrors on the walls, the chandeliers, and the provocative art hanging on the walls.

Deb sees his wonder and waits. She smiles when his eyes land on her and she signals for him to come into the storage room with her.

"We'll start in this corner. These crates have been here for so long that I don't even remember what's in them."

Daniel, soon covered in dust and cobwebs, moves the first crate to a table. Deb hands him a hammer and a crowbar. He pokes at the curled end of the plank and soon pries the lid open.

Deb dives in, but before she unearths anything, she says, "Get the next one will you, pet?"

While he pries the second crate open, she removes a fifteen-inch statue of a naked woman from the first crate. Just the sight of the figurine reminds her that it is part of a matching set. She carefully places it down on the table and digs in to see if the second one is in the same crate but alas, the crate is empty. She moves the empty box to the outside of the storage room's entrance and digs into the second one where she gleefully finds the twin.

She says excitedly, "Can you put the two crates outside in the back? I'll take these pieces. I know exactly where I want to display them. Then we'll come back and find more treasure."

Crates are opened, a few are shut and re-stacked, the rest are emptied. More items are put on display and more wooden boxes are discarded. Deb is delighted to find two crates full of decorative drinking glasses as, more often than not, glasses become an expensive casualty almost every day at the brothel.

"How come you never went through these before, Deborah?" asks Daniel.

"I forgot about them, I guess. Most of these belonged to the madam before me," she admits.

Deb doesn't hide the nature of her business from Daniel like Emily does. She believes that honesty and transparency on her part will help Daniel develop his own fair opinion. She didn't see Daniel blush or stutter when the naked statues came out of the crates so Deb concluded that Daniel's new friend had likely introduced him to some aspects of adulthood already. She is grateful that Vera, a kind and gentle girl, opened his eyes to that reality.

"Aahh!" Daniel yells.

His ear-piercing screams wake up both Deborah and Emily for the fourth time in one week, always at three o'clock in the morning. Three months into his sixteenth year at the brothel, he has seen something his young mind can't deal with.

Both women rush to his bed while tying up their housecoats. They find him sitting upright, drenched in a sweat and panting. "I'm all right now. I'm sorry if I woke you. Please, go back to your beds. I'll be fine," he insists.

Deborah catches Emily's arm before she sits by his side and says, "Let me try this time."

Emily nods and gladly turns to go back to her room. She hasn't yet come to terms with the fact that her son has slept with one of the girls! He isn't a boy anymore and she can't process this new information. She also feels inadequate to help him as she slept through the whole thing on that forsaken night.

Deborah reasons, "Daniel, maybe it would help if you talked about it."

"Why? You were there. You know perfectly well what happened. I'll be okay, Deborah. You can go back to bed."

"I'm not leaving. This is my house!" asserting herself unnecessarily. "I want you to tell me what you saw. To be honest, there were people blocking my view and I didn't see it like you did. Please, tell me Daniel," she demands as gently as she can. "Maybe by telling me about it, the nightmares might end."

He shakes his head no. She leans in to hug him as she bends to sit on the side of his bed and he rests his head on her shoulder. Pretty soon, his arms go around her waist and he weeps.

Momentarily, he straightens back up and says, "Hank was one of Vera's new regulars. That's what Vera told me, but honestly Deb-Deb, I thought he looked at her with stars in his eyes. He was always hungry for her. Just her," he emphasizes. "I wish I knew last week what I know now about the business. I would've warned you, or—or someone, about him. He was her last customer that night. I noticed that he was timing it that way a lot lately.

"I was going to sneak into her room after he left, you know, like we planned. As I was approaching, I heard her muffled cries. Then I heard furniture break and then everything went still. That's when I opened her door and rushed in. It was dark, so I turned up my own lamp to find her.

"I saw him on top of the broken bedside table," Daniel gulps. "He had a knife sticking out of his stomach and he was covered in blood. He was dead! I searched for her and couldn't see her anywhere. Then, there she was, on the floor halfway hidden underneath the bed. I softly called her name and tugged on her arm. She'd pulled a blanket over her face. I pulled it down, away from her eyes and she was trembling with fear. I tried to soothe her but she wouldn't stop shaking. I lifted her up to her bed and that's when I saw all the blood on the blanket and pillows. She couldn't speak. When I turned around, you and Jim and all the other girls were in her room.

"Now, you tell me when these nightmares are going to stop, Deborah! Because they'll never stop for her. He carved part of her cheek out for heaven's sake. Her beautiful face is all cut up and she'll never be able to work or go out in public again. What kind of monster does that, Deborah? He ruined her life," says Daniel, exhausted.

Deborah now knows exactly what happened. She explains, "Men like Hank are beyond jealous, Daniel. They're possessive, dangerous, and unpredictable. They lose control of their senses. My profession sees more men like this than any other line of work. Vera was probably his first lover and she was most likely gentle, encouraging, and everything that he'd never gotten from anybody else. It often happens that a fellow will fall in love with a working girl that way.

"Normally, when I see a customer repeatedly asking for one specific girl, I make sure she is busy with someone else. Usually that encourages a man to choose another girl. Vera was certain he was harmless and I'm sorry she was wrong, Daniel.

"Maybe he wanted her to go away with him. But you have to know that no matter what request she would have replied no to, it would have angered him. I guess that he was the kind of man who thought that if he couldn't have her all to himself, no one would have her at all. Then after he hurt her, he couldn't stand to live without her, so he turned the knife on himself."

Deb lied. She told Daniel that the deranged young man had fatally stabbed himself. She knew that Vera had to live with the realization that she killed a man but Deb didn't know if Daniel could handle the whole truth.

"I don't know what Vera will do with her life now," Deborah reflects, "I'm going to visit her in the hospital next week. I promise to stay in touch with her, Daniel. I promise to take care of her as long as she needs me. She's very sweet and so full of life but he's changed her forever and I'm truly sorry about that."

She pauses and then adds as she strokes the back of his head, "I'm glad you told me. You know, now that you've shared this with me, I believe you'll be able to rest easier real soon."

She was right.

"It's too fast, Deborah," Emily cries as they both watch Daniel embark the train to Philadelphia.

"Time does that, Emily. Wasn't it just yesterday that he wailed when he fell down trying to walk upright?" asks Deborah.

"I guess, but was yesterday sixteen years ago?" she says, picturing the one-year-old boy taking his first steps.

Both women wave their handkerchief when Daniel pokes his head out of the window of the second last caboose. He smiles in anticipation of adventure and waves back as he watches them get smaller and smaller, standing there on the platform.

He's on his way to work in the biggest mining company this side of Lake Michigan. Deborah has been reassured by an old friend that he will hire Daniel and mentor him. If the young man shows promise, there would be a secure future for him in science and geology.

27
Lilith

Mr. Trolley thanks Emily and turns to Lilith. "I believe this is where you come in. Can you tell us about your life before you met Daniel?"

"I'm glad to," she replies softly.

Graham observes Emily reach for Lilith's hand as she knows what's coming. He's chagrined to think that for the couple of months that they spent time becoming friends they hadn't talked much about their past. He wishes he could be the one giving her this comfort that she will apparently need.

On the second Tuesday of September 1852, in the small town of Bolder in the State of Ohio, the teacher of the one-room school asks, "Does anyone know what the word orphan means?"

Noreen Chant, currently the oldest student at twelve-years of age, raises her hand.

"Yes, Noreen?"

"I believe it means someone whose parents are no longer living," she answers.

"That's correct. We have a new student starting with us today. Her name is Lilith Green. She's eleven years old and an orphan. She's staying with the Masseys down the road to help Mrs. Massey look after her six children."

The teacher turns to Lilith and says, "Go sit next to Noreen, dear."

That is the extent of Lilith's introduction to her classmates and new world. Later during recess, when talking out loud is not punishable with more homework, Noreen says, "Tell me about yourself."

"No please, you go first," the polite Lilith insists.

"Oh, all right. I have one older brother, two younger ones and one younger sister. We have a dog and a cat, three horses, one cow, four pigs and I don't know how many chickens. We all live on a farm three-quarters of a mile up that road to the east," says Noreen, pointing. "Okay, your turn."

"My mother's aunt, Miss Rosanne Beckley, took me in after Father died. She was a sweet old lady and I was well cared for. I got schooling at her home by a tutor. Every day after classes, my great-aunt would teach me to play piano. My school days started at nine o'clock and ended at four in the afternoon."

"Gee! A tutor! I've never heard of any such thing. Tell me more. What were your parents like, how did they die?" asks a curious Noreen.

Lilith replies, "Aunt Rosanne told me almost everything I know about my family. I don't remember much because I was only six when my father died. She told me that Mother had given birth to my brother, but he died, then Mother died right after. Three months later, there was a terrible accident in the barn where Father was working. The barn caught fire, Father and two horses died. Aunt Rosanne told me that I couldn't sleep for a month after I came to stay with her because I missed my father so and kept dreaming about the fire. But over time everything got better."

"How come you're with the Masseys now? Couldn't your great-aunt look after you no more?"

"No. She was old and died too. There's no family left to look after me. The minister said that I should go live with a family—with people who needed me as much as I needed them."

"Oh, that makes sense. When's your birthday? Mine's August 15. I just turned twelve," says Noreen, easily dismissing the sadness of Lilith's life.

Lilith replies, "Aunt Rosanne said that my family's Bible recorded my birthday as January 18, 1841. So that makes me eleven and a half."

"Where did you live before coming here to Bolder?"

"I was raised in a little town west of Westlake called Birktown. That's in Ohio too, about seventy miles from here.

"Is that where your Ma met your Pa?"

"I don't know. Aunt Rosanne said that my mother, her name was Helen, ran off with my father, Fred, when she was twenty or so. I forget exactly. Anyway, my mother's father, Aunt Rosanne's stubborn brother, Gavin Beckley—stubborn was her word, not mine—anyway, he thought that my father's age should be closer to my mother's so he wouldn't even give them his blessing for them to court. Well, she was in love! So of course, she ran away. Grandfather Gavin disowned her. He'd already planned on moving back to Europe by then and he was so angry with my mother, that he decided that if she ever wanted to see him again one day, she'd have to find him. He didn't even tell my aunt exactly where he was going."

"Europe? Gee!"

"My great-aunt never heard from him again. Not even a letter to say he made it there safely. She was disappointed with him, and regretted that he would never meet me and know me or see for himself how sweet and polite I was—her words, again." She shrugs. "His loss, I guess. He doesn't even know my mother is dead. His own daughter!"

"Why do you call her your aunt when she's your great-aunt?" asks Noreen.

"Even though she wasn't, she insisted she was too young to be called a great-aunt and soon it just became a habit to omit the word great."

Noreen nods and is in awe of Lilith's very different life. "You're very pretty," she says, as if just now discovering that.

"Oh, thank you. What a nice thing to say."

"Are you lonely?" asks Noreen. She can't imagine not seeing her parents and siblings every day.

"I don't miss anyone or anything from when I was little. It's all confusing actually," says the stoic young girl.

Miss Beckley, a spinster, didn't have the knowledge to raise a girl-child. From the very beginning, she taught Lilith things that she should have learned as a mature young woman. However, it enriched Lilith with keen social graces, and fine etiquette skills. She can also find her way around a kitchen and a garden, and is passionate about sewing.

Lilith didn't inherit money or goods, not even in trust. If Miss Beckley had anything of value to leave behind, she had made arrangements for the distribution of her possessions several years before Lilith came to live with her. At the time, and because of her spinsterhood, she wanted the church to receive everything she owned.

Miss Beckley didn't make changes to her Last Will and Testament after taking in Lilith. The elderly great-aunt didn't think that she would die while Lilith was still so young so she failed to plan for the girl's future. She came to like the child and felt a responsibility for Lilith's nurturing, but she never considered her anything more than a ward.

Lilith didn't grieve for Miss Beckley. The woman had kept her emotions at arms length and Lilith never really warmed up to her only living relative. Lilith felt alone, like she belonged to no one and that no one really cared for her well being beyond basic necessities like water, food, clothing, and shelter.

Lilith had her own room at great-aunt Rosanne's home but now she shares a room and a bed with three young girls at the Masseys' place. She never feels happy until she befriends Noreen.

Lilith's living arrangements specify that she can stay in school as long as she also cleans the busy house, which she does on weeknights. She bakes bread on Saturday mornings, followed by doing any laundry left undone by the mother of six. On Sundays, Lilith mends clothes after the church service. If she can't handle all these chores, she'll have to quit her schooling. So even on days when she is physically exhausted, she won't admit it, not even to herself. She is determined to get the most education the school has to offer. She's already learned at a young age that she only has herself to depend on.

Lilith's ambition is just like Noreen's—to become a school teacher. Even while she cleans and bakes, Lilith recites mathematical equations and practices spelling complicated words.

When Lilith is fifteen years old, she leaves the Masseys' home for Mrs. Kate's Boarding and Lodging House down the road. Mrs. Kate agrees to provide Lilith with one room that is furnished with a bed, a chair and small table, in exchange for Lilith cleaning on week nights, baking bread on Saturday mornings, and doing laundry in the afternoons. For a little bit of pay, she can mend the other borders' clothing on Sundays after service.

Noreen, who has one more year left of schooling, wonders out loud, "Why would you walk away from the Masseys for a lonely place like this boarding house, Lilith? Don't you like being with a family and living a normal life? Why do it and still end up doing all the same work? I don't understand."

Lilith doesn't have the words to describe a life where she doesn't feel a sense of belonging. The only physical contact she's had is an occasional hug from Noreen, or when one of her bed partners kicks her while she slept. She tries to explain, "I never fit in with the Masseys, you see. They always treated me like a servant and a stranger. Besides, the older children are helping out now and can easily do all my chores. At least here at Mrs. Kate's place, I'll make a bit of money for all my hard work and gain some independence. And, most importantly, have a bed to myself."

Almost overnight, Lilith develops into a full-figured young woman. Mrs. Kate leans toward treating her more like a daughter needing protection than a hired hand. Lilith and Mrs. Kate aren't the very best of friends, but they do have a relationship that provides Lilith with a small taste of a motherly presence.

The school year following Noreen's graduation is a lonely one. However, Lilith is determined to become a teacher and focuses on her last year of studies, instead of making new friends.

Noreen writes as often as she can. The most exciting letter Lilith receives is read so many times, it is memorized.

When I last wrote, I told you about meeting a delightful man, Jared Pessant and how very sweet he was to carry my suitcase from the train station in Gooseville to my new schoolhouse where I have a bedroom and sitting room at the back.

Well, Jared found all kinds of reasons to come by every other day after school hours—to look in on things, you know, to fix this or that. Eventually, he asked me if I would escort him on a walk to the only restaurant in town, for coffee and a slice of pie.

FINALLY, he asked me to marry him, Lilith. I said yes, of course.

We will be wed next week Wednesday. It's all so dreamy. I love him very much. I can't wait for you to meet him next year when you come to visit. Please write as soon as you can.

Lilith sighs and thinks, *Noreen is living the life I have dreamed of for myself. I want to teach, I want to be a married woman, and one day become a mother—even if marrying is the end of a teaching career. Noreen must love him more than teaching, I guess. Unless this small town has trouble finding a replacement teacher? Then maybe they'll let her teach until she becomes a mother. Hmm.*

Lilith's reciprocating correspondence over the rest of the school year involves her telling Noreen about finding employment as a schoolteacher in Erinsberg, another small farming town in Ohio about forty miles further south than Noreen's home in Gooseville. A few weeks later, Noreen's letter brings a smile to her face when she reads that the town folk of Gooseville decided to keep Noreen on as a teacher until she announces the arrival of a baby. Both women celebrate the news of Noreen's pregnancy privately.

In no time at all, it's Lilith's turn to graduate. She unceremoniously leaves Mrs. Kate's and with the few dollars she's earned, she purchases a stagecoach ticket to Gooseville. She is finally free to go wherever and whenever she pleases.

Lilith is overjoyed to see her only childhood friend and is happy to finally meet Jared. Noreen's letters contained endless paragraphs about her husband and Lilith feels she has *known* him almost as long as Noreen has.

Jared is an upstanding young man who already holds an important position as the assistant to the manager of the railroad division in charge of transporting grain and other goods. He has the potential to do remarkable things for his hometown and he involves himself in all kinds of civil activities, even planning on joining a political party and making a name for himself.

Lilith stays with the Pessants for the next three months until it is time to take up her teaching post in Erinsberg.

28
Lilith and Daniel

Daniel had started at the bottom of the ladder with the THR Mining Company, and learned the hardships of coal mining. After a few years of hard labor, the early demise of the foreman provided him with the opening to move ahead. The other miners rejoiced on his promotion as he was well liked and known for his fairness. Both company and employees would profit from Daniel's smart and hard work.

Daniel didn't see himself working in the pit for the rest of his life, even as a foreman. He befriended prospectors and learned from them what it took to work for the company above ground. His studies paid off when he was promoted once more, now as a manager prospecting new claims.

Counties for miles around Gooseville have a tradition of holding a dance after a new barn is built. Now twenty-four-years old, a confident and worldly Daniel watches the entrance door, on the lookout for the appearance of young, attractive, and single women. He isn't alone in his excitement for the dance to begin. Several men from the prospecting crew are in attendance this evening for a well-deserved night off after the past month's prospecting for coal and other valuable minerals.

Daniel's anticipation of female company is soon deflated as he sees only couples and families enter the new barn. No, wait, there appears to be an unattached young woman with that couple, but when she twirls to look at the room, his hope is deflated by the tall girl's obvious adolescence and Daniel turns his gaze away.

Daniel gives up trying to find an available woman who will make his evening enjoyable and surrenders himself to the wall of onlookers, his fellow prospectors. He might even consider dancing with one of the men—several of whom had noticed the shortage of women, and were already arguing about which one would dance in the place of the girl.

The gala is in full swing by the time Jared, Noreen and Lilith arrive. A lively piece has just finished playing and folks are catching their breath while the musicians take their first break. Ladies reach for their fans and men line up for the punch bowl.

Suddenly, a hush comes over the crowd and all heads turn at once. Whoever had looked first toward the entrance started the motion with a loud intake of breath. The silence following the gasp makes Daniel turn to see what everyone else is gazing at.

Lilith is used to the staring and averts her eyes from the people gawking at her, pretending to straighten a ribbon on her skirt. Noreen has forgotten strangers' reaction when they first lay eyes upon Lilith. Jared is certainly not used to the swift, eerie attention.

Not only is Lilith one of the most beautiful women anyone in the room has ever set eyes upon, the etiquette lessons her aunt Rosanne insisted she endure as a young girl resulted in perfect posture and a certain confidence.

However, today, in a new town with strangers' eyes watching her, she is highly aware of her exceptional looks and starts to feel uneasy. It always takes a while for people to warm up to her—even women are reluctant to approach her to just talk as they are threatened by her beauty.

A few moments later, the curiosity dies down as people check their manners and continue about their business. Jared brings the two women each a glass of punch. The music starts up again and he asks his bride to accompany him to the dance floor. For the duration of the waltz, Lilith reflects on the fact that she's never attended a barn dance before. The small town of three hundred people where she and Noreen grew up was fairly established and not many new families moved in or had to build new stables.

Lilith snaps out of her day-dreaming when the music ends and Noreen returns to her side. A couple of minutes later, Jared joins them accompanied by three older gentlemen. Jared's ambition and career aspirations leads him to befriend everyone he meets.

Jared introduces his wife and Lilith to the owners of a Philadelphia-based business, Mr. Tibbent, Mr. Hankley and Mr. Rowan. Lilith is immediately asked to dance by the senior, Mr. Tibbent, who has the misfortune of being three inches shorter than her.

Lilith is sure he is old enough to be her grandfather but what she finds most unattractive is the fact that he smells of dirty socks. She doesn't relish the thought of having to be polite to the other two, if they also emit odors that make her nauseous.

She's never danced before and follows Mr. Tibbent's incompetent lead. She becomes very uncomfortable when her bosom bumps into him. Of course, he doesn't seem to mind and gives her a most ridiculous smile at the accidental bumps and beads another ripple of sweat from his brow at every mishap.

No sooner has she been returned to Noreen that Mr. Tibbent asks, "Well, that was most enjoyable. Miss Lilith, would you like to have another go?"

She doesn't know where her head is at when she replies, "Oh, Mr. Tibbent, I'm afraid I've promised someone else this dance."

Lilith is sure she will be caught in this lie as no one else has talked to her since her arrival. She is painfully aware that she will have to lie again and say something like she can't see him in the crowd or that he hasn't arrived yet.

But since the trio's appearance, Daniel has made his way to their side of the room. He had observed Tibbent's fumbling and he overhears the conversation. He approaches closer and interrupts, "There you are. Would you like to have that dance with me now?"

Lilith blushes, reaches for her fan at the end of the cord around her wrist but decides against using it. She nods and does a short curtsy toward the older gentleman and quickly accepts Daniel's request. She takes his extended hand as they walk toward the center of the room together.

Lilith is fair in hair and skin color; her dance partner is dark in contrast from spending his days outside. He's a few inches taller than her which is just the right height for dancing. She is delicate looking with an incredibly small waistline whereas he has great square shoulders that taper to a V just above his hips. He is lean yet fits his clothing well.

Noreen wonders where they have met as Lilith hasn't mentioned meeting such a good-looking man. She watches the pair walk away and concludes that they compliment each other. *Hmm*, she wonders.

Both Lilith and Daniel know that she has accepted the dance to cover her lie. She has no idea if he is spoken for or not. She certainly doesn't want to start any trouble and would rather accept egg on her face and be caught in a lie than be accused of husband stealing or of stealing a promised husband-to-be.

The music isn't fast paced and they can easily hold a conversation while dancing without risk of being overheard.

Daniel is the first to speak, "Please forgive me. I don't often interfere in other people's affairs but you looked so uncomfortable dancing with old Tibbent that I had to see if you needed, ah, saving. If you walked away right now, I'd fully understand and not blame you for any embarrassment it might bring me."

Lilith laughs easily at Daniel's confession and replies, "I do forgive you. Though I'm not sure it was appropriate for me to so readily accept to dance with you. I don't know you."

She's relieved that she has yet to uncomfortably bump her chest up against his. He's a good dancer.

"Oh dear, I'm putting you in an awkward position now, aren't I?" He pauses. "Let's see, how did we meet?" he asks. He sways to the music and she follows suit. As he is pondering the dilemma, she answers it for him by borrowing from Noreen.

She replies, "We met at the train station. You carried my possessions into the station."

He smiles, nods, and says, "Yes, of course. I introduced myself to you as Daniel Breat, best looking, single, gentleman of the THR Mining Company—oh, that's Tibbent, Hankley and Rowan by the way. I asked if you needed assistance and I carried your fifty-pound crate into the station." He asks, "Anything else I need to know about our first meeting?" His big brown eyes gleam at the fun the two are having dancing and embellishing on their deception.

"Yes. It was only a twenty-five-pound box and I could carry my own five pounds of books," she says and can't help but smile back at the best looking, single man in the room.

She adds, "I'm Lilith Green and a new school teacher. I'll be reporting to my first post in September." Lilith is secretly hoping she hasn't divulged too much information to a stranger—even if he does appear to be a decent enough man who won't cause her any harm.

By now, the music has stopped and Daniel knows he had better escort her back to her friends—he has made the best impression he can and hopes that she will be interested to learn more about him.

Even before she dances with any the other single men in the place, she knows she wants to get to know Daniel better. She dances every dance of the evening, but only one man is considerate of her comfort. Daniel asks if she wishes to get a refreshment, or sit when it's their next turn to dance. She appreciates his attentiveness and doesn't realize that he would rather sit and chat than speak a few words in between steps. His motive is to impress her enough that she won't think of anyone but him when she remembers this evening.

In the following months, Daniel often makes his way over to the Pessants' home after the week's work. He courts Lilith and treats her like a friend. She doesn't have any parents or chaperone and is only seventeen years old, but she's old enough to make decisions for herself. He asks her out for lemonade and cake or pie at the local restaurant, and invites her for walks in the park. Sometimes they just sit in the back garden under the trees and talk about their hopes for the future.

Lilith learns so much from Daniel. He is the first man who has ever shown any interest in her and she easily falls in love with him. She's never been treated with such respect and tenderness by any other human being. Except for Noreen, no one has ever cared what she says or thinks about anything. Lilith has never shared her hopes and dreams with anyone, until him. With the lack of affection she experienced as an orphaned child, she doesn't know if she can ever show him how grateful she is to have met him, and wishes for a lifetime with him to do so.

Daniel doesn't know what it is about her that keeps him coming back. It might be her innocence, her attentiveness to his every word, her beauty, her gentleness, or even her eagerness for any kindness he shows her. Maybe it's a combination of those characteristics. Daniel is very fond of her and soon comes to realize that he's in love. Won't his mother be surprised?

Daniel tells Lilith, "Mother is very prim and proper. One would believe that she's high society, but she's a bookkeeper on the south side of Delton." He tries not to fib; but he knows not telling the whole truth of his mother's work situation is just that. The omission is partially for his own worry that Lilith may not understand and partially to protect his mother. His mother would be mortified if he ever told the truth about her place of employment.

He continues, "My father went to work in England when I was two and she never saw him again. He and his father died in an accident there."

At this revelation, Lilith does not hold back. She tells him everything about her lonely past. It is in those moments of raw truth that they sense each other's need for friendship and affection. They are certainly friends, nevertheless, the importance of friendship is obscured by their youthful and natural attraction to each other.

There is no need to drag the courtship into a long, drawn-out affair. Daniel cannot imagine life without her so he proposes. Lilith agrees, and they marry.

29
Lilith and Daniel

The memories of Lilith's wedding day and night wrap their warmth around her. She is grateful for another ten-minute break to think about Daniel and then continues her story.

After the brief wedding ceremony in late August, at a table for four in the only restaurant in town, Daniel orders a bottle of bubbly wine with dinner. Lilith thinks the gesture romantic and that the drink is delicious.

Jared tastes and accepts a glass. Noreen takes a sip but decides the wine isn't to her liking and declines a glass of her own. She thinks that her pregnancy may be causing her to dislike the strange new taste.

After Noreen and Jared leave, Daniel pours Lilith another glass and finishes off the bottle himself. He says, "A toast—to us," and they drink.

He smiles, "A toast to our delightful witnesses, oh, they've left already." Lilith giggles and they drink anyway.

"Ah," Daniel continues, "a toast to our waitress." They drink as the young woman picks up dirty dishes and walks away.

"And finally, a toast to an empty bottle." He is being silly, but so is Lilith who's kept up with him. She thinks herself to be the luckiest woman in the world and that she is fortunate to have found true love.

She is the first woman Daniel has ever wanted to marry and as he respects the sanctity of marriage, he's kept their carnal relations for their wedding night. It has not been easy as she is so desirable.

Lilith is nervous in her anticipation. She doesn't know her husband is skilled in the art of love making and that his upbringing has contributed to that aspect of his education.

After he pays for the meals, he takes his new bride by the hand and leads her to their room. She is apprehensive of this part of her becoming a married woman as Noreen had told her there will be pain but it will go away and that she will eventually enjoy the coupling.

Lilith doesn't understand what is going to cause her pain. Although Noreen knows what to expect, she couldn't explain it to Lilith. Not only did she not have the words, she was also uncomfortable discussing such a thing openly, even with her best friend.

The only exposure to sex either Noreen or Lilith have ever had was when they had come upon a pair of dogs, seemingly locked in the act. Several of the Jackson kids were shrieking with excitement at witnessing the oddity. The dogs suddenly separated when the children's mother threw a basin of cold water on the canines. And that is the extent of Lilith's knowledge of sex.

Noreen's mother, like her mother before her, couldn't put into words the events of a wedding night either. So, before their marriage, neither woman thought the act of sex was going to be anything exciting or different for them. They just had no clue as to what to expect. Many women relied on their husbands to explain the deed that leads to becoming a mother.

Even though Daniel has been exposed to all kinds of debauchery, including sex with wanton women, drinking alcohol and smoking cigars, he never considered sex as sinful, not even the premarital kind that many men from all walks of life afford themselves. He never believed that it is bad or wrong, only natural.

Daniel was taught that a woman worthy of marriage should be a virgin and, like his mother, truly believes that the prostitutes at the brothel chose that way of life. The prostitutes had been like older sisters to him until the time he came of age. Then they began to look at him differently, no longer acting like sisters; and more than one taught him the pleasures to be had in between a set of sheets.

Daniel can sense Lilith's apprehension so he tenderly kisses her until he feels her relax. Kissing is all the physical contact they have shared thus far and he knows he wants her to like what is going to happen next. He takes it slow and easy and senses when she is ready to move on to something new.

He steadily undresses her while making sure his lips never leave her face or neck. He encourages her to explore beyond the kissing they have shared over the summer by placing her hands on his shoulders and beyond. She follows his lead and takes his shirt off. She stands staring at his magnificent shoulders that are inviting caresses from her inexperienced hands. She closes her eyes and stretches her neck back when he lays hands on her breasts. He continues to kiss her and with one arm, he brings her close to his bare chest while he fondles her with his free hand.

She briefly recalls Noreen's advise that she would inevitably get over the pain, but still cannot understand what pain there is to be had. All she feels is light-headed and waves of energy all over her body. She can't explain what's going on inside her as a flood of emotions release—she just knows that she doesn't want the feelings to stop.

Her heavy breathing and soft moaning tell Daniel that she is enjoying the foreplay. He is excited to finally have her in his arms like this. He releases the string that holds Lilith's underskirt and it drops to the floor. She unconsciously starts to sway her hips toward Daniel's and on occasion tilts her head back exposing herself even more. He bends over to kiss her in the hollow between her breasts.

He remembers being told that virgins will experience pain their first time unless the man is very attentive and takes it slow. The prostitutes had further explained that pain can possibly be avoided if the woman reaches a climax just before penetration. He didn't know the talk had been crude and vulgar. He was inexperienced at the time and he only knew that if he were ever to make love to a virgin, he would try his best to make it pleasurable for her.

He lifts her up off her feet and gently places her on the bed. Lilith's senses are elevated and she is oblivious to everything around her except for the kissing noises she hears coming from the strangest of places on her body as it rubs up and down in a sweat underneath Daniel's. She runs her fingers through his hair, then caresses his shoulders, massaging them with the same rhythm of their naked, gyrating hips. She moves her head side to side on the pillow, tangling up her hair.

The sight of her like this is beyond exciting for Daniel and just as he thinks that he can't hold back much longer, she starts quivering, gasping and moaning. He instantly penetrates as deeply as he needs. She lets out a small cry, moves her hips even more to accommodate him and he promptly experiences his own release.

When the euphoria dies down, she once again wonders about the pain that Noreen had made such a point of mentioning but figures that she can deal with it when it happens.

Daniel opens his eyes to see her looking back at him. She smiles, raises her head up ever so slightly and kisses him.

Daniel, still virile from the absence of a woman in recent months, doesn't remove himself from Lilith's warmth. Within five minutes of kissing, he starts the rhythmic motions once more. Lilith is eager to experience again the overwhelming ecstasy of their coupling as she has never felt such free abandonment.

Daniel is relieved that she enjoyed the act. He would hate it if she felt otherwise. He cannot imagine himself being a miserable married man who frequents brothels for satisfaction.

One honeymoon night at the hotel is all they can afford. Come September, Lilith will start her employment as a school teacher in Erinsberg about forty miles away. The Pessants put them up for a week until they hear from the town of Erinsberg that a home for them to occupy is ready.

Daniel had written his mother about his upcoming nuptials, but the short time between the wedding and Lilith's first day of teaching negated an opportunity to travel to Delton for a visit. The last paragraph he wrote …

My request for a transfer to practice my trade in Erinsberg was kindly accepted by the THR Mining Co. As you know, my work comes to a halt when the ground is frozen and that's usually when I come home to see you and Deborah. But being newly married and with Lilith's teaching, I don't know when exactly that's going to happen. I will find work with the local farmers in the meantime and when children bless us and Lilith stops working, we'll make plans to visit.

The house that was made available for their use is on the old Clayton homestead two miles away from the main street. Mr. Clayton, a childless widower, had passed away a couple of years earlier and the place has been unoccupied since.

Daniel and Lilith soon get accustomed to the commute to town. Their plan to build a home closer to the school is abandoned. Not only do they live rent-free at the old farm, they also value the privacy the remoteness gives them from the prying eyes of students' parents and other townspeople.

In July 1862, the twenty-one-year-old Lilith is enjoying a leisure bath after a hot day's work. She baked bread early in the morning so the oven wouldn't heat up the house during the hottest part of the day. Then she refreshed the bed with clean sheets, counting herself fortunate to have a second set of sheets to use while the wet ones were hanging on the clothes line. Not all her neighbors have such luxuries.

While sitting in the tub, she reflects that Sunday mornings, on the way to church, she makes it a habit of giving away loaves of bread to friends. Lilith and Daniel can never eat a dozen loaves of bread in a week, but she is used to making twice that many loaves and doesn't feel the need to cut back when she can share the much-appreciated staple with others.

Even after four years of marriage, their home is not yet busy with little ones. Doctors who specialize in determining why any couple has yet to conceive are located far away in cities like New York. Lilith and Daniel decide to hold off from such an expensive trip. For now, they both have an income and put away all extra funds as they plan for the future, including an eventual move to Philadelphia or Boston as they near old age.

Lilith loves children and is the only teacher in this remote community of two hundred people. In three months, classes will begin again as the school season starts late in September as the children are needed to work in their family farms' gardens and fields. For the same reasons, the classes end late in April or early in May as soon as it is planting time.

Lilith doesn't mind, she easily takes up from where she leaves off with the students. She loves to teach and never tires of holding the same lessons year after year.

Lilith now pokes a toe out of the water and then the whole foot. The breeze coming in through the kitchen window easily cools the exposed limb. She smiles and admires her lovely foot. Well, according to her attentive husband, the whole leg is admirable and she chooses to believe him.

She daydreams and doesn't notice a shadow cast on the wall. Just before she pulls her foot back into the water, a grimy hand reaches up and grabs her by the ankle.

She yells out!

Daniel had sneaked into the house, anticipating catching her bathing on such a hot day. He'd gotten down on the floor and slithered his way over to the tub but didn't expect to fully surprise Lilith. He quickly sits up.

The expression of fright on her face and shock on his throws them both into a fit of laughter. Playfully, she splashes him.

Still laughing, he says, "Well, I guess I have to remove my wet shirt now."

She grins and replies, "Don't stop with the shirt. This water is still warm enough to wash the dust off you, too." She folds her knees up and invitingly says, "There's enough room in here for the both of us. Come on in and I'll wash … "

She doesn't have a chance to finish when he leans over and while unbuttoning his shirt, plants a salty kiss on her mouth. He quickly takes his shirt off and starts undoing his belt and pants. The boots and socks come off next. He removes his underwear, lifts one foot over into the tub followed by the other and they soon discover that there isn't enough room for the both of them after all.

He reluctantly helps her up and she awkwardly tries to keep her clean body away from his dirty one. She places one foot out of the tub while he holds her steady. She bends over to reach for the towel and takes the other foot out of the tub. He lets go of the hand steadying her and bends down to wash off the day's dirt.

Lilith decides that it is too warm to put any clothing back on, so she remains naked and turns her attention to cleaning his back. After she washes away the grime, she moves closer toward the tub, reaching over to his upper chest from behind. He rests his wet head conveniently in between her soft breasts.

After four years of marriage, he is still surprised to feel desire at the slightest advance from her. The lack of children allows them many opportunities to explore sexual adventures whenever they want. The absence of influence from elders allows Lilith to behave without inhibitions. She would have been mortified to learn that her freedom to parade naked in front of her husband is considered scandalous, or worse—whorish.

Lilith never turns him down. She is never too busy if he is willing. Whatever she is doing will still be there to do afterwards. He makes her want more all the time—she is satiated for only as long as he is. Lilith doesn't know these feelings are unusual as she has no one to talk to about her needs and desires, nor someone to compare her experiences with. Daniel doesn't focus on his emotions, he only knows that she is exciting, lovely, and reciprocating.

After he splashes one more round of water on his face and combs his hair with his fingers, he grabs a hold of the sides of the tub and pushes himself up. She rises as well with towel in hand. She motions for him to stay in the tub while she starts to wipe him down. The wind briefly picks up and leaves goose-bumps on his wet buttocks and thighs, but she soon wipes those areas once she gets passed his wide shoulders to the small of his lower back.

He steps out of the tub facing her and neglecting his wet feet, he leans to one side and picks up his young wife. He carries her over to the freshly made bed just a few feet away in the small house. He kisses her deeply on the mouth, and passionately begins making love to her.

Often times, Lilith is happy that she isn't yet a mother because her friend Noreen once told her that sexual interests normally dwindle with the birth of a child. Lilith isn't sure she wants that to happen to her. No matter how much she wants a child, she hopes she will feel the same way toward sex as she does at this very instant for the rest of her life.

Lilith hesitates to speak after allowing herself to relive her happiest memories. The summary she just provided doesn't fully describe her husband's loving touch, his mischievous smile, his whispers of affection, their shared dreams …

With an encouraging nod from Emily, Lilith recounts to the others, the most difficult time of her existence thus far.

30
Lilith

Life becomes routine for Lilith and Daniel with respect to the seasons and chores. Lilith never wonders how her existence could be any better or different because she's never been happier.

There was a time when Daniel wondered if children would ever come and if he could be happy staying on this meagre homestead with Lilith. He lived a different kind of life before meeting Lilith and always had ambitions to become wealthy. But when he discovers that working in the fields is therapeutic and that married life is blissful, he concludes that if babies ever start coming, he will stay here in the serene prairie land. If they don't come, well there will always be opportunities for c hange and growth.

They have surprisingly been able to survive off Lilith's wages and stow away all of his. Lilith has never had much money and she never acquired a taste for spending it. Daniel is at liberty to toy with the idea of owning his own company one day and earning more money than he could ever spend, but he doesn't feel pressured or rushed to change their current situation. In the autumn season of 1862, he is readily hired back at the Lowe's farm for the duration of the months when prospecting is impossible because of the frozen ground.

The day starts out particularly warm for mid-October and Lilith hurries to get her wash on the line to take advantage of the sun's heat. Suddenly, from a distance, she hears her name being called. She turns toward the sound and sees dust flying up on the dry road behind the young man assigned to work with Daniel for the day. The fellow appears to be frantic about something.

Lilith's heart drops to her stomach as her mind races—something must have happened to Daniel! Dread envelopes her and adrenaline pushes her to run toward the wagon.

"What's wrong? What is it?" she asks quickly while still approaching. The man jumps down from his seat, motioning for Lilith to go to the back of the wagon and see for herself.

"Daniel!" The sight of her husband lying in a pool of blood shocks her. "What happened?" She looks up at the driver who doesn't take the time to answer.

"Quickly, go to him," he says as he helps her up into the wagon.

Running towards the barn, he yells back, "I'm taking your horse to fetch the doctor. Keep your hand on the wound. I'll be back as soon as I can!" He soon rushes away on the unsaddled steed.

Blood is seeping through Daniel's fingers where he clutches the wound in his gut. Lilith places a hand over Daniel's and both apply pressure on his stomach together. She leans in toward the love of her life, her one reason for being. Her mouth dries up, her heart races loudly.

Daniel forces a smile to his lips and says, "A stupid accident really. I'm sorry I'm getting your dress all bloody."

She shakes her head, "It doesn't matter. What happened?" she gently asks.

"We were working on the barn today. We'd put our tools away when I saw one nail sticking out of a top board. Well, neither one of us wanted to take the ladder out again, so I stood on the seat of the wagon to reach it. That's when the brake let go. It's sudden drop," he inhales deeply and resumes while exhaling, "motioned the horse to move forward. That caused me to fall backwards on the seat. One leg landed on top of the seat and the other one was sticking out of the wagon. My head was bobbing up and down on the hard floorboard. I tried to straighten myself up while that mare, I swear she has a mind of her own, just kept on going. The real trouble began when she stepped up from a trot to a full gallop. The wagon hit a deep rut and I went flying off the wagon. By then we were too close to the cliff and I flew down into the bushes below. I impaled myself on a stump. It was a good thing that I wasn't alone."

He closes his eyes as relief comes over him. He'd had a chance to tell her what happened and to say one last time what he said every day. Speaking more slowly now, "I love you, Lilith Breat. You've changed my life. I didn't know how lonely I was until I met you."

Lilith doesn't interrupt Daniel as she doesn't know what to say. Should she shush him to maintain energy that he might need later? She can't see through her tears while she leans down to lie beside him, one hand on his wound and the other under his head. She's propped herself up on one elbow afraid to take her eyes off him.

He wraps his free arm around her waist and continues, "I don't want to die, Lilith. I love you. I love our life together. I'm too young! I don't want to go yet. Please Lord, don't let me die." He cries out loud and suddenly stops as he feels himself weakening.

All too soon, he can no longer see her but doesn't tell her so. His bloodied hand leaves her waist and moves up to touch the back of her hair and the side of her face. His breathing becomes shallow.

She instinctively knows this may be her last chance, "I love you too, Daniel. So much. I couldn't imagine my life with someone like you because I never had it this good. And now I'll die if you die. I'll be so lost, Daniel." Her body convulses with every sob. Her tears mix with the blood his hand has smeared on her cheek.

He doesn't close his eyes. He can't feel the motion of her sobbing body but he can still hear her speaking. As if she knows, she continues, "I love everything about you, Daniel. Your crooked tooth, your teasing smile, oh, how I wish I'm pregnant so I can have your child to remember you by. I hope he has your big eyes and your strong chin. You're a handsome, gentle, wonderful man and I thank you for the privilege of having been loved by you."

He passes away while she is still talking. As if on cue, the wind dies down and instantly, the leaves stop falling to the ground. The dead silence registers the absence of his breathing, "NO!" she wails, and the birds take flight at her sudden outburst.

Then she whispers, "Daniel, don't go. Daniel, my love. Daniel … " She starts cooing and rests her head on his shoulder until the doctor's arrival.

The lawyer loudly clears his throat, not because Lilith is crying and a tearful Emily is consoling her, but because of the sob he's heard coming from the sixth occupant.

Graham is itching to leave the room. He never would have imagined such a tragic life for Lilith. She never let on. He hates that he can't reveal his feelings for the weeping, distressed woman or provide his sympathetic arms to console her. He wonders about the four women's history and asks himself, *When is all of this going to make sense? How are we all connected?*

Mr. Trolley says, "Thank you Lilith, for sharing your story. I think we are done for today. We will pick up from this point tomorrow."

Lilith says to Emily as they head out, "I'm often surprised by my emotions, even after all this time." Emily's reply is lost in the hallway.

Graham rushes out of the room in an effort to fight his strong desire to embrace her in his caring arms. He has dinner plans with his father and doesn't mind showing up early.

Mr. Trolley shuts the door after his secretary leaves the room. He walks toward the chair that faces the books and asks, "Bourbon?"

"Yes, please." He takes a deep breath. "It's not that I didn't know she was a widow, it's just ... "

"I know. I'm sorry. I should have warned you." He hands him a glass, then walks over to the desk, picks up a package and says, "Here. These are advanced copies of the agents' reports. Read them so you don't have any more surprises."

"Are there any more?"

"Not as tragic as this one."

They both drink.

31
Lilith

Graham is more than an hour early for his supper rendezvous. He heads to the bar of the Palmer House for a drink while he waits for his father.

The Lestor men greet each other with a hardy handshake and a pat on the shoulder. They have both agreed long ago to only hug in private as their usual display of their affection for each other, makes too many onlookers uncomfortable.

"How was your trip, Father?"

"Uneventful. I arrived yesterday because I finished in New York City early."

"Are you anxious to go home?"

"I haven't thought about it, especially since I discovered a steel mill for sale here in Philadelphia. I'm planning on heading out there to see how they run things. When you're done here, we should go together."

"Yes, I'd like that. How is it that you're finished with business in New York already? I thought we'd have to go back there for the final sale of your father's land before going back home to England."

"One of the buyers of another property decided to buy the last one."

"So, does this mean we're heading home earlier than expected?"

"Why, are you in a hurry?"

"No. No, I was just wondering what your plans are after Philadelphia," Graham replies. He's not sure what he wants to do. *I'm not going to make a decision until I talk to Lilith, he thinks.*

"I haven't decided yet. How was your day? How's the reading of the Will and have you found out how you're related to her?"

"I would rather talk about your business, if you don't mind. It's been a confusing day."

"Sure, of course." His father's topics of conversation center on their businesses, pushing the matter of the Neustat estate out of his mind.

The following morning at precisely ten o'clock, Lilith resumes her story and Graham braces himself for more tears. He hates to see her this sad.

The funeral and the week following are a blur to Lilith. She vaguely remembers neighbors dropping in to say a kind word and to bring a dish of food. She does what is required of her—visiting with folks and eating a bit of food to satisfy onlookers—but she can't shake the empty darkness.

She wonders, *Is it me? Am I bad luck? My mother, my brother, Papa, Aunt Rosanne—they're all gone. And now, Daniel. Can anyone ever love me and live?*

A week later, classes resume and she continues teaching. She doesn't have the same enthusiasm for her work and doesn't do much more than teach, weep and sleep.

Lilith stops doing all the things she had once joyfully done. She no longer bakes bread to share or takes the time to make delicious meals. She doesn't add a bow to her hair, she just pins it back. She even ceases going to services on Sundays because a church service was the last event where she was happy and accompanied by her vibrant, loving husband.

She can't think of any reason for being. She has no purpose except to teach and anyone can easily replace her at that.

By mid-December with the school break around the corner, a sense of panic takes over. What will she do with her life now? Will she ever enjoy teaching as she did before Daniel's death? Should she move somewhere away from these debilitating, gut wrenching memories? Yet, this place holds all her happy memories too. Can she leave that?

Almost in answer to her questions, Lilith receives a letter from her best friend. Lilith vaguely remembers writing Noreen during the worst of her depression following Daniel's tragic death. Noreen knows that she is now the only living person who loves Lilith and that Christmas will be a time when Lilith will need a friend the most. Noreen's letter invites her to come spend the holiday season and to get acquainted with Noreen and Jared's newest daughter.

Absentmindedly, Lilith packs her clothing, and locks up the house. Her offer to leave the horses with a neighbor in exchange for a ride to and from the train station is readily accepted. Lilith takes the train to Gooseville on an overcast Thursday morning, one week before Christmas.

Noreen hardly recognizes Lilith when she sees her step off the train. Her friend looks gaunt, her face expressionless, her smile and beautiful, straight teeth buried beneath a grave sadness. Noreen wants to help Lilith find a reason to live again but she doesn't know how to do that. For now, she shows her that someone cares. Yet, despite Noreen's best efforts, their reunion lacks its usual warmth and giddiness.

A few days after a most quiet Christmas, Lilith's mind snaps to attention. She hasn't spent a breath without Daniel in her thoughts, but somehow, she has neglected her duties to his memory.

She thinks desperately, *I must tell Daniel's mother! I need to find her.*

She doesn't know about her son. How could I have let so much time pass by?

"Noreen," she calls out from her room. "Noreen, I need to go to Delton. I'm leaving tomorrow morning. I haven't told Mrs. Breat about her son."

Noreen knows she can't stop her, but she can at least delay her leaving for such an adventure without a plan. She asks Lilith a series of very good, sensible questions that Lilith doesn't know the answers to.

"What's her name?" Noreen asks.

"I don't remember her first name," Lilith replies.

"Oh well, what's her address then?"

"I don't know that. Maybe if I found one of her letters to Daniel."

"Yes, that's smart. But what if she's moved, what then?"

"I don't know."

"What about the horses back home? What about your students? Are you going to write to the town of Erinsberg and tell them they need to find a new teacher, two weeks before school starts up again?"

Lilith doesn't have answers to any of these questions but isn't deterred in her quest.

"Mrs. Breat most certainly deserves to be located and told about Daniel," Noreen reassures. "But instead of just showing up in Delton and not knowing where to go, how about you write a letter and ask the city to assist you in finding her?"

Lilith exhales and says, "Oh, that's a good idea, Noreen. I'll get pen and paper and start working on that right away. Will you read it and tell me if it makes sense to you before I send it off?"

"Of course, bun," a pet name, short for bunny, usually reserved for one of her children. "I'll gladly do that for you."

Noreen breathes a sigh of relief. She can only imagine her friend wandering the streets in the City of Delton when the only other big city she's ever stepped foot in is Westlake, Ohio. Lilith would be lost with no clear agenda in mind. Noreen doesn't want to think about what could happen to her sad friend without some definitive plan.

December 29, 1862

To: *Sheriff's Department*
The City of Delton, Michigan

Dear Officers:

I am writing to you today because I need your assistance in finding one of your city's citizens. She is Mrs. Breat, a widow. I do not know her first name. I believe she has always resided in your city and is employed as an accountant in Madam Deb's Fabric shop on the southeast side.

I hope you can find her for me and write me back with her address and full name. I have to sadly inform her that her only son, Daniel, has passed away.

Please find it in your hearts to help me accomplish this heavy task.

Yours truly,
Mrs. Lilith (Daniel) Breat
Erinsberg, Ohio

"That's a very good letter, Lilith. I wouldn't change a word. Let's send it first thing tomorrow morning. After we do that, do you want to go for a walk by the river? I heard they want to put in a bench and start making it look like a park. There's promise of a clear day tomorrow," Noreen says pleasantly.

But Lilith freezes at the mere thought of going for a walk. Gooseville had been the town where she and Daniel courted after they met and she could see him everywhere. Quite suddenly, she feels a need to leave.

The next morning, Noreen and her growing family walk with Lilith to the train station after they post the letter. Lilith wires ahead to Erinsberg asking her neighbors to come meet her at the train station with the horse and wagon.

Even though Noreen was glad to see her friend, she isn't sorry to see her go. There is so much gloom surrounding her. Even Noreen's children sensed it and had an unusually quiet holiday as a result. Lilith thanks Noreen and Jared for their incredible generosity and gracious hospitality and for looking after her so well.

"I love you, Lilith. Write to me when you're settled in. Take care now."

Noreen wipes a few droplets off her cheeks as the train pulls away. Jared puts his arm around his wife as they wave their goodbyes. Noreen wonders if she will ever see her friend again and how soon she will hear from her.

The neighbor picks up Lilith from the train station with her team of horses. At the sight of the team, Lilith knows she should sell at least one horse and possibly the wagon too. She will only ever have need for the one horse and the buggy until it is time to leave for Delton. She realizes all the decisions that she will have to make, alone, and dreads the weeks ahead.

The void left by Daniel's passing fills her surroundings with a stillness. It seems she can never escape the silence. Other than the friendship she cherishes with Noreen, Daniel had been the only other person who knew her well.

Lilith mechanically goes through their possessions and packs away keepsakes and non-essentials into crates. She gives away Daniel's clothing and anything else she can't make use of. All the paper money they have stashed away is sewn into the hem of her winter coat. As soon as she hears from the City of Delton, her plan is to leave Erinsberg. She can't live here anymore.

She cries every day. Daniel's memory is in everything and everywhere. She is anxious to leave Erinsberg and sometimes decides that she won't wait any longer. Then by the next day she comes to her senses and knows she must wait for word about Mrs. Breat's whereabouts.

When school starts up again in early January, her classroom is bursting at the seams. Her life's daily routine is busy and she is grateful for that.

Lilith's thoughts constantly drift to memories of Daniel, making her neglectful of herself and careless of her surroundings. One morning, she wakes and finds a frozen bucket of water that is sitting next to the stove. Lilith chides herself for forgetting to feed the stove with enough kindling to last the night and then she notices that she hasn't even replenished the wood box. She dreads facing a dark, freezing morning to gather the logs piled up by the side of the house and vows to not make that mistake again.

Everybody notices her detachment. With downcast, unfocused eyes, Lilith stops greeting her neighbors and even her students can feel her sorrow.

One day at the mercantile, Lilith comes upon a couple who are engaged to be married. She congratulates the two and wishes them well. She stops short of wishing them happiness as she is afraid she might lose any happiness she once knew if she wishes them the same. She hurries home before tears obliterate her vision.

She will never forget Daniel's tender demeanor, the hope she felt for her love-filled future, their shared happiness, joy, and dreams. Her fond memories and the resulting smile that graces her face dissipates when she recalls the weight of his head and his bloodied hand on her face. She throws herself on her bed with great misery remembering the death in his eyes.

While packing, Lilith finds Daniel's letters from his mother and vows she will go search for her immediately instead of waiting for the response from the Sheriff's Department in Delton. Disappointingly, the return address is that of the Post Office. *If I go to the Post Office, I wonder if they could tell me where her home is,* she thinks. *How many fabric stores could there possibly be in Delton?*

Lilith certainly has enough money to pay for lodging while she searches. Determined to go, she finishes packing, crating up her belongings except for travel necessities. The next afternoon, she receives a letter from the Sheriff's office. By the end of March, on what would have been Daniel's twenty-ninth birthday, she leaves Erinsberg for good.

32
Lilith, Emily and Deborah

Lilith tells the small group that after she placed her crated belongings in a short-term storage building near Delton's train depot, she hired a cab to take her to the police station.

Emily and Lilith recount how they finally met.

When Deb hears a knock at the front door one morning at nine-thirty, she thinks it is a client who is still drunk or one who's had a fight with his wife and is coming to seek sympathy. She opens the door and sees the loveliest creature standing there and thinks to herself, *What luck! I wonder how many men would give their week's pay to spend quality time with this shapely young wench.*

Deb's greeting is pleasant, "Oh my. Hello there."

Lilith replies with a question attached, "Good morning. Is Mrs. Breat here?"

Deborah's glee is dampened at the question but she doesn't let Lilith stand outside for long. If this young, beautiful woman is here for Emily, she is probably a respected member of society and won't appreciate the stain on her reputation just for having stood at the madam's front door.

"Yes, of course. Please, come in," she answers, stepping aside to let Lilith in through the front entrance. "I'll get her for you. Won't you sit down and wait here?" she asks, pointing to the sofa in the boudoir.

The young woman nods and Deborah turns to leave. "I'll return shortly with Mrs. Breat. May I tell her who's calling?" Deborah asks, dying of curiosity as to who the young woman is and what her connection is to Emily.

"Certainly. I'm Mrs. Daniel Breat."

"Oh!" Deborah nods and hurries to get Emily. Deborah meets Josie in the hallway and asks her to get the tea on. Emily is in her office upstairs working on last night's accounts when Deborah bursts in to tell her that a young lady has asked for her.

Emily ponders, "She came in through the front door?"

"Yes. I guess she didn't know to go to the residential side," replies Deborah impatiently.

"Who is she?"

"Mrs. Daniel Breat," Deborah emphatically announces.

At Emily's startled look, Deborah places her hand on the younger woman's arm and continues calmly, "Josie is getting the tea on. Do you want it brought into the parlor?"

"Oh, yes please. How very thoughtful of you, Deborah. Thank you."

Emily rises from the desk and hurries to the parlor as Deborah goes to fetch Lilith.

While she waits, Lilith examines her surroundings. Her eyes jump from provocative wall hangings to statues of naked men and women. Rich fabrics cover the sofas and chairs that adorn the large room. The chairs are all very elaborate in their velour coats and the colors on the walls, floors, furniture and even the ceiling is impressive. The rich decor inside the building is well disguised by the ordinary brick exterior.

The pictures on the walls however, hint at the true story of the ill repute house.

What an odd room. Maybe the fabric store is adjacent? Lilith thinks.

When Deborah reappears, she invites Lilith to follow her, "Emily is in the parlor and we have rung for tea." Lilith follows Deborah to the residential side of the building and immediately registers the difference in decor. The shades on these walls are all a pale yellow, the floorboards are well worn, and the furniture is ordinary. A woman is waiting in the parlor, her hands tightly clasped in anticipation. The room holds comforting and personal possessions like framed pictures, unfinished sewing projects, books, and plants. Lilith inhales deeply in the hopes of subsiding the butterflies in her stomach. Deborah turns and closes the door behind her, leaving the two women alone and taking her overwhelming curiosity with her.

Emily smiles as she approaches Lilith. Lilith extends her hand and says, "I'm Lilith. Daniel's," she pauses briefly, "wife."

Emily ignores the hand, opens her arms, and gives Lilith a most welcoming hug. Her first comment has a question attached, "I'm so happy to finally be meeting you. So where is my handsome son?"

Lilith's sucked in breath and the stricken look on her face tells Emily more than she wants to believe. "No. No! When? How?" she sobs freely. "Oh, Lord. My sins have finally caught up to me. I'm being punished."

Although Lilith is puzzled at the statement, she leads Emily to a sofa. She sits next to her and painfully describes everything about the horrifying accident.

She says, "I apologize for not finding you sooner. I didn't know your first name nor your address. I found a letter from you to Daniel but your return address is just the local post office. Finally, I wrote the Sheriff's office and they provided me with the information that led me here to you."

Emily wipes tears and says, "I was getting a bit concerned that I hadn't heard from Daniel in so long. He was never this neglectful. Here

I thought the two of you had probably left to go prospecting for the summer and that usually makes it difficult for letters to find their way."

"Yes, I can see that," says Lilith. She just blurts out, "He died peacefully in my arms." Both women weep anew, consoled by the word *peaceful*.

In the silence following their heartbreaking conversation, they drink their cold tea, each wrapped in a memory of the young man. Lilith interrupts the stillness in the room and boldly asks, "What did you mean when you said you were being punished for your sins?"

Emily's posture stiffens. Other than Deborah, Lilith will be the last living person who Emily can consider as true family so she divulges the whole truth. With Daniel gone, the truth will harm no one, and it might set her free from her own guilt.

"I'm not Daniel's birth mother. He never knew my sister as she died giving birth to him. He was such a beautiful boy, full of mischief and laughter. He filled my life with joy. I didn't deserve such joy."

"What did you do that was so terrible to deserve losing Daniel? After all, you took in your nephew and reared him," says Lilith. "Did you raise him all alone? Where was his father?"

Emily has revealed more in the last minute than she thought she would ever tell another living soul but she tries to explain, "My dear Lilith. I hope you don't think less of me after I tell you this. I would hope that you'd want to be my daughter-in-law regardless of my faults and weaknesses."

Lilith gives her a nod and Emily takes it as consent and continues. "My own mother died when I was seventeen. In the year following her death, my grieving father became a drunk and gambled himself out of the rich lifestyle that my sister and I had been brought up in. He sent me here to work for Deborah as her accountant. He sent Adeline, Daniel's mother, to a neighbor to become their maid. Can you believe a father would do such a thing?"

Lilith certainly has her own story about the loss of family and nods.

Emily continues, "Adeline had enough strength left in h
that she was wooed by the sole heir to the Gateway Estate. Wh
parents discovered the courtship, they banished him overseas t   and
to finish his studies. He left without knowing that Adeline was with
child. When Adeline's pregnancy started showing, his family sent her to
work for another wealthy family. They didn't treat her well and eventually
her loneliness drove her to seek me out. She exhausted herself getting
here in the middle of a winter storm and died giving birth to Daniel. I've
always wondered if I should have tried to find David and tell him about
Adeline and his son, but I never found the courage."

Emily's handkerchief is too wet to be of further use. With disgust, she
uses the back of her hand to wipe her nose and cheeks. Everyone she has
ever loved is gone now. Lilith is also wiping wet cheeks. She doesn't have
any family left either.

"Over the years, I became protective of Daniel and tried to shield
him from the shame of my working for the madam of a brothel. Oh,
don't get me wrong. Personally, I'm not ashamed, but people can be so
cruel and I badly wanted to protect Daniel, so I told him lies. I was never
married! I didn't have a husband who went overseas and died there."

Both women sit for moment, silently in their own thoughts. Emily
relieved to share her feelings, Lilith amazed that her husband had actually
been raised in a brothel!

Emily breaks the silence, and asks, "What did he tell you about where
and how he was brought up?"

Lilith can't help the small smile on her face and says, "He told me
you had found an accounting position with a fabric company on the
southeast side of Delton. That was the only detail I had to work with
when trying to find you. I sought help from the Delton police officers
when I found one of your letters without more of a return address other
than the Post Office. Then one day, I decided I was going to write you
regardless, but before I had the chance to mail that letter, I received a
reply from the Sheriff's office. They asked that I come here to Delton and

they would escort me to you. When I got here, I told them I didn't need an escort, they only need tell me the address. They were reluctant, but I insisted and here I am."

"I'm glad you didn't come here with the sheriff or his men, especially later in the day. That would've scared some of the customers away and Deb wouldn't like that," says Emily.

"Oh, I'm sure," replies Lilith, raising her eyebrows. "It wasn't easy to get the address from them and I fully understand why now."

They spend the afternoon getting to know each other. Lilith tells her about having lost her own parents and brother, of moving in with her great-aunt, and of Rosanne's death five years later. She tells her about Noreen and about her menial life up until the time that she became qualified to teach. She rejoices when she tells her about meeting Daniel and how he made the evening of the barn dance turn into the best day of her life.

"So, you're all alone too?" asks Emily.

Surprised by the reality of the question, Lilith replies, "Yes. That's right. I am."

The women look into each others' eyes, lean forward and hug once again. Emily says, "Well, let's make sure to stay connected no matter what."

Lilith very much agrees.

The women each take a deep breath, picking up their cups of cold tea.

"Tell me more about Daniel," Lilith implores. What was he like as a child?"

"Oh, dear. Well, he was forever a happy boy. He'd make us laugh all the time. It was almost uncanny that he knew humor at such a young age. One day when he was almost two-years-old and being potty-trained, he ran to the room where we kept his pot but Deborah hadn't seen him go to that place. That was his signal that he needed to pee. By the time she figured out where he was, she had missed the opportunity to help him get his pants down and found him standing on a wet floor. She cleaned him up, changed his clothes and then went to take out a pail and a mop. He wanted to help clean up his mess and took hold of the mop. It was much too unwieldy for such a small child and he quickly became frustrated. In order to avoid a tantrum, Deborah said, 'I don't have the right size mop for the height of a little boy like you.' To which Daniel replied, 'Well Deb-Deb, get one.' He would always say the darnedest things. We figured out what he meant was that he fully intended on peeing on the floor again in the near future." They laugh.

"Did he tell you that he had scarlet fever when he was five?"

Lilith shakes her head, no.

"He almost died. He had such a sore throat that he couldn't speak. The sides of his throat were swollen and I remember being frightened by how feverish he was. There was a red, hot rash on his little body that scared me more than anything. I didn't know what was happening to my son. A doctor came by and we had to isolate the residential side of the house because his illness was contagious. Those were two long weeks full of worry."

A comfortable pause followed and then Emily continued fondly, "One time he had rushed home from school because there was something very important that he didn't want to forget to tell me. 'Guess what Mama,' he said. 'We have a new boy who just started today and his name is Richard Richardson. I think that's marvellously fun, don't you? Can I change my name to Daniel Danielson? Can I?'"

Lilith soon sighs with subdued laughter. How she would have loved to have seen the interaction between Daniel and his mother, especially sharing stories such as these.

Emily invites Lilith to stay for supper. In the kitchen, Deborah and Josie meet Daniel's widow and learn more about the last four years of his short life. Lilith has finally met the two women of her late husband's childhood that he spoke of constantly—Emily and Deborah.

When it comes time for Lilith to head back to her hotel, Emily is apprehensive for her safety. Deborah agrees and asks her to please stay the night. As Lilith doesn't understand the dangers of city life, she trusts that these women do and she stays. She settles in her husband's old bedroom, thinking about all the memories of Daniel the walls were witness to.

The next morning, Emily insists that Lilith stay in Daniel's old room for as long as she needs until she decides what she wants to do next. So, with the watchman as capable carrier, Lilith returns to her hotel to collect her things and then on to the storage building near the station for her crated items.

The watchman carries all of Lilith's possessions up the stairs. She wants to put her things into longer-term storage, but Emily convinces her to save the effort and expense and tuck the crates in the corner of the bedroom where they will be out of the way.

Emily also thinks that the sight of the unpacked crates will speed up Lilith making a decision about her future. She is right. But before she can make a plan, Lilith is presented with an unexpected job offer.

33
Lilith

As she ages, Deb becomes more determined to find a madam to replace her. She isn't going to live forever, and she is worried about the future of the women under her roof. Although they all do their work well, not one has the ability to run a business. Emily would be an excellent manager, but she wouldn't set foot in the boudoir.

But now, there is Lilith who is both smart and beautiful and has additional qualities that would make her an ideal replacement. Deb starts to list them off:

- Lilith, being a school teacher, has a good head on her shoulders.
- She likely enjoys sex, knowing Daniel.
- She may be lonely for male companionship.
- Her beauty and physique will attract most men and new business.
- She may be needy in a monetary way.

Deb knows that if she can convince Lilith to get into the business, she will make a huge success out of herself. Deb has an instinct about these things and hopes that she can help Lilith realize that her obvious sensuality is made for such a career.

Deb waits for a Friday afternoon when she knows that Emily will be spending at least three uninterrupted hours with the books. She then boldly asks Lilith, "Do you want to come with me? I'd like for us to spend the day together, if you don't mind."

Curious, Lilith agrees. *This should be fascinating*, she thinks.

Deb opens the French doors in between the business and residence side. Lilith finds herself once again in the room of rich colors and fabrics on the walls, floors, and furniture. There are men inside with the working girls. Deb attempts to entice Lilith by showing her what she presumes is the glamor of such a life as hers. Deb never knew anything but abuse as a child and prostitution as an adult, so a good life in Deb's eyes is the one she is offering Lilith.

Lilith looks on at the women in their expensive dresses, moving in sensual ways that speak—without using words—to the eager men. She can't explain why her body is reacting to the suggestive scenes. She hasn't felt any sensations like this since before Daniel's death. Even her breathing is becoming deeper. Deb observes Lilith and knows her instincts are confirmed and she smiles with hope.

Taking turns, one of the Madam's fashionably dressed girls offers the visiting men a choice of drinks and provides them with a list containing the names of the girls and the cost of each service. Of course, a verbal menu is discreetly spoken out loud for the illiterate. The customer exchanges payment for his drink and his choice of services and is led upstairs by his chosen girl.

Deb has not stopped talking since they walked into the room. "This is how it works in most brothels. The men are served with a liquor of their liking. The girls walk around and stop to chat. They discuss whatever the gentleman wants to talk about. It's all about him and making him feel good about himself. We find that if we pay particular attention to new clients and are especially gentle with those who are here for their first sexual experience, they'll come back. However much the gentleman is willing or able to pay dictates the girl who will service him and how long his stay at the establishment will be."

"So, some men come here for their first experience with a woman?"

"Oh, yes. In fact, many of the young virgin men who come here are brought by their own fathers. Many of those fathers believe that had they been provided with such an experience themselves at that age, they might never have married into such boring lives, void of love and passion; lives that drive them into the arms of the women here."

Lilith's eyebrows raise and Deb continues, "Of course, the fathers also use what we have to offer while they wait for their sons. At least the women here know how to treat a man and make him feel like his life is worth living and that there's excitement to be had. It's very beneficial, for everybody, I assure you."

Lilith doesn't think men are so insecure that they need such flattery and attention from women who work in a brothel. She also doesn't think that most wives become cold and unfeeling toward their husbands, but she keeps an open mind.

She thinks, *Perhaps my marriage was an exception.*

Deb tries to show Lilith that the work is noble and provides a necessity. "Sure, there are men who become regulars as they're either not married or not being satisfied at home. Oh, I'm not blaming their wives as some have failing health and can't perform their wifely duties. Some don't have the know-how and their husbands certainly weren't capable of teaching them either. Men that come here have all different kinds of home situations and come from all kinds of work and business. But as much as men are all different—when it comes to sex, they are all the same."

Lilith says, "Oh, I doubt that."

Challenged, Deb calls one of the working girls over to her table, "Would you tell Lilith what kind of work the men you've had as customers in the last few weeks do for a living?"

"Certainly. Let me see, I've had a couple of politicians, a teacher, a preacher, doctors, miners, an editor, clerks, a bank manager, a deputy, a store owner, a train conductor and … "

"Thank you," interrupts Deb. "Now get back to the customers." Lilith has no choice but to believe that plenty of men use brothels for pleasures they do not get elsewhere.

"It's not hard to understand when you know that most men think about sex all the time. When men aren't getting it and can afford to pay for it, there's no better place than a brothel to get what they need. We are discreet. If the men want to sit and visit with each other, they can. If they want to remain anonymous, they can ask for privacy and they'll get it. You can tell which ones aren't married because they have no fear of being seen here. Those who come after dark are usually married. You'll even find that a lot of the gentlemen callers don't even live in Delton. They're here on business and are free to indulge outside of their hometown's watchful eyes."

A different girl brings a tray holding a bottle of brandy and a couple of glasses to Deb's table. Without seeking Lilith's consent, Deb pours them each a drink. Lilith hadn't tasted hard liquor before and expects to find it distasteful but she finds that she rather likes it and soon relaxes in its warm glow.

Deb hopes that in time, Lilith's curiosity might just finally be the ticket to her retirement. Deb watches Lilith look on as seductions unfold and she can't tell if Lilith's cheeks take on a rosy hew because of the liquor or the scenery.

Deb's favorite and newest girl, Tina, walks in just then. More than one set of eyes watch the young beauty. She is wearing a black dress with bright yellow trim and the dress shows cleavage which Tina expertly exploits. Lilith's eyes almost pop out of her head and she gulps the remaining brandy at the sight of this sultry woman in action. Lilith watches Tina lead a man past the bar to the room of poker tables at the back.

Deb refills Lilith's glass and smiles as she watches the younger woman enjoy the show. Men walk around the place with ease where they can comfortably place an arm around the working girls and squeeze arms and buttocks, knowing that they will not be rejected, shamed, or scolded. Lilith becomes frustrated and pines for Daniel's loving attention.

Just then, a gentleman is let into the room. Calvin is of medium height but he is a man who is so sure of himself that he appears taller. Gifted with wide shoulders and a flat stomach, he is certainly handsome with his square jaw, dark hair, and brown eyes. He scans the room and his eyes rest on Lilith. He makes his way around the room, kissing the girls hello, his actions catching Lilith's eye. Everyone appears to know him and he is bold enough to openly fondle all the girls.

Finally, he approaches Deb's table, bends, and kisses her hand when she places it in his. "Calvin, darling. How good to see you. It's been too long. Let me introduce you to my niece, Lilith." She winks at Lilith in the hopes that she will go along with the white lie.

Calvin bows and doesn't take his eyes off Lilith's. He takes her hand and kisses it. "Deb, where have you been hiding such a lovely, ah, niece?"

Lilith decides to find her voice, "How do you do. I wasn't hiding as I just arrived in town. I'm here visiting."

Calvin puts his right hand on his chest like he's wounded and says, genuinely, "You mean you're not going to stay?"

"I haven't decided," she responds, unsure how she feels about his apparent sincerity.

"Well, until you do, I'd love to spend some quality time with you, starting right now. Deb! Tell me how much I have to spend for this beauty's service," he blurts as his eyes focus on Lilith's chest.

His hungry stare strikes a yearning in Lilith's core and she feels her breathing deepen and her heartbeat quicken. Calvin can sense her body's response to his own lusty needs and is encouraged. She stutters, "I, ah, that is to say, I'm not for hire."

"Really? You look exquisite, delightful, dare I say, even delicious.

Please let me shower you with jewels and furs. Let me help you shop for the perfect gown and come to the theater with me. We can forget all about this place. Just be with me. What do you say?"

Deborah, worried that Lilith will bolt right out of the room, interjects, "I'm afraid you're out of line, Calvin. Lilith's only visiting with me. She truly is my niece."

Calvin looks at Deb first, then back at Lilith, and sighs. "I have insulted you. I'm terribly sorry. Please forgive me. Let me buy you dinner and I'll make it up to you."

Lilith exhales and is about to decline when he suddenly picks her up by the waist, right out of the chair, and swings her around in a full circle. He lets her down gently but before her feet touch the ground, he places his left leg securely on the floor in between her thighs and tilts backwards. The movement makes her bend forward, chest first into his, and makes her fully aware right through her skirts, of his muscular leg in between hers. As she slides down to the floor, her weight, even as light as she is, gives the momentum of being massaged on every part of her body that touches his, but especially her voluptuous chest and her pelvic region.

Out of breath and blushing, not quite knowing what to say, Lilith shakes her head back and forth and pushes her hands up on his chest as he straightens up. Solidly back on the floor now, he cups and kneads her left buttock as he lowers his face to kiss her neck where his warm breath produces goosebumps.

All the while Deb is saying, "Stop it, Calvin. Calvin, don't do that. Watchman! Tina! There you are. Come meet Calvin, please."

Finally, the watchman lays a hand on Calvin's shoulder and he releases his hold of Lilith. Speechless, she averts her eyes and walks as quickly as she can out of the room. She closes the brothel's adjoining door behind her, leans up against it and fans herself from the heat of her unexpected desire.

Calvin keeps his gaze on the departing beauty then turns it toward

Deb, "Pity. How could you tease me like that? Who's going to be able to satisfy me this evening after seeing her?"

Deb replies, "Don't be so dramatic, Calvin. Let me introduce you to Tina."

There's no point berating Calvin for his instinctive actions as the two women were, after all, in the brothel side of the building. What else could they expect?

Safely behind the closed doors, Lilith still fanning herself with her hand, makes her way to the empty parlor. She sinks into the first chair, still feeling the heat on her cheeks.

Initially, Lilith is confused by her body's response. Then shame follows. *What will Emily think of me being seduced by the first man who looks me in the eyes with such lust?*

Five minutes later, Deborah enters the parlor and places her hand on Lilith's shoulder. "They're not all like that, you know. Calvin knows that he's good at seduction, he knows what he likes, what he wants, and goes after it. His reputation here among the girls is that he knows how to use it too. Most men need a bit of persuasion because they don't realize that they're free to be themselves here. Calvin is actually quite exciting. Oh, if only I were thirty years younger."

Lilith agrees in part to some of what Deb says and voices, "I know. But some men are more like Daniel. He was so kind, gentle, loving, attentive, and everything wonderful."

"Now, Lilith. There was bound to be at least one man who would stir up those feelings in you that only Daniel once had, so don't fight them. Not only can you use those feelings to remember him by, you can use them to remind yourself that you're a vibrant woman, still alive and with blood flowing through you. Daniel didn't expect you to die with him."

Shocked, Lilith replies, "How can you say that? I don't want to forget Daniel. He was everything to me, still is. I miss him very much, I love him so completely. I feel like I'm being unfaithful even if only my mind wanders. Deborah, he just died!"

"Yes." She pauses and adds from her own experiences, "Sadly pet, one day you'll forget the feel of Daniel's arms around you. Oh, you'll never forget how he was the one to awaken the woman in you and you'll never forget the love. I promise. Just don't be too hard on yourself."

Deb could sense that Lilith wouldn't know how to listen to her own body so she vowed to help her make the right choice. Maybe Lilith's choice wouldn't meet Deb's and the brothel's needs. If it did though, Lilith would be the queen of madams for counties around, Deb would make sure of that.

34
Lilith

The following afternoon, Deb asks Lilith, "How would you like a chance to make a little bit of money each week by sewing, washing, and mending the fancy undergarments that have suffered a mishap?" Lilith jumps at the proposition and they head toward the girls' quarters.

Deb observes that Lilith is very mindful of the delicate and easily torn materials she has picked up from the mending pile. Mostly, Deb sees that Lilith's curiosity is being challenged anew.

Just then, Tina pokes her head out from behind a curtain and says, "Deb, you'll have to help me. Oh, hello. You must be Mrs. Breat."

Lilith looks on at the woman from yesterday who is three years younger than her, has jet black hair and fair skin. She wears powdered makeup on her eyes that gives one the impression that they tilt upwards and the rouge lifts her cheekbones beyond where they really are. Lilith thinks she looks exquisite.

"I am, Miss?"

Deb interjects before Tina can say anything. "Lilith, you should know that we don't use our last names much in here."

"Well then, Tina, please call me Lilith."

"That's a very pretty name," she says, hiding behind the drape. She continues, "Deb, I'm having difficulty with this thing."

"Come out and let us see. Apparently, Lilith here is very good with sewing challenges. Now did you find a tear?"

"No, I don't think so. I'm just having a hard time trying to figure out how to make it fit my body," she explains as she walks to the center of the room with her arms around her middle. She adds, "Wherever did you find this? It's beautiful."

"I honestly don't remember," replies Deb.

Lilith raises an eyebrow and blushes at the sight of her. Tina's full-length dress is the brightest red possible. The shiny satin is glued to the whale bone underneath. The corset is the shape of a heart at the front with material finely draping over each breast. It doesn't have any shoulder straps or ties at the back. The top of her chest and over her shoulders to as far down as her buttocks are bare! The entire dress relies on the woman's ample shape to hold it up as it is solely supported by the curves of her bosom and derriere.

"Oh dear, Tina. You're not enough to fill it up with. Lilith, can you tell if there is any way it can be altered?" asks Deb knowingly.

"I will need to have a closer look. Tina, could you slip it off?"

"Sure. Actually, if I do this," she inhales and twists to the right, "it just falls off."

"Oh, I see. It is too big on you," Lilith giggles to hide her discomfort at seeing the naked young woman.

Tina doesn't bother to cover up. She just stands there and hopes that Lilith has a magic needle and thread so she can be the one to wear the most sensuous gown she has ever seen.

Lilith turns the dress to examine the inside where the material connects with the whale bones. Then, she turns it to face away from her and holds it up to her body as she approaches the looking glass.

She concludes, "No. I'm afraid that any alterations would destroy the fabric as it's too delicate. See how the hem here has unraveled? That would happen throughout the entire dress if I took it apart. I believe it was made for one woman only and that it was actually sewn together one inch at a time as she was standing in it."

Deb remarks as she reaches for the hem, "How very clever and difficult to make, I'm sure."

"That must have taken a lot of patience on everybody's part!" exclaims Tina. She continues, "Lilith! While you were holding it up next to you, I thought it might fit you properly. Go on, give it a try."

"Tina! No. I—I couldn't. I'm not one of Deb's girls. I've—never. It's too provocative!" she stammers.

"No one else is here! Please? No one but the three of us will know what it looks like on a woman with the right body shape," Tina answers back, encouragingly.

Deb agrees and tries to sound nonchalant and not too anxious or hopeful. Out of curiosity more than anything, Lilith acquiesces.

"Do you want to go behind the curtain to put it on?" asks Deb.

"Ah, no. I'm sure I'll need your help with it," she says as she starts to undress and blushes the entire time.

Deb is right—Lilith could have been Aphrodite. If she wanted, Lilith could have men offering to buy her the moon with a figure like that!

Tina says, "It is easier I think, if the garment starts from the floor. Here, like this," and she places it so Lilith can step into the circle she made.

Tina starts to lift it up. "You have such shapely hips compared to mine. Lucky you. Oh, well this is where we differ considerably," pointing to her chest and all three women laugh. Lilith pulls the dress into place, running her hands down the fine material covering her hips. It is breathtakingly sensuous.

Tina is overjoyed. "How I wish this was in my size. I could turn a lot of tricks in this Deb. Lilith, see for yourself in the mirror."

Lilith almost faints at the sight. "This sure does not leave much to the imagination, does it?" she gasps.

Both Deb and Tina sigh. Deb says, "Tina, please be a darling and go check on things downstairs."

"Sure Deb," she says, putting her day dress on and leaving the room.

Deb says, "Well, I don't think I'm ever going to find a working girl who will fit this as the original owner did or as you do."

Lilith starts to remove it and Deb decides to help her out of it.

"You know, I really have no use for it. If you want to keep it Lilith, go right ahead," says Deb.

"Oh, I couldn't. I'd never have an occasion to wear it."

Deb laughs. "Nonsense. Don't you think you'll meet and marry someone one day and show him what you're made of?"

A flabbergasted Lilith answers, "What? Don't you think a new husband would think me a—sorry to say this—but a whore for wearing something like this?"

"Personally? No. I would think a husband would be excited that his wife isn't a prude but a willing sexual partner."

"I can't have this conversation, Deborah. I'm sorry but … "

"Oh, of course not. It's too soon, especially after yesterday. Please just take over the work with the girls' wardrobes. Leave this in that armoire by the corner over there. Now let's forget all about this." Deb leaves the room, cheerful at the thought that she has succeeded once again, in awakening feelings that Lilith can't deny.

Lilith's nimble fingers make quick work and the pile of outfits needing mending is down to an empty basket by the end of the week. Lilith doesn't make a large sum of money from the work, but feels good to be of use again.

Emily isn't entirely oblivious to the goings on in the house. She knows Deb is forever on the lookout for a replacement and Emily figures that the misguided Madam has targeted Lilith as that person.

When the two are alone together, Emily has a heart-to-heart talk with Lilith. "Let me tell you about the ugly, dark side of being a prostitute that Deb likely hasn't divulged."

Emily tells Lilith about Daniel's friend, Vera. "The poor girl took her own life about eight years ago. She just couldn't face all that darkness. At one point or another, all the working girls suffer a beating at the hands of some angry man and more than one has ended up in the hospital.

"These girls also worry about unwanted pregnancies. Then there are days the lawmen come around and arrest everybody. Oh, they release them usually the very next day, and most of the time the watchman is freed the same day, but we're never sure what's in store.

"Then there are days when some customers come here straight from work and don't take the time to bathe and change from their smelly clothes. I don't know how the girls put up with it. Well, that's not true, I guess I do know in part. One girl told me once that she would indulge in opium every chance she had so she could tolerate all those men and what she does with them and to them. It did help me understand how they continue to have one sexual experience after another throughout the day and pretend they're enjoying themselves just to please the man they're with. How anyone would choose that over a fulfilling marriage … well, I wouldn't, is all I have to say."

The life of a working girl is hardly pleasant, and Lilith doesn't have to be told twice. She had a slight temptation at the beginning—a piqued interest rather, but she knew she'd never seriously consider it. She now knows exactly what she wants to do.

The following week when she once again stubs a toe on a crate of her belongings, she decides to venture to the northern side of town, where the closest school is located, in search for a place to stay and to find employment. She will teach in this city if they have an empty post for her.

She also knows that in time, she will want one man who will love her as much as Daniel had. She doesn't want to have sex with different men because more than anything, she aches to feel that complete rewarding comfort of a good marriage again.

35
Graham

Graham is most uncomfortable with the conversations thus far and asks, "When is all this going to make sense, Mr. Trolley?"

"I understand how frustrating this is for all of you. Please bear with me for a while longer. We have a few minutes before we take a break. Could you tell us what brings you to America, Mr. Lestor? I'm asking because had you not been here in our country, I had instructions from Mrs. Neustat to pay for your voyage."

"Certainly. Of course."

In early July 1867, Mr. Graham Lestor steps off the train in Delton and is welcomed by a refreshing breeze that almost gives flight to his top hat. He reaches up and pushes it down tighter to hold back the locks of brown curls.

For the past four years, Graham worked as a manager in his father's steel mill business headquartered in London, England. This is his first trip to North America and his first stop was New York. He couldn't resist spending several days sightseeing in the impressive city before boarding the train to take care of business in Delton. He's not there for the steel end of their business enterprise though. He's there to sell his father's American real estate holdings and Delton is the first city with property he is tasked to deal with.

He's excited to begin the process alone. At twenty-nine, he's eager to prove his worth beyond the steel side. His father will be coming to America next month after he handles pressing business matters that keep him in England and Graham is determined to have made progress in the real estate transactions before he arrives.

Graham inhales deeply of the fresh air once more. Delton will be the first place where he will spend two months by himself and he's looking forward to it. He collects his belongings and heads to his hotel room to rest until the first meeting at ten the next morning.

Before Graham left home, his father had repeated his instructions. Graham knew them well and even made a list to put his father's anxiety at ease.

- Observe and listen first.
- Keep an account of all the information you are provided with.
- Ask follow-up questions until everything is crystal clear.

"Knowing more about our holdings in Delton will help you ask better questions." His father took out a map of the area and pointed, "We own this land, from here," he started on the outskirts of the southwest side of Delton, "including this park, to all the way over here—a couple of avenues passed the trees there. They call it a park but it's not fully developed; it's more like a wild forest, if you ask me. They do tend to the grass in an area where neighboring children play.

"Now, across from our land, here," he continues as he points, "there's a brothel that faces this cluster of trees in between Bronson and Chester.

The location of the brothel is ideal for that type of business because there aren't many neighbors to make complaints about the comings and goings. But any plans for development need to take that business into consideration because, if it were me, I'd keep my businesses that attract ladies away from that area. For now, hear what the land developers have to say and wait to see what plan they have come up with. Of course, once the land passes from our hands to theirs, what they wish to build is their business, however, we don't want them to invest unaware of the situation."

Graham didn't really hear anything new from his father and said, "It's not like I'll make a final decision without you anyway, Father. I assure you I'll investigate the value of the area thoroughly if I don't get a feeling that a better deal may be on the table."

"Good. I was hoping you'd say that. I'm really looking forward to your report and especially your recommendations. I'm anxious to find out how much you'll learn from all this."

"Me too. Thanks for your confidence."

"Don't mention it, son. I trust you, Graham. Always have."

"So, I already had plans to be in America before I received my letter from you, Mr. Trolley." Graham had stuck to his travel and business details and stayed away from mentioning anything about his personal life back home in London. He didn't want to invoke any resentment from the present company. His life was certainly peaceful and full of love compared to the stories he had heard in the last day from the two women in the room and those of the two older women.

36
Lilith and Graham

During the break from the reading and the shared stories, the memory of a fun summer spent together flashes by in both Lilith's and Graham's minds.

While Lilith daydreams, Emily fills the quiet in the study with comments about the art on the walls, the exquisite workmanship of the furniture and even the designs of the carpets.

Out in the hallway, Graham paces and wishes things hadn't ended the way they did with Lilith. It had been such an enchanting time until ...

In mid-July of 1867, Lilith is enjoying the summer break from teaching and leaves *Alice's Dress Shop* after purchasing three yards of cotton fabric and a pattern of the latest professional woman's fashion to add to her teacher's wardrobe. As she's only one block north of Madam Deb's, she decides to go visit her mother-in-law for afternoon tea. She knows that she can just drop by unannounced as her company is always welcomed by Emily.

Lilith feels eyes following her but this is nothing out of the ordinary. Due to her breathless beauty, people often stop what they're doing and watch her walk by. Today is no exception. One onlooker decides that he will do more than stare, and just as she approaches the spot where he is peering in a display window, he turns suddenly, knocking her package right out of her hands. She stumbles at the movement, stepping on his foot.

"Oh, I'm so terribly sorry. How clumsy of me," Graham says as he bends to pick up the package. He immediately finds himself appreciating the etiquette lessons his grandmother insisted he attend as an adolescent, even though he has just purposefully bumped into the loveliest woman he's ever seen.

"Hah!" Lilith inhales through her mouth when their eyes meet. *Daniel!*

Lilith shakes her head and finds her voice, "No, I'm the one who's sorry, sir. I hope I didn't hurt your foot."

"Not at all. You're as light as a feather because I didn't feel a thing. You must be an excellent dancer," he chuckles. "May I escort you somewhere, Miss?"

She is enchanted by his British accent and smiles at him. "It's Mrs., and no thank you. I'm on my way to surprise my mother-in-law for tea," replies Lilith, pleasantly.

"Very well then. Good afternoon, Madam." He thinks, *of course she'd be married.* Disappointed, he walks away.

Lilith immediately chides herself for sounding rude. She hasn't made many friends in Delton outside of work and hasn't met a man yet who interests her. Maybe it's because of his accent or his uncanny resemblance to her late husband, but she finds herself calling out, "Excuse me, sir."

"Yes?" He turns slowly, uninterested now in the possible flirtation.

"I was wondering, if you don't mind, would you escort me to the corner café after all. I don't usually do this, but I feel compelled to tell you something."

He doesn't know if he should. Her attractiveness is alluring, yes, but she's married. His curiosity wins in the end. It's just for a cup of tea—or coffee? Can you get tea in a café?

"As you wish," he replies.

They sit down and introduce each other. Both order tea with cream, no sugar.

Lilith begins, "I must apologize, Mr. Lestor. You see, I lied to you earlier. Well not really, I just didn't … oh brother! Ahem. Let me start again. You see, I was married once. My husband died four and a half years ago. Then when I first came to Delton, I lived with my mother-in-law for a couple of months until I found a very nice apartment north of here near the school where I teach. I've been living there ever since."

Graham has been drinking his tea quickly as he intends on excusing himself as soon as she's done telling him what she needs to confess. However, he hasn't waited long enough for the tea to cool and it burns his tongue. He guesses he deserves that and makes a face just then.

Lilith thinks. *That's Daniel's face all right.* She grins.

Graham doesn't know what he did to earn her smile and can't help but smirk back. *What a magnificent visage she has and then the corners of her mouth go up like that and it's even more so. How is it possible that one woman has been gifted so abundantly?*

He reaches to lightly touch her hand and says, "Thank you for wanting to tell me that. I'm new here in Delton and I was hoping to run into someone who could show me around. A teacher on her summer break is the perfect kind of person to introduce me to what this town has to offer. I think it's fate that I literally bumped into you—a school teacher. Don't you agree? What do you say? Will you accompany me around town?"

Oh my, he's also brazen—just like Daniel. Lilith snickers softly because of his effortless ease of speaking his wish. She replies, "I suppose that would be fine. There are many places I'd like to visit again and to especially see them through a new pair of eyes—yours, Mr. Lestor."

"Then it's settled. So please, call me Graham."

"Very well—Graham—and you can call me Lilith."

They finish their beverage and agree to meet at the café the next day. "Are you sure ten in the morning is a good time?" he asks.

"Yes, the museum opens at ten-thirty. We'll walk over there from here."

"I bid you a good evening, Madam. I mean, Lilith. What a perfect name for a gentle lady such as yourself."

Lilith senses renewed energy the next morning. She doesn't deny that she's looking forward to seeing Graham again. She hurries out of her apartment toward the café. Graham does the same thing, quickening his pace so he can spend as much time with her as possible.

Anxious for the morning to begin, they quickly make their way to the museum. "Oh, look Graham. How lucky that we came here today. There's a display on dinosaurs. Why, just a few weeks ago at school, my lesson was all about what has been discovered of these giant animals that lived on earth before us. I'm so excited."

He feeds off her enthusiasm but discovers he doesn't have to. He's just as captured by these historic creatures as she is. They spend the better part of the day learning all they can on the topic.

"The only thing I didn't enjoy about today was the food," says Graham.

"I agree. We won't eat at the museum tomorrow, I promise."

"I must attend a meeting that will last past lunch and won't be able to meet you until two in the afternoon. I hope that's acceptable. Unless you want to skip a day, that's fine too."

"Two o'clock it is. Where's your meeting? I can meet you there."

"Well, that would save us time. My meeting is on Fourth Avenue and the building number is five."

"Then it's all arranged. I'll show you our library. It's not far from Fourth." Lilith places a hand on his arm when they approach the park.

"Ah, there's our café. This is where I bid you good day Graham. Until tomorrow."

He takes her hand, brings it to his lips, kisses it and says, "Until tomorrow my sweet, Lilith." Their eyes lock before she veers north toward her apartment, and he turns back toward the library as his hotel is located half a block west of it.

As it's still early in the day and nothing needs Lilith's attention at home, she changes direction and heads south to Madam Deb's to visit with Emily.

The next day, the young couple's late tour of the library leads to a shared supper meal. "I feel like I've known you my whole life, Lilith, even though we've lived thousands of miles apart."

"I know what you mean, Graham. I feel the same way," she girlishly giggles as she looks onto his handsome face. "How did you like the library's selection of books by women authors? That special section is my favorite part of the library."

"I daresay it's a bold move but it appears to attract a lot of attention."

Later, the two young people part at the same place—halfway between Madam Deb's and Lilith's apartment.

They agree to skip meeting on the Friday as Lilith has commitments— her attention to new sewing projects at Madam Deb's. Graham doesn't want to delay seeing her again, but convinces himself that their next rendezvous will be even sweeter because of the time in between.

They go for a walk on Saturday and watch a game of cricket in the park. "I didn't know Americans knew how to play!" exclaims Graham.

"I think those men are immigrants and that most Americans don't know the game. I, for one, don't understand it," confesses Lilith.

Graham takes this chance to come near her when he points to a player and explains what the man is doing and why. Then he brings her attention to another player, leans his face in closer to hers, as if whispering, and tells her what that player is doing and why he's waiting his turn to play.

His hot breath in her ear gives her the shivers.

"Are you chilled?" he asks as he dares place an arm around her shoulder to provide warmth.

"No, I'm perfectly fine now. Please tell me more," she encourages. He smiles when he considers that he likely enjoyed explaining the game to Lilith more than the players who won it.

Graham notices that people stare at Lilith wherever they go but that she never seems to care. When he mentions it, she replies, "Oh, yes. That happens often. I'm used to it and I try not to let it bother me. Is it affecting you in any way? Do you want to not be seen out with me anymore?" she asks, disappointingly.

"Not a chance. I want to be seen with you, everywhere and always."

She blushes and smiles.

"Will I see you tomorrow?" asks Lilith, when their day ends at the café.

"If you love the theater, and even if you don't, will you come with me tomorrow evening? I'll hire a carriage and I can drop you off at your home afterwards. It'll be dark outside and I'd feel terrible if you didn't make it back home safely," he begs.

She raises her long eye lashes and smiles. She leans in and places one hand on his chest when she replies, "I'd love to go to the theater with you. Where shall we meet?"

"Give me your address and I'll be at your door to pick you up at seven."

"All right." Now that he knows where she lives, she feels that they've just moved up a step in their relationship.

He's surprised to learn that she lives two whole blocks further north than their usual meeting and parting place, but surmises that she enjoys the exercise.

The theater is featuring a play, *Romeo and Juliet*. Lilith hasn't had an opportunity to see it until now. Graham reserves his feelings on the production as he's seen it once already in London. He doubts that it will be as delightful here in America, but as the evening progresses and as he watches Lilith become more emotional with each scene, he decides that it is the best rendition he's ever seen.

They are both in a romantic mood on the way to her apartment and inside the cab of the carriage, Graham boldly turns his body toward Lilith. She hasn't wished for such an advance from a man in a long, long time and for a moment she isn't sure about her feelings. He places an arm around her shoulders and pulls her close to him. She quickly dismisses her hesitation.

"Lilith, you've brightened my days and invaded my dreams. May I kiss you?"

She doesn't speak. Instead, she leans in closer to him, tilts her head to his and the action invites his lips to hers.

How sweet it is to feel the softness of a man's lips on hers once again. She can't help herself and kisses him back with confidence that she won't scare him away. If he noticed her boldness, he didn't mind as he returned with a tighter embrace. Only when the carriage stops do they stop kissing. Graham can tell that Lilith is blushing by the heat of her cheeks beneath his palm. He steps out of the carriage to help her down and is reluctant to release her tiny waist.

"Tomorrow?" she asks.

"I'll send you word on the time. At this very instant I can't recall what I'm doing tomorrow. We'll meet at our usual spot. Wait for my note?"

"I will. Goodnight, Graham."

"Goodnight, my dear." He watches her walk up the stairs, open the door and step inside.

Once the door is closed behind her, a flushed Lilith leans up against it and decides that she will tell Emily about Graham soon. But for now, she's very happy to only share her adventures with him in her letters to Noreen.

Graham's suggested activities postpone Lilith's visit with Emily as the couple's plans occupy the remainder of late August. There is poetry reading at the Library on Tuesday, ice cream tasting on Wednesday, and visiting the pond on Thursday to witness hundreds of mallard ducks.

Each parting is sealed with a kiss on Lilith's cheek. They both want more than a mere peck, but they're mature enough to know that they need to discover their true feelings for each other and that more passionate kissing will only cloud their judgment.

Friday will once again take up Lilith's time with sewing, so reluctantly they agree to wait to meet on the Saturday. "Let's make it earlier. Say eleven? At our café?"

"That sounds delightful. Instead of meeting outside of it, let's stop in for tea," offers Graham, reaching up to her face to play with a stray strand of hair.

"Agreed."

37
Lilith and Graham

With no specific place or project needing his attention early Friday morning, Graham goes for a walk. He by chance sees Lilith walking down Chester Street toward Malloy Avenue. He decides to follow in the hopes of spending time with her even though their next date is not until Saturday. But just walking with her for half a block will be better than not seeing her at all.

I'll try to catch her before she goes to her sewing job, he thinks. However, she doesn't turn to cross the street to the building on the east. She enters the brothel from a side door that he presumes is the employees' entrance!

An eerie feeling envelopes him as he stands there, gaping. *Sewing? Is that really what she's doing in there? Has she lied to me all this time? And to think I was flattered by her blushing at my kiss after the theater. What is she? Is she really a school teacher on summer break? As attractive as she is, she could easily be a working girl. Hmm. Since we've met, we've only seen each other twice in the evening and those could have been her nights off. She's smart, could be conniving too, and definitely sensual.*

He tries to convince himself that she has a positive motive or purpose in being at the brothel, and decides to wait until she comes out to ask her to clarify her deed. As the morning passes, he crosses the street and leans against a tree. After the noon mark, he sits against the tree, keeping an eye on the side entrance door. But she doesn't appear even after the sun sets and the trees in the park to the south have given up their shadows to the night. It begins to rain and he takes shelter underneath the awning of a building on the east side of the street in order to watch the door while he waits out the rainstorm. The longer he waits, the more he suspects. He spends the night there, watching and occasionally nodding off.

The next morning when she comes out with the early sun, he doesn't follow her to her apartment. Instead, he heads back to his room. He dashes in between the puddles and crosses the street in front of the house of ill repute to take advantage of the wooden sidewalk. As he passes in front of the brothel, he notices a sign announcing a masquerade ball is being held on the upcoming Saturday—tonight. All gentlemen are welcome and for a fee of $10.00, they can enjoy the company of the ladies in full costume. Refreshments will be served.

He decides he'll attend as surely the madam of the place will want all her girls working. No doubt Lilith will be there and then he'll know for sure. He'll need to purchase a mask. He doesn't know what he'll do when he sees her there but he has time to think about what he might say. He sends her a note.

> *I regret I will not be able to meet you this morning at eleven after all. I will let you know about tomorrow. G*

He sleeps the remainder of the morning into late afternoon.

Lilith is so excited for the ball that she has no qualms about canceled plans with Graham. She goes back to Madam Deb's and spends the rest of the day there. Deb had given her the go ahead to make a unique costume for each working girl.

Over the past several months, Lilith spent time with each woman so she could design and sew a unique dress for each wearer. All eight frocks are of the same style—excessively low necklines and ruffled skirts that daringly end just above the knees, but the masks and skirts vary in the colors of black, crimson red, bunny-pink, and royal blue. The dresses are adorned with shapes of heads of bulls—also known as toros—white cottontails, cut out shapes of Siamese cats and even white swans. One has a tiara attached to her mask and another has Blackbeard's hat. The most unique design is for Tina. Her costume is that of a Sheriff; her mask looks like a badge, and so do the cut out navy-blue trimmings sewn onto her light grey dress.

Lilith helps the girls get ready. Once they have entered the boudoir, she leaves the establishment with Emily as the pair is going to spend the night at her place where they can enjoy a quiet sleep.

As they leave through the side door, Lilith is excited and curious to see if there's a line up of men waiting to get inside. She looks around the corner. What she sees at the entrance to the brothel shakes her to her core. *Can it be? Is that Graham putting on a mask before entering Madam Deb's?*

All the way home she replays the scene in her mind. It is him! There's no doubt about it. Emily knows Lilith is distracted and decides to not say anything until Lilith is ready to mention what's agitating her. Lilith is relieved that she hasn't yet told Emily about Graham, otherwise how would she explain what she's just seen?

There has to be a reason, thinks Lilith. *Graham didn't seem the type, but then again, right from the beginning of my knowledge of this brothel, I would never have guessed the types of men who do pay for sex. What was he doing there? I thought we had something special between us. Am I mistaken? Can he not stay away from other women? If we are to get serious, will he be the type to step out on me until we're married? Or worse, will he continue with that infidelity even afterwards?* She has to get answers before letting the relationship develop further. Alas, she knows it's too late for her heart and she can only hope to keep a level head.

Graham is surprised and relieved to not find Lilith among the masquerading women. He's certain he would recognize her if she was. He breathes out easily as he leaves ten minutes later. Nevertheless, he still has unanswered questions.

As promised, a note awaits Lilith when she wakes Sunday morning, inviting her to meet him at their usual place at two in the afternoon.

At one-thirty, Lilith walks Emily home and turns back toward the café to wait. He's also early. She's so wrapped up in what she needs to discuss with him that she doesn't notice that his face clearly shows his shock and disappointment at seeing her coming from the direction of the brothel.

As he remains quiet, Lilith suggests they take a walk in the park. He nods and they stroll in silence toward a bench by the pond.

Stoic and deeply concerned, Lilith asks, "What were you doing at Madam Deb's last night?"

Instead of replying, he defensively asks, "How do you know I was there?" Had he missed identifying her? Maybe the madam didn't put her full staff of working girls on the floor at the same time after all. He adds, "Did you see me? Do you work at Madam Deb's brothel?"

Her voice slightly elevated, replies, "I saw you go in. And as a matter of fact, yes, I do work for her on Sundays, mostly after the church service. I mend garments for the girls."

"Ha, I'll wager that's a lie. How is it then that I saw you go in when it wasn't a Sunday?" He doesn't know what upset him more, the fact that she caught him going in the brothel or that she replied that she did indeed work there.

She argues somewhat louder, "I already told you what I was doing, but you don't believe me. So, why should I repeat myself?"

He isn't listening and asks sternly, "How could you deceive me like this!"

"Deceive! Deceive—you? What do you mean by that? I could ask the same of you. Do you frequent brothels? What kind of a man are you?"

"Don't judge me! I don't think you have that right!" He's angry now and lowers his voice accusingly. "I've heard about women like you. It all starts off innocently enough but you prey on rich men like me and threaten to expose them to society unless they pay you a lot of money. Some of you even trap us into marriage."

"Haaa!" she inhales, surprised and hurt that he would think anything like that about her. She may have been tempted once by the life at Madam Deb's, but she prefers to teach children any subject than teach grown men anything.

She rises from the bench in a huff and says repulsively, "At what point did your disgusting mind ever think that I'm capable of doing something like that?" and walks away. Confused, he stands and leaves in the opposite direction.

She knows she isn't out of his sight yet, but doesn't care. She starts running toward her home, tears flying off her face.

He doesn't watch her leave as he's too upset and appalled by what has just happened. How could they have had so much fun these past few weeks and be so angry with each other today? How could he have so misjudged her character?

Two days later, he leaves for New York, relieved that there is no possibility of bumping into Lilith ever again.

Graham soon meets with his father at his place of business on Madison Avenue. "Oh Graham, this report's very thorough. Well done, son. So, tell me all about Delton."

Assuming his father wants to know the business end, he finds he can speak on that topic for hours.

"This is wonderful. And how did you pass the time outside those meetings? Did you meet new people? Where did you go? What did you do all those weeks?"

"Well, I've seen their library and the museum which had an exhibit on dinosaurs. I've been to their theater and I've even seen a group of locals play a game of cricket."

"Cricket? Did that make you homesick?"

"No. Not really. Hmm." He thinks, *I didn't get homesick at all.*

"Hmm," copies his father.

For the next five months, Graham helps his father with their businesses of steel and real estate in New York City. On the third day of the first week in January 1868, his father calls him into his office and says, "This letter came for you."

"For me?" Graham sits and opens it. He reads it and says, "That's odd."

"What is it?"

"Apparently, I'm an heir. I'm to inherit from some woman who lived in Philadelphia. Do we know anyone in Philadelphia?"

"I don't recall. Maybe someone that we know moved there?" He lies. "Are you going to go?"

"Well, it says I only need to get myself there and everything else is paid for—a room and all meals are included. They don't expect the reading of the Will to last more than a day or two and I must admit, I'm curious," replies Graham.

"Then you should go. You've worked so hard in both Delton and here in New York that I think you deserve to see more of this country before we go back home."

The younger man shrugs his shoulders with indecision.

"Go. I'll join you there. I'll make arrangements to stay at the closest hotel to where you'll be. We'll plan on having dinner together and see what else the city has to offer. What do you say?"

"Well, if it means I get to spend more time with you exploring a new place, then I say yes. I'll go. I'll leave the address with your secretary. Thanks Father. I'm looking forward to it now."

38
Emily and Lilith

Mr. Trolley asks, "In one of the investigator's reports, it's discovered that Madam Deb passed away and left the business to Madam Tina. What did you do afterwards, Mrs. Emily?"

Emily and Lilith share the telling of the answer.

Deborah dies on September 4, 1867. Even after the years she spent grooming Tina to do her job, she still feared that Tina was too young and immature to keep the brothel going successfully, but resigned herself to the fact that it wouldn't be her worry once she was gone.

Emily decides to retire and rent a suite of rooms near Lilith's.

She often thinks about the long conversation she had with Deborah where the older woman shared her life experiences and wonders why they hadn't spoken freely like that years ago. She would have enjoyed knowing more about the woman earlier, but was grateful that it was later than not at all. She's saddened to learn that not many people acknowledged their association with her friend, so as a gesture of kindness and respect, Emily pays the newspaper for an advertisement space to report the madam's passing.

The newspaper company is always in search of new customers and knows that many people are curious to read anything remotely scandalous so they don't hesitate to publish the obituary. Many people probably think it obscene to print anything about someone as shameful as a madam, but they can't help themselves and buy a copy. Emily never regrets making the news of her long-time friend's passing public knowledge.

A few months later, on the second Saturday of January 1868, Lilith—still stinging from the last encounter with Graham—pastes a fake smile on her face when she brings the teapot to the table and sits down across from Emily. "We deserve a rest after all this unpacking." She looks around Emily's new sitting room. "You know, I'm amazed at how many things your new cabinet can hold. Tea?"

At Emily's lack of response, she nudges her friend. "Emily? Are you daydreaming?"

"I'm just thinking about a strange letter I got in this morning's post. It's from a lawyer in Philadelphia."

Before she can say any more on it, Lilith says, "Me too! I haven't opened it yet." She retrieves it from her coat pocket and the women compare them. The content is identical, concluding with:

In order to collect your inheritance, it is of the utmost importance that you attend this meeting.

For your convenience, the reading of the Last Will and Testament will be held at the same place where you will be staying. Mrs. Neustat has made available one of her guest bedrooms for you. You need only pay for your fare to travel here.

Please wire me the date and your estimated time of arrival at the train station. A hired cab will await to deliver you to 142 Michigan Avenue, in Philadelphia, Pennsylvania.

"What do you think this means?" Lilith asks.

"I'm not sure. I don't know any Neustats. I wonder though, if you have one too, this inheritance must be related to the Breats. But as far as I know there aren't any living Breats in the State of Pennsylvania. Have you decided if you're going?" asks Emily.

"Well, I'm curious. And perhaps the inheritance is significant enough to make the fare for the train worthwhile. I'll need to arrange for another teacher to take care of my classes, but yes, I think I'll go, that is, if you come too."

"It's been a long time since I set foot in Philadelphia. It's been many years since the deaths of my parents and the family's financial scandal. I don't think anyone would recognize me. So yes, if you're going, I will too."

"Great." Lilith pauses and then smiles, "You know, I was going to buy myself a new dress for my birthday coming up but I'm in the mood for a bigger change. We can both benefit with a whole new wardrobe for the trip, Emily. Oh, and a new hair style. What do you think?" asks Lilith, welcoming anything that diverts her thoughts away from Graham.

Emily can't see herself spending money unnecessarily, but when she thinks about all the conservative, outdated and worn dresses hanging in her armoire, she decides, *Why not show up in Philadelphia like I never left?* "Yes, lets. We can start this afternoon."

Both, thrilled with a new adventure that they will experience together, quickly make plans for the rest of the day and the following week. They will shop for clothes, shoes, luggage—and anything else that strikes their fancy.

Monday, Lilith will advise the school board that she will be away on family business for a minimum of two weeks starting on the twentieth. Emily will purchase train tickets and send a wire of their arrival date and time.

They reserve Tuesday through to Friday evenings for fittings on their new clothing. On Saturday next, they will see about getting new hair styles and start packing. Sunday will be the last day to clear up anything left uneaten, unpacked, and undone.

Just making plans excites the two friends and they feed on each other's enthusiasm. Emily feels like a seventeen-year-old again, and Lilith's eagerness overshadows her unfulfilled yearnings of Graham.

Lilith has never purchased more than one new dress at a time and can't wait to get started. On the way to one of the shops, she says, "I still have money that Daniel and I had put aside for our future. I find that I can afford to spend hundreds of dollars, Emily. I probably won't, but I can if I want to."

"Oh dear. I've never spent a dime on myself, especially after Daniel left. And then Deborah left me some as well, so I guess I can say I can afford to spend thousands and I know I won't spend that much!" Both giggle at the prospect though.

The day to travel is finally here. Lilith decides that this will be the right time to inform Emily about Graham. Regrettably though, there is an elderly couple sharing their train car and polite conversation occupies the entire trip instead.

As promised, a carriage picks them up from the station and brings them to Mrs. Neustat's home on Michigan Avenue.

"Good afternoon. I'm Mr. Reynolds, the butler. This is Mrs. Harper, Mrs. Neustat's housekeeper. Please come inside and Mrs. Harper will show you to your rooms."

Once they pass the spacious entrance, Emily notices three evenly spaced doors on both sides of the grand staircase and envisions a study next to the library, a piano in the music room, a parlor for guests as they wait, a ballroom too perhaps, and a private family room.

As they climb the stairs, Mrs. Harper points out the direction to access the gardens and the dining room below where they will have supper shortly.

At the top of the staircase, Mrs. Harper doesn't turn in either direction. She walks straight up to the set of doors in front of her, opens them and says, "You're in here, Mrs. Emily Breat. This was Mrs. Neustat's room." The maid enters to check whether everything is in order.

Out of curiosity, Lilith follows Emily inside. They are welcomed with tasteful light and dark-green trimming everywhere. In the center of the room, there is a very large canopy bed. It is dressed with half a dozen pillows and a duvet that contains a double down-filled quilt. Emily runs her fingers over it. She can only ever remember touching something as soft and silky once before—the coverlet on her own parent's bed, decades ago.

The room holds classic tables, a lounge chair, a desk, four Victorian high back chairs, a couple of armoires, and lamps. Lilith marvels at the full-length mirror in a corner and Emily admires the craftsmanship of the intricate designs carved into the legs of the bedside tables. The delicate decorative work on many pieces of furniture is unlike any Emily has ever seen.

The room lacks knickknacks or evidence of the personality of the owner. Almost as if the hand maid can read their minds, she says, "Mrs. Neustat's personal items have been removed until the Will has been read and things have been decided. Please don't hesitate to inform me, by just pulling this rope here, if you need anything that isn't already provided in your room. Now, this way please, Mrs. Lilith Breat."

"Please call me Lilith."

"And me, Emily," she says a step behind them.

"I couldn't possibly do that!"

"But it will become tedious to always add our last names. We won't mind," Lilith says.

"How about if I call you Mrs. Emily and Mrs. Lilith? Will that be acceptable?"

"Definitely. Please do so," Emily answers.

Back in the hallway, the women turn to the right. They enter a smaller, but pleasantly decorated bedroom. The bed sheets, pillows, curtains and towels are white, and smartly trimmed with dark velvet lace.

After checking the room and brushing imaginary lint off the bedspread, Mrs. Harper says, "If there's nothing else for now, I'll leave you ladies to rest. The rope to summon a maid, Mrs. Lilith, is located there next to the bed."

The women change from their travel attire to warm tweed skirts and jackets, and minutes later meet in the garden. Even on this chilly winter day, a walk is exactly what they need after sitting for so long on the train.

Lilith decides against telling Emily about Graham and is glad that only Noreen knows of the ups and downs of that unfortunate relationship. She determines it may be better to just forget about him, and says, "I feel so spoiled, Emily. I don't know what this inheritance involves, but if I end up with more money than I can spend, I swear I'll buy a house and fill it with furniture like the pieces in my bedroom upstairs. It's absolutely breathtaking."

"Oh, Lilith, I couldn't agree with you more. I feel young again now that I've returned to the beloved Philadelphia of my youth."

The dinner bell rings seconds after they return from their walk. At dinner, the ladies are well provided for by the kitchen staff. They're eager to follow the butler to the sitting room for their after-dinner tea just to see how their deceased hostess had decorated it. The peaceful quiet of the room and the warmth of the huge fireplace finds the two women yawning before too long.

The large mansion and the distance in between rooms provides a noise-free rest for both ladies. They never hear the sounds made at night by the maids cleaning the common areas that are used during the day. They also don't hear Graham's footsteps on the south east side. Nor, a half hour later, the footsteps of yet another man who will occupy the bedroom several rooms farther down from Graham.

Breakfast has been brought to the bedrooms of the late arrivals upon their requests, while Emily and Lilith happily enjoy a buffet consisting of omelets, bacon and sausages, fruit, pastries, a variety of cheeses and clotted cream. A table has been set for them by the window of the terrace on the east side. Although, it's closed to the outdoors for the winter, the inviting space provides plenty of sunshine and warmth.

"What time is he expecting us?" Emily asks.

Lilith is surprised that Emily hasn't remembered. She smiles and replies, "We don't have to go anywhere. He comes to us and we'll be meeting at ten."

Emily says, "Yes, of course."

"Shall we go then?"

"Let's."

With a spring in Emily's step and anticipation in Lilith's, the newly attired ladies sway down the hallway toward the study, the middle door on the right of the grand hall.

39
The Breats

So much was said yesterday, then after Graham's explanation on how he arrived in America and during the break that followed, Emily finally turns to Lilith as she pours herself a cup of tea and asks, "Do you think that Graham has an uncanny resemblance to Daniel?"

Lilith looks down, takes a bite of her pastry, and chews it thoroughly. She decides to not answer Emily's question, and diverts her mother-in-law's thoughts by saying, "Graham and I know each other."

"What?"

Lilith whispers everything to Emily, right up to the part of him accusing her of being paid for servicing men and tricking him into marriage.

Emily is appalled. "He didn't believe that you were just sewing costumes for the girls?"

Lilith shakes her head. "I wanted to tell you about us and many times I came close."

"Well, I know now," says Emily.

"Yes, finally. I find it astonishing that he's somehow related to Mrs. Neustat and possibly to me too. I'm quite anxious to find out how we're all connected so Graham and I can go our separate ways and be done with each other," states Lilith.

Mr. Trolley welcomes them back after the short interval. "I want to thank everyone for sharing your stories. Back to Mrs. Neustat now. In summary, yesterday we learned of Delilah's youth, her upbringing, her pregnancy and the loss of it, her marriage to Martin, then her relationship with Victor, and finally, her marriage to Mr. Neustat. Let's return to her letter now."

The letter continues …

Sometime in 1835, before I knew of Daniel's birth, I realized that I needed to find someone to inherit my estate. My death would be of a benefit and of importance to someone of my choosing. But who? I had purposefully lost contact with everyone in my family. I never set foot in the State of Maine again. And anyone who knew of my existence didn't know I had returned to live in this country and had been since 1800.

I never searched for an heir on Mr. Neustat's side of the family, because he married me for my money. I was truly relieved when he passed.

In early July 1836, I overheard my chambermaid talking to a maid of the Clarkson household. These two maids were sisters and were gossiping outside my library's window. Before I had the chance to reprimand their idleness, I overheard them mention the name Breat. I was not going to let the chance slip me by, so I came upon them suddenly and ordered them both into my study.

I demanded they repeat the entire story. Clarkson's maid insisted that she had heard part of it second-hand herself and couldn't be sure of its authenticity. As I wasn't aware of any other existing family with the last name of Breat for hundreds of miles around, I made her repeat what little she knew. It wasn't much.

There had been a young widow by the name of Adeline Breat who came to work for the Clarksons in late December of 1833. She was already six months pregnant at the time of her arrival. The story was that her husband had died in some terrible accident. The maid said that Adeline suddenly left the Clarkson's home in her ninth month. Everyone assumed that she went to her sister's home in Delton.

So that was the first time I hired Benson and Decker. The private investigators showed up at my door the very next day.

I told the gentlemen what I had learned from the Clarkson maid and that I believed the Breat child was born in 1834 in the town of Delton. They were tasked with bringing me back any information they could find on the child and its mother. Being discreet in their investigation was of the utmost importance to me.

Agent Benson planned to speak to the maid and Agent Decker headed for Delton. Decker's investigation resulted in little progress until he moved his search to the south side of the town. His progress was entirely due to luck. He observed a Miss Josie at a local bar one evening. For a whiskey, she would tell stories of the goings-on at Madam Deb's. What he overheard from the adjoining table one evening spurred him to buy her a drink, or two. She came to his quiet corner of the saloon and told him enough to provide me with a very thorough account.

The report from Mr. Benson's visit with the Clarkson's maid also revealed new information. She gladly repeated everything she had told me and divulged to the investigator that she had heard this gossip from the gardener at the Gateway Estate. Benson immediately set off to find the gardener in the vineyard off Randolph Street where this Curtis fellow knew more details than the maid but was reluctant to tell for fear of retribution.

It took some convincing but the agent had plenty of experience in that area and assured the gardener that the information would never be traced back to him. This man was soon telling Agent Benson everything about his employer's son.

Apparently, the young David had taken quite a shining to the girl, Adeline Thordeaux. You could even say that they were courting. When his parents found out about their son's attraction to someone of inappropriate *social standing, they put a stop to Adeline and David's courtship.*

The gardener easily overhears the conversation heightening to an argument drifting out from an open window of the drawing room.

"Mother, Father! How can you say such things? You do not even know Adeline."

"Watch your manners. You will refer to her as Maid Thordeaux, David."

He ignores his mother's demand. "Adeline is lovely, very well-mannered, intelligent, and too delicate a lady to be working as a maid—here or anywhere for that matter!" David argues with his parents and defends his relationship with the beautiful Adeline, but they can't see past her father's shameful actions and the family scandal.

He continues, "She is a victim of unfortunate circumstances. Have mercy and pity, after all she has lost her mother and been separated from her oldest sister who has been exiled to some insignificant town somewhere. At the very least, give yourselves the gift of getting to know her."

They can't allow that to happen. What if they like the girl? What will the neighbors say? No, they've made their decision. The best thing for their son is to send him to a university in England to complete his studies of Business and Management. He will have until the end of the week to say goodbye to his friends and to pack up his things.

Later, David tells Adeline, "I am being punished just because I am in love with you. It is so wrong, Adeline. Please say you will wait for me. I will come back for you, I promise. They will not be able to keep me in London forever."

A mature Adeline senses what time and distance can do. She says, "It is true. In time you may forget me, David."

He shakes his head in denial.

She continues, "Well then, if you do come back to me, whether it be months or years, I will still be here." She smiles and he is appeased.

David leans in to kiss Adeline. Knowing that this may be their last opportunity to be alone together, he lets his overwhelming feelings of passion wrap her close to him. She feels his desire and his need to communicate his love. She denies him nothing.

David's parents intercede any mail to Adeline knowing that she cannot write their son without knowing his return address. They feel appeased now that the connection between the pair has been severed.

Months pass and the change in Adeline's growing belly announces to everyone a distasteful reality. David's parents fabricate a false story to pawn her off to the Clarksons. They lie about Adeline's make-belief husband having died in a farm accident and about how they can't keep her on as a single mother. The Clarksons are kind enough to give Adeline a home. When she disappears a couple of weeks before she is due to deliver her baby, they too are relieved that they won't have to support a young widow plus her child.

No one cares that Adeline has disappeared. She has befriended no one at the Clarkson's residence except the maid Katie, and even they aren't very close. At least the maid remembers to tell Mr. Benson that when Adeline came to work for the Clarksons she had introduced herself as Mrs. Breat. Adeline had divulged her true name to Katie, who assured her she'd keep the secret. But Katie tells her lover, Curtis, and gossips with her sister, the Neustat's maid.

One last letter addressed to Adeline arrives after her departure from the Clarkson's residence. Its return address is Delton and is promptly remitted to sender by Katie. Even though Mrs. Neustat knows this already, Katie tells the investigator anew that she doesn't remember the name of the sender, only the city.

Months after Adeline's disappearance, David came home for the duration of the school break. He is frantic to find Adeline but no one seems to know what happened to Miss Thordeaux, not even the servants in his home. He becomes unbelievably angry with his parents for allowing his first love to vanish and vows to never talk to them again.

His parents don't believe he will do such a thing. But they do not want to feed his wrath any further and withhold the news that they sent the young maid to work for the Clarksons. Telling him that she was with child—his child; would never be spoken out loud.

At the time, the Clarkson's maid and the gardener are too afraid to tell David what they know. The pair has shared more than this information, they have indulged in a forbidden alliance which would cost them their jobs.

Only the passing of years, a split in the relationship between the maid and gardener, and assurance from the investigator that the source of the information will never be divulged, provides Curtis with the courage to tell the agent what he knows. His willingness to share this knowledge is also helped along when he discovers that Katie has been the first to gossip about the Breat girl.

The letter continues …

This brings me to the Breat connection. In 1829, Victor's parents, Gertrude and Henry Breat had been kind enough to write that they were spending a week visiting in Philadelphia, but felt compelled to see me and asked if they could stay with me. I wired them back stating that I'd be delighted to receive them.

I told them and I'll tell you now that I was elated to have them stay with me for the duration of their visit. I was grateful that they needed to share their troubles and humbled that they felt comfortable enough to do that with me.

It was during the first day of their stay that they revealed their learning of my separation from Victor and how the news had saddened them at the time. It wasn't any easier for them to tell me about Victor's early demise either. The three of us spent the afternoon sharing our fond memories of

Victor. At least I didn't have to pretend how I felt about him anymore, how I always felt about him, how I still do to this day.

Emily, they then told me that their daughter, your mother Elizabeth, had married well, but moved to Philadelphia and estranged herself from her family and friends in Delton. This bothered them very much and they couldn't stand the pity demonstrated by their friends, or the gossip it birthed.

Your mother had attended the best boarding schools your grandparents could afford. She was almost fourteen years younger than Victor so that made her sixteen when we married. She was eighteen when we divorced and thirty-five when he died. We didn't know at the time that she would be dead herself the following year.

I didn't know that she passed away until the maids' gossiping led me to hire the private investigators to learn what they could about people with the last name of Breat.

I compared the dynamics of siblings like Victor and Elizabeth's to mine and Frederick's and concluded that the members of many wealthy families were actually strangers to each other. Although I was tutored at home, I didn't know my brother! Even if we had grown up together and I would have known him as an adult, I daresay I might not have recognized him had I passed by him at the concert hall. Likewise, Elizabeth hardly knew of Victor's existence.

In all likelihood, neither you nor Adeline knew you had an uncle Victor. So, when I first started putting my affairs in order, I couldn't find any living Breats other than your grandparents. I think you should know that they both died of natural causes, in their home, a couple of years apart from each other. Your grandmother died first.

Of course, Agent Benson's report alerted me to the sad fact that Adeline passed away giving birth to David's son, Daniel.

Emily, may I extend to you my sincerest condolences on the loss of your sister. She was brave when she packed up everything she had and left the only city she'd ever lived in to come find you.

40

Frederick

The letter continues …

 For years, the investigators have provided me with very thorough updates on Daniel. He had done well at grade school followed by further studies in Philadelphia. I was proud to learn of his employment with THR Mining and of his promotion to lead prospector.

 What a coincidence that the company was prospecting in Ohio where he met Lilith. You see, it was around this time that I learned of another relative and that Daniel wouldn't be my sole heir.

 As you know, my brother was born in 1799, when I was sixteen years old. I don't know all the details surrounding the end of my parents' lives, but I will tell you what I have learned.

Portland, Maine - August 1803

 With his nanny close by, a three-year-old Frederick plays in the garden at the back of his home. He spots his mother, spreads his arms upwards and gleefully starts running toward the patio door. The nanny also turns to greet the boy's mother but screams in horror instead when she sees blood streaking Beatrice's dress and the woman holding a knife in her right hand.

The nanny dashes after the boy, grabs him and flees to the stables. She has heard about Beatrice's past episodes of violence toward her daughter but she had never witnessed it herself. Beatrice drops the knife and then falls to her knees, rocking and humming tunelessly.

One of the other servants summons the authorities. As the dumbfounded Beatrice is unable to speak, the officers follow the drops of blood up the stairs and come upon Alfred's dead body located on a bed next to one of the servants. Both had been stabbed while in a state of undress. Beatrice is charged with double murder, judged to be insane and is sentenced to spend the rest of her life in prison.

The nanny, a childless married woman, promises the court that she and her husband will watch over the boy until a family member can be located. She fears for his future if vicious gossip attaches itself to his last name so she wisely changes it.

Frederick is raised by this kind woman who becomes a widow herself five years later. She treated the boy as her own son, leaving him the farm when she passes.

In Portland, thirty-nine-year-old Fred's oldest friend says, "You should get married. Who are you going to leave your farm to when you die if you don't?"

"Well, I would marry, if there was a woman who'd want me."

Both men look each other in the eye. Wagging a finger, the friend asks, "Why don't you hire one of them matchmakers?"

"Pshaw. That's not for me."

"Why not? I heard that old Benny found himself a good woman and she's already with child."

"Gee. You think I should?"

"Can't see why not. Can't hurt except maybe in your wallet."

"Fine. I think I might," Fred declares, deciding to put an end to his bachelorhood.

For a fee, the matchmaker has him attending barn dances, picnics, and other events where he is promised he'll meet eligible women. The unmarried women, many in their late twenties, are referred to as old maids. The women's fathers also pay the matchmaker a fee as all are eager to marry off their daughters.

Twenty-year-old Helen has several reasons why she is attending the barn dance. One is to help her friends serve food and beverages and another one is to irritate her father. She once declined to marry a man of her father's choosing. The merger would have benefited her father financially and she refused to be used in that way. Her scorned father then retaliated by discouraging other suitors, who were more to her liking, with lies of her distasteful character.

Helen is unlike the other young maidens. Her beauty, grace and privileged upbringing provided her with the pick of the litter as a young debutante. But the games that her and her father played in the last four years have negated her finding a suitable husband. Thus, the third reason why she attends these events is to meet someone.

Fred likes Helen and chooses to dance with no one but her. Helen takes a shine to him too. They start courting against her father's wishes who disapproves of the man, a mere farmer. This only strengthens Helen's resolve to marry Fred.

Helen's father threatens to shun his daughter and cut her off from any of his money or inheritance but as she is of legal age to make a choice for herself, she chooses Fred. Her disgruntled father makes life in Maine truly difficult for the newlyweds, so much so, that Fred and Helen sell their farm and head west. They eventually settle and make a home in Ohio.

The letter continues …

Luckily for all concerned, I looked for relatives with the name of Breat. Had I not wanted to write a Will and leave my estate to Daniel, I would not have informed my lawyer that my maiden name is Greensley. I then told him about my name changes to Fowler, Dentz, back to Fowler, then Breat and finally to Neustat.

Had my lawyer not known that my true maiden name is Greensley, he would not have known to ask me about the outreach from a lawyer in Maine who was looking for Greensleys who resided there between 1780 and 1803.

My brother Frederick Greensley became Fred Green in 1803 when he was four. He married a young Helen Beckley when he was forty. The one true gift of themselves, is my most beautiful niece, Lilith. Helen died in 1847 while giving birth to a son, who died with her. Then three months later, Fred accidentally died in a barn fire.

What you don't know Lilith is that sadly, I found out that Fred Green was my missing brother only after he had passed away and you had left to live with your great-aunt Rosanne. I doubt Frederick even knew he had an older living sister.

When your mother died, Frederick wrote to her parents informing them of her passing. As he didn't know where they resided, he sent the letter to a lawyer in Maine who had assisted with the sale of his farm years earlier. That lawyer was acquainted with the lawyer I hired after my parents' death. They connected somehow, and that's how I ended up with this information.

My father never changed his Will, but because Mother was responsible for his death, she would receive nothing. I was named the sole heir. Their home had been sold after the murders, and the proceeds were added to their vast estate. Thankfully, I didn't have to go to Maine to claim what was rightfully mine. The lawyer took care of all that nasty business for me and just like that, I had become even wealthier.

I soon received several crates that contained my parents' personal belongings. I never opened them. I almost had them burned. Fortunately, I was wise enough to put them in storage in the attic instead.

At the time Lilith, I must admit that I was puzzled by the fact that Frederick never came forward to claim what was rightfully his. I wasn't aware that my brother didn't know his rightful last name was Greensley. I know in my heart that I would have tried harder to find him had I known.

At the mid-day meal that is once again shared only by the two women, Emily asks Lilith, "How does it feel to know so much more about your parents and your grandparents?"

"I feel incredible, Emily. It's hard to believe that I still had a living relative. I'm disappointed that Mrs. Neustat never told me who she was until after she died. She told me everything she knew about my family, which in essence is really not that much. She wasn't close to either of her parents and she was only in love that one time—with your uncle! She kept the company of many men during her travels and yet she was a loner, that's for sure. And she didn't know my father—her brother! Truly, sad."

"Hmm, bitter maybe? Have you noticed how she cleverly omitted telling us her maiden name when she started writing her story and Victor's last name—until now? I did," Emily says with a sense of adventure.

"That's right! Very astute of you to notice, Emily," says Lilith.

"I can't wait to find out how Graham fits in."

"I can. So now, it's my turn to ask. How does it feel to know so much more about the Breats?"

"I was overwhelmed. I didn't know I had an uncle and I don't recall ever having met my mother's parents. By the sound of her descriptions, they were loving, regular people that I should be proud to call family. I was surprised to learn that my mother distanced herself from them though. You see, growing up, Mother always made it a priority for Adeline and I to be the best sisters we could be. Listen to me, look how that ended up. Adeline didn't even tell me she had met David, let alone gotten in the family way."

"I'd say that was more your father's fault than your mother's."

"You're probably right," Emily admits.

"So that makes us cousins by marriage?" Lilith exclaims and both giggle at the fact.

41
David

The letter continues …

I now move on with my story.

My first husband, Martin Dentz, left America with his first love Valerie and moved to England in 1806. I don't know much about his life. They married and tried to have children for many years before finally having their first child, a son born in 1813. I'm sure they were both overjoyed with this child after trying for ten or eleven years.

All I have left to say on this matter can be summed up in dates and places. Rather than boring you with all those facts, I now ask that someone else inform you on the details of the lives of Martin, Valerie, and their son—someone who knew them very well.

The lawyer stands. "We've had a sixth person in the room with us since our meeting began yesterday."

Graham nervously shifts in his seat.

"Before he reveals himself, I ask that you withhold any questions until he has had an opportunity to tell his story in full. Do I have your promise that you can keep your questions until he is ready for them?"

"Yes. Certainly," the women say in unison.

Graham feels a heaviness in the pit of his stomach but nevertheless, he says, "Of course."

The lawyer walks the few steps to the hidden chair facing the wall of books and says, "Please come and introduce yourself. We are all anxious to hear about your connection to Mrs. Neustat's first husband."

When Graham sees who stands up, and before the man can mention his name, he says, "Father! What are you doing here?"

Surprised by the outburst, the lawyer interrupts, "Mr. Lestor! You promised."

"Yes, I did. I'm sorry."

The ladies are puzzled.

Graham's father crosses the floor to the middle chair where Emily is sitting. Emily's feelings confuse her. She has never felt an immediate attraction toward a man before and she's baffled. He extends his hand and out of politeness she puts hers in his. He kisses the back of it and says, "My name is David Lestor of the Gateway Estate. I am Daniel's father."

The women gasp, "Oh," and both stand up.

Graham is deflated. The past couple of days have been full of revelations and now he finds his father too has been withholding information about his past. *I just saw him last evening. How could he not tell me that he too was part of this affair? He could have even told me weeks ago when I first received my letter from Mr. Trolley! Or last night at supper—he could have told me!*

Lilith is visibly upset to learn that Graham is obviously Daniel's half brother.

Emily is truly pleased to finally meet the father of her nephew—her son—and be done with decades of lies.

David ignores Mr. Trolley as the lawyer moves another chair closer to the group. He focuses on addressing Emily, "I want to say to you,

Miss Emily Thordeaux, that I loved your sister, Adeline. I still do. I came back for her as soon as I could and was shocked when I found that she had disappeared. No one seemed to know where she had gone. Of course, now I know my parents' role in her disappearance and their efforts to keep us apart. Yesterday brought back so many memories. She was the love of my life and I hope it gives you comfort to know that she was so loved."

"Yes, it does. I'll be able to rest knowing that she hadn't been taken for a fool. I'm truly sorry that your parents never wanted to get to know Adeline as the fine young lady she truly was. They would've loved her, I'm sure," says Emily.

David still holds her hand in his when he speaks. "Yes, if only they'd given themselves that privilege. My sincerest of sympathies, Emily, on the loss of your sister and Daniel," his voice falters, "our son."

Her eyes sting with fresh tears as she notes that formalities are set aside when he calls her by her first name, so she does the same, "Thank you, David. My condolences to you as well. I also want you to know that I'm truly sorry that I never tried to find you and tell you about him. You see, I always thought your last name was Gateway. It would have been difficult to find you too, I'm sure."

"Yes, I'm sure too," he says with a sigh, releasing her hand.

Emily slides back into her chair, stunned by the new developments.

David bows his head when he greets Lilith. He also takes her hand in his and kisses the back of it, then says, "I would've been proud to have you as my daughter-in-law, Lilith. I could never have imagined a lovelier daughter-in-law than yourself. I was happy to learn that before my oldest son died, he had the joy of loving someone and being loved back. I want to extend my sincerest condolences on your loss."

Lilith can't help herself and throws her arms around him. He hugs her back. "Thank you for your kind words and I too give you my most heart-felt condolences."

"Thank you." Moved to tears, he then turns to his son and says, "I only learned yesterday that I had another son. You know how much I love you and I'm truly very proud of you. I can only imagine that Daniel would've been your best friend and you his. Forgive me for not telling you about all this, but if you'll indulge me, you'll know why shortly."

David lets out a huge breath of air when Graham reaches to hug him. Even without knowing all the truth, Graham forgives his father everything. He loves him that much. They hold onto each other for several seconds, pat each other on the back once, and pull apart.

Emily and Lilith glance at each other, surprised at the unusual display of affection between father and son. The men sit down next to each other, Graham giving his seat to his father and sitting in the farthest chair.

David smiles then and starts, "Although I never met her, it just so happens that I personally knew Delilah's first husband, Martin Dentz and his second wife Valerie—and their most precious son. His name was Jonathan and he was born the same year I was, in 1813.

"I met Jonathan on my first day at the university in 1833 when my parents had banished me from my home in Philadelphia. Jonathan didn't reside on campus because his parents lived nearby. We became the very best of friends.

"We were closer than friends. We were brothers. I was always over at the Dentz's home because theirs was a happy one. It wasn't at all like mine. Mine was a strict and sterile environment, whereas Jonathan and his parents spent a lot of time together. He and his father went fishing and hiking, they built projects, they did all kinds of things together really. I watched from the outside of this close-knit family and envied them. I'm sure that they would've forgiven Jonathan anything, even for bringing scandal on their family by falling in love with a girl who'd been ousted out of society's circle." His bitterness shows through.

"Their welcoming family unit gave me the determination to continue with my schooling. I had come very close to quitting after I returned from Philadelphia after that first school break.

"I was so angry with my parents for sending Adeline away and with the Clarksons for letting her go, that I said some pretty nasty things.

"Then yesterday, I discovered that Adeline had all these decisions to make without me. I'm sure she had no choice but to seek out her only living relative, her sister Emily. Worst of all, I had no way of tracking down either of them. No one told me she was in Delton. I was looking for Thordeauxs. Even if I would have known that I should have looked for Breats, I wouldn't have found any in Philadelphia.

"After I completed my degree, I was still blind with rage. I defied my parents and stayed in England.

"The Dentz family gladly let me stay with them. I had no money and no job, but what I did have was a degree in Business and I soon found a decent post." He takes a deep breath and lets it out slowly, not happy to share the next part of his story.

"Well, the summer of 1835," he gulps just at the mention of the year, "Martin, Jonathan and I were on the lake, in their sailboat, fishing. We didn't catch anything, but just spending time together after a long week at work in downtown London suited everyone just fine. Quite suddenly, the winds picked up. We thought nothing of it as it wasn't our first time on rough waters. But then the skies darkened so we decided to head home, disappointed and empty handed.

"The weather worsened and even though it was only mid-afternoon, visibility was quickly diminishing. The water was rocking us terribly and fog overtook us. It even started to rain, then thunder and worst of all, lightning. Just like that, we could no longer see each other clearly, never mind the shore. We were forced to leave the sails down and drift. We each went to different sides of the boat to watch out for rocks, armed with an oar for pushing away from the danger they presented. We had to wait out the storm and pray that we would continue our choppy drifting toward land.

"When we came upon the rocks, I pushed on them and from my position on the deck, I saw an opening to get to shore. I got out of the boat, grabbed the rope, and let the waves push it toward a patch of sand.

Mr. Dentz had seen me jump out of the boat and from his view point, he could alert me of any other rocks that might damage the boat. He was more concerned about getting home safely, but why let the boat get damaged if it could be avoided, right?

"He too jumped out when the boat was almost all out of the water, helping me pull the boat further onto the grassy patch of beach. We both looked at each other and smiled when we realized that Jonathan had let us do all that hard physical work while he conveniently stayed on board. I yelled at him, 'Okay you weakling, you can come out now.' But there was no response."

He forced out a chuckle, "You know how it is. We jumped back on the boat to tell him it wasn't funny and that he could come out of hiding from the deck below. But he wasn't there—he wasn't there!" he repeats, alarmingly, even now, decades later. David takes out a handkerchief and wipes his eyes. No one says a word.

"I lost my brother that day. I lost my way and my will to live. I recall thinking that grieving was not for the faint of heart. I thought I had grieved once when I lost Adeline, even though I didn't know that she was dead—I had hope that we might meet again one day. The permanency of a sure death makes you experience a totally different kind of grief.

"I focused on the pain left by Jonathan's tragic drowning and sank to a state of depression. Yet, it was somehow comforting to know that I wasn't alone in my grief. Both Martin and Valerie were hurting beyond comprehension. Their only son had died! Their reason for living, their hopes and dreams, their future—all gone."

David accepts a glass of water from Lilith, takes a big gulp and is able to go on. "A couple of months passed and life found its way back into our emptiness and stirred things up. At breakfast one day, Martin and Valerie asked me to consider staying on in their home with them because they didn't think they could handle more losses. They told me that throughout the past couple of years, they had grown to consider me as their son too. I was glad to accept because I had nowhere else to go.

Leaving them would be worse than losing Jonathan. Thinking that the only people who showed me any kind of love wouldn't be there, on hand, whenever I needed them? Well, it was unthinkable. It would have driven me into madness.

"Life changed for the three of us. They sold their home in Cambridgeshire, partly I think because that was where Jonathan had died, and we moved to London. Jonathan, Martin and I had rooms in the city, but now with Valerie in London as well, they purchased a large house with plenty of room for just us three. We never forgot Jonathan, but we did gradually acknowledge our blessings every day. That's something I learned from them. For all my parents' wealth, I never once saw them be grateful. I watched Martin and Valerie lose a son and thank God for me. I became a man who would value virtues over money, love over power, and humility over greed.

"But it didn't happen right away," he turns to look at his son. He inhales and exhales a couple of times. He nods his head, and everyone waits for what he will reveal next.

42
David

"I'm afraid lies surround your birth too Graham, just like Daniel's. I've never been married. Unlike Daniel, your mother didn't die giving you life. On the second anniversary of Jonathan's death, I got drunk. So drunk, that I couldn't walk. I remember stumbling and getting picked up by a young woman with no name. A couple of days passed before I sobered up long enough to realize that I was in her bed.

"With empty pockets and wearing shoes that weren't mine, I left her place and walked home. Martin and Valerie treated me like they would have Jonathan—relieved that I had returned home safely. They only raised their eyebrows when they noticed my dirty and torn clothing, but they said nothing. I was an adult after all and should be able to figure things out for myself.

"Weeks passed and became months. Precisely nine months later, a baby in a basket with a note was left on the Dentz's doorstep. The baby was mine. The mother was giving him to me because I could provide for him much better than she ever could. You didn't even have a name.

"I didn't know anything about babies, or how to be a parent. But

Valerie did and she soon took over the role. Martin too. He easily accepted his role as grandfather. As you grew, Graham, I knew in my heart that I would never love anyone as much as I love you. Oh, I'm not saying I couldn't fall in love again, I'm saying that a father's love for his child cannot be fully defined or replaced. My love for you has no limit.

"I found time to reflect on my life and decided that my goals and my desires were to become the best at all I could be. As a child, I was raised by nannies. I was *allowed* to visit with Mother and Father once a day. Their faces were those of my parents, but the faces I loved belonged to my nannies. As I grew older, I was *privileged* to join my parents at meal times. As I grew older still, I was provided with an excellent education. I know I should have felt grateful, for it was a good education, one that set me up for a successful future. But I always knew that they used the excuse of furthering my education as a convenient way of separating me from Adeline.

"I didn't want to raise any of my children like I had been. I didn't want to make my earning a living and acquiring possessions and power more important than my offspring. When I first met Adeline, she told me stories of her parents and her sister and I envied them! Up until the time her mother passed away, Adeline knew she was loved. It was unfortunate that her father didn't see beyond his grief until, well, you all know how that ended. There was a happier time when Adeline was secure in her parents' love, as I'm sure you were too, Emily."

Emily nods.

"I wanted all of that—I wanted to be able to put my hand on my child's head and brush his hair. To feel his tiny, sticky arms around my neck when he had enough of play and was ready for bed. For him to not be afraid to cry when he skinned his knee and come to me to make it feel better."

Emily nods again.

David smiles at her and continues, "I would be the one to teach my son about fishing, sports, and hunting. I wanted to earn the title of father. It wouldn't be right for a nanny to get all the glory that comes from the innocent, pure love of a child unless it was her own."

Graham gets up from his chair and David automatically rises too, "You did, Father. You did." Father and son give each other a loving hug. Emily and Lilith can't help but look at each other again and silently they know what the other is thinking—any child would be lucky to have David as their father.

The men sit down once again. "The year my father passed away, his obituary appeared in the business section of one of London's newspapers. By then, he and I were strangers but Martin convinced me to come back to America to claim my inheritance, and to decide if I wanted to warm the relationship with my mother. But when we met, she was as cold as when I saw her last. Right then, I vowed to not live life as my father had lived his—void of love for his spouse and his child. He loved money, power, and land, and part of me regretted returning to my original home. But I wanted my share of his estate to go to Graham, not to lawyers and such so I stayed as long as necessary and then returned home. Home to England." He cleared his throat, looking quickly at the lawyer. "Pardon me, Mr. Trolley."

"No offence taken, Mr. Lestor."

Mr. Trolley picks up from here, "Before we go on to the reading of the Will and disbursement of assets, there's one last piece of Mrs. Neustat's letter and the agents' reports that I'll read."

43
Delilah

The letter continues …

I can only determine that the writing of this long letter has made my mind wander to my youth. I had yet another dream of a long-forgotten memory.

Portland, Maine - 1793

"You do not understand, you ungrateful child," yells Beatrice. "You are the most unreasonable ten-year-old I have ever known. Your twin sister is so smart while you are such an imbecile. Dance! Together!" Beatrice is asking her daughter to do the impossible as the dead sister is obviously not there to dance with.

"I'll show you." Beatrice approaches her daughter who curls into herself, becoming smaller as her mother gets closer.

"Stop that, Delilah. Straighten up. Now, come here. Take my hand. Look, Charlotte is doing it right. Why can you not be more like her? She has such talent." Beatrice takes the smaller hand and squeezes hard with frustration.

"Ouch."

"What?"

"Nothing, Mother. Like this?" asks Delilah.

"Oh, never mind. You have made me forget the steps. Again! Maybe they should have taken you instead." Then she mutters, drifting off into her own confused mind as she walks out of the ballroom into the hallway.

With slumped-over shoulders, Delilah slowly leaves the room to go to the library. Her tutor will not be expecting her until two o'clock for her lesson, but she doesn't want to dance by herself, nor play. Her mood is made grey by her exhausting, confused mother.

No sooner has she exited the room does she fall to the floor, in pain. Her mother's back hand to the mouth had been waiting for her.

Delilah immediately scrunches herself up into a ball and protects her head with her hands and arms. She doesn't cry out. It is her experience that loud noises make her mother angrier.

Before Beatrice can apply another beating, her husband Alfred comes running down the hallway toward the pair. He slows down and gently catches Beatrice's raised fist in his hand.

"There, there, darling. All is fine, now. Everything is going to be alright," he says, leading her away before she can inflict more pain on the young girl.

Alfred leads Beatrice to their room unaware that his curious daughter followed them. Delilah observes her mother sob into her fatigued husband's shoulder.

He says, "There, there my dear, Beatrice. Everything will be alright now."

"How can you know that? She is gone, Alfred, and it is all Delilah's fault. That Delilah is responsible for the death of our children, Alfred. Why do we keep her? Why can we not send **her** away?" she whispers.

Alfred shakes his head at his befuddled wife's tale. What will she say or imagine next? She is being unreasonable to believe that an infant would have killed her twin sister, or that a six-year-old would have planned the disappearance of her sibling.

Alfred never mentions their other child's name out loud. Beatrice will have to be medicated if he does. Even the eavesdropper, Delilah, is confused by her parents' conversation—our children?

The letter continues …

This time when I wake up, I am crying. I remember my mother's overwhelming, constant distress and I remember my father's—what? Love? Certainly not. A father doesn't bond with his children, and most certainly not with his daughters. At least that was not my experience.

And yet, my father must have cared enough about me to rush to my rescue from my mother's swift fists.

There is another memory. It isn't just a flash from a dream, it is another memory.

I'm writing the words STOLEN SISTER. Not dead sister, but stolen.

I can't help myself. I'm crying out loud. How could I not have remembered? Everybody told me my twin sister was dead and that's all I ever focused on. But over the years, my mother often muttered on about her stolen two-year-old child. I just never paid attention to her rantings and forgot all about the incident especially when they never mentioned Eleanor's name again!

Four years earlier, in Portland, early November of 1789, Beatrice is having a good day and enjoying the walk in the park. She is outside with her two daughters and their nannies.

The cool breeze makes the two-year-old Eleanor fall asleep in her pram and Delilah is skipping ahead toward a swing. Beatrice watches Eleanor's nanny nod off on the bench nearby and decides to run after Delilah and push her on the swing.

As she nears the older child, Beatrice sees her trip and knock her head on the swing as she falls. The six-year-old cries out at the injury and Beatrice then does something that is unusual for her. She places a hand on the nanny's arm and holds her back as she moves to console her own hurt child.

That was the incident that broke Beatrice's thin thread of sanity. While she soothes Delilah in her arms, Beatrice glances over to the sleeping nanny. The pram is gone, along with the child in it!

No one remembers how they got home, but an hour later, a detective asks, "Are you sure no one followed you to the park, Mrs. Greensley?"

In a trance-like state, she answers, "Well, I am not so sure now. I guess we could have been followed, I just did not notice. One does that when one is not aware of the dangers that lurk, does one not?"

Alfred hopelessly watches an officer ask his six-year-old daughter, "How badly did that scrape on your knee hurt? When your mother bent down to comfort you, were you not looking right at your sister's pram when it was taken? So, tell me, how can you say you didn't see anyone there?"

The officers' questions almost infer that the girl is responsible, in some way, for her sister's disappearance. When Delilah starts crying, he quickly puts a stop to the inappropriate line of questioning.

"Very well then," the officer says, directing his questioning to Albert, "Do you know of anyone who might want to bring harm to your family, Mr. Greensley?"

"What? You think we were targeted? That is impossible! Why are we being asked all these ridiculous questions when there is someone out there getting farther away with my daughter as we speak?"

The officer in charge diffuses the situation and explains that they must explore all possibilities but for them to rest assured—the officers who stayed behind at the park are already in search of the missing child.

"Do not ask my wife about having any enemies. She is fragile, to say the least. She will have nightmares and imagine all kinds of people wanting to do us harm."

"Very well then, you answer. Do you or your family have any enemies?"

Alfred tries to think of any business associates who might be his enemy and can't think of any. "No," he replies.

The officer has follow-up questions, "How about here in your home? Have you reprimanded an employee recently? Or possibly, fired someone unjustly?"

Alfred can only think of the chamber maid who Beatrice accused of stealing. "She was released of her duties two weeks ago. Her name is Maggie, oh, I forget her last name," he says. "I should have that information in my files. This way please."

Regrettably, the document had never been completed properly. It only had Maggie's first name and a name of a previous employer. Maggie was referred to them by another of their employees who unfortunately had since vanished. Beatrice cannot remember the last name of the young woman, or at least can't remember in her distressed state. Despite the scant details, Alfred is certain that this information will lead to his missing daughter and urges the police to investigate at the previous employer's home.

Later, when the officers have finally left his house, Alfred approaches Beatrice who is still distraught.

In his weary and pathetic state, he says something stupid, "They think you may have angered Maggie when you fired her. Maybe she is responsible for all of this."

Beatrice is crushed to think that Alfred lays the blame on her. In her presently unstable mind, she in turn lays the blame on Delilah. After all, who had preoccupied her while the baby was stolen? Thus began years of festering hatred and unjust blame.

44
Delilah

The letter continues …

    Waking up from that dream and the rush of memories that came with it made me do something that I never thought I would need to do. I tasked my butler to open the crates in the attic and find my family Bible.

    Well, there it was, in black and white. My mother certainly did not have an easy time holding onto her pregnancies. She must have suffered greatly. It is no wonder that she went mad.

    Listed on the first page were my family members.

Alfred Greensley	*1755 -*
Beatrice	*1758 - (Married July 4, 1780)*
stillborn	*June 27, 1781*
Charlotte	*August 1, 1783 - died November 2, 1783*
Delilah	*August 1, 1783 -*
stillborn	*November 30, 1785*
Eleanor	*May 4, 1787 - disappeared November 7, 1789*
stillborn	*December 13, 1794*
Frederick	*November 22, 1799 -*

Emily, it was around this time that my agents presented me with a quarterly report, which is when I learned that your employer had passed away and that you had moved to live closer to Lilith.

I always felt that the least I could do was to ensure that my heirs were not in danger, or in Deborah's case, that you Emily, had not been cheated by the new Madam Tina.

Per his usual method, Agent Decker located and questioned Miss Josie for the information. I was glad to hear that nothing about Deborah handing over her business to Madam Tina withheld anything that belonged to you.

Miss Josie is always revealing more than what was asked of her. She is such a delightful source.

Mr. Trolley pulls out the last report and says, "This is dated October 12, 1867. The agents wrote:

> We were assigned by our client to find out more about Mrs. Emily Breat's state of affairs; especially if her former employer (Madam Deb) had left her in a favorable situation. The client requested personal details, including photographs, of Madam Deb and the new Madam, Miss Tina—if possible.
>
> Miss Josie indicated that according to Madam Deb, the name of the woman that raised her was Maggie. Miss Josie believes Maggie and Deb's last name was Seevers.
>
> A local private investigator could not find anything in Delton on a person by the last name of Seevers. The search has been extended to surrounding towns. As luck would have it, an old school record from the mid-1780s was located. The actual date on the document was worn out, but the last name Seevers belonging to a couple of brothers, Harvey and Luke, indicates their hometown was Tootleberry.
>
> The school record had a newspaper article clipped to it. It was dated 1799 and stated that Harvey Seevers was once arrested

for being drunk and disorderly. He was accused of setting fire to an old hut after a fight broke out. Nobody was hurt in the fire so he was only sentenced to serve an undisclosed amount of time in prison.

No records were found on a Maggie Seevers. It is believed possible that Seevers is not an accurate last name.

Emily's pulse quickens. Mr. Trolley resumes reading.

The letter continues …

I have you to thank Emily, for the newspaper article about Madam Deb's death. Otherwise, I would never have gone in search of her background, nor received a most precious gift from Miss Josie. Mr. Trolley will now show you what I'm talking about.

"Here's a picture. Emily, Lilith, who is this person?" asks Mr. Trolley. Both women reply, "Madam Deb."

"Here is another picture. Who is this person?" asks the lawyer, again.

Emily is puzzled by his question but she shrugs her shoulders and replies, "Also Madam Deb."

Mr. Trolley places the pictures next to each other on top of the desk, facing the heirs. David and Graham lean in to look. The lawyer asks, "What do you see in the background of the first picture?"

Emily picks it up and takes a closer look. "Why … that's her brothel."

"That is correct. Now what do you see in the background of the second picture?"

Neither Emily nor Lilith know the location, but as the men lean in once more, they both say at the same time, "That's the Tower of London."

"Very good, gentlemen. Tell me Emily, has Madam Deb ever left the country?"

"No. As far as I know she never wanted to travel abroad because she had a fear of water," replies Emily, puzzled.

"So, how can this be?" asks Lilith, pointing to the two pictures.

Mr. Trolley nods and says, "Indeed. How can this be? The second picture is that of Mrs. Neustat. It was taken in the mid 1850s on one of her many trips overseas. She was very excited when Deborah's picture was obtained by the investigator and delivered to her. She even left me instructions to return it to Miss Josie with a note and five thousand dollars."

"Does this mean ... ?" asks David.

"Despite legal proof, it is my strong opinion that Deborah was Eleanor, Delilah's stolen sister. Her real name was Eleanor Greensley. Emily and Lilith, you both lived with one of your relatives. Madam Deb was your aunt Lilith and your uncle Victor's sister-in-law, Emily. Regrettably though, it was another discovery after death."

"So, that's why!" exclaims Emily.

"Why what?" asks the lawyer.

"Why Deborah was disguised as a boy when she was a child. This Maggie woman probably thought correctly that the lawmen would be looking for a woman with a girl child, so she cut the girl's hair and dressed her in boy's clothing."

"Oh, poor Deborah," sympathizes Lilith.

Mr. Trolley says, "How devious. And now, finally, the last page of Mrs. Neustat's letter which is just as legal a paper as her Will."

The letter continues ...

I bequeath to my niece Emily (Thordeaux) Breat, fifty thousand dollars and my house, including all the contents. I give you full permission to start living carefree. Get back onto society's pages if that is your wish. Meet interesting people. Travel. Enjoy your life, especially now that you no longer have any monetary worries.

I've spoken before of having regrets so do not be surprised when I say again that I regret never having introduced myself to you, to all of you, until now. Emily, I'm sorry I didn't approach you to let you know of Daniel's demise. I'm sorry that I let Lilith go through all that trouble to find you when I knew your whereabouts all along.

Can you imagine Deborah, or rather Eleanor, and I meeting had I approached you? You would have seen our resemblance then. Like I said before, regrets.

I bequeath one hundred thousand dollars to my niece, Lilith (Green) Breat. It is my wish that you will want to live with Emily in her house. Of course, inheriting this money is not dependent on it. You may live wherever you please. I know that under different circumstances I would have liked you, I daresay, even loved you. I have watched you grow up to be someone I would have been privileged to know. I'm just truly sorry that we never met.

After I found out about you, Lilith and your great-aunt's death, you could have become a part of my life but I was too set in my ways and afraid. You see, after I lost Victor, I always believed that I didn't deserve to love someone, and especially to have someone love me back. I didn't want to become your guardian because I sincerely thought you would grow to hate me one day.

So, it was easy for me to sit back and let you live the life that I thought you needed to lead. Besides, you may never have met Daniel and married had I uprooted you to Philadelphia when you were eleven.

I bequeath twenty-five thousand dollars to Graham. I can only say that I was pleased to learn that Martin, my first husband, innocent in all my cruel games, achieved what he truly desired in life—to have a grandson like you.

45

Lilith and Graham

"Lilith, wait. Lilith!" a discouraged Graham says loudly in the grand hall.

Unlike her generally quiet demeanor, Emily also calls out, "Lilith, come back here!"

Lilith has reached the door to the gardens but stops, turns slowly and shakes her head. She just stands there, so Emily and Graham approach her together.

"Don't run away Lilith. Hear him out. Don't leave things like this. Promise me you'll both have your say. Promise?"

Lilith inhales, exhales slowly and acquiesces. Graham breathes out.

Emily nods with satisfaction and then motions that she's going to go and sit on one of the chairs by the window facing out into the terrace, where the last of the sun's rays is still reaching.

"Lilith, we so quickly became good friends when we met. I enjoyed touring the sites of Delton with you. I can't imagine how truly boring my being there would have been without your pleasant company. It didn't take me long to realize that you're someone special and that I wanted to get to know you a whole lot better.

"What Mrs. Neustat's long letter has taught me is that I would have preferred to learn about your youth directly from you, months ago. I regret never hearing about your earlier life before now. I'm sorry I never asked you to talk about yourself when we first met."

Finally, he blurts out, "I never would have thought those things about you had I known about your past. I'm so sorry for what I said and thought of you, Lilith. Can you ever forgive me? I was so afraid that you might be, well you know ... "

"A harlot?"

"Yes. I apologize and please know that I am very shocked by my thoughts back then and that I didn't listen when you were telling me otherwise. I'm ashamed for making you feel—inadequate or unacceptable, to be worthy of my attention—especially because I'm so very fond of you and I so want to see you again."

Lilith holds up her hand to stop his speech. "That's enough, Graham. I accept your apology, but I'm not interested in resuming our friendship."

"What? Why not?" Graham mistakenly thought that his accepted apology would fix everything. He adds, "It can't be because I knew the place you walked into that Friday was a brothel."

"I didn't know that your father's business and his land holdings made you aware that Madam Deb's place was on that street. But no, I'm not mad about that."

"What is it then?"

"Did you use Madam Deb's services that night?" she blurts.

"No! I only went inside to look for you. I left after about ten minutes when I didn't see you there. But to be honest though, I have, ah, visited a brothel. Once. I was with a few of my university mates. We were young, drunk, and stupid. I spent my entire week's money on a working girl and then had to beg for food until the following week's allowance came in. I was too embarrassed to tell my father that I had squandered away that much cash because he would've demanded details on the reasons why before opening his wallet. I decided that I could wait out the seven long days, but boy did I get hungry!"

She laughs at his meek confession and he laughs with relief. Lilith is certainly pleased that she gave him the opportunity to speak up and clear the air.

He approaches the woman he loves and puts his arms around her. A sense of security and familiarity envelopes her. *These are Daniel's arms.*

Graham is puzzled by what he sees on her face, nevertheless, he bends to kiss her cheek. She moves her face toward his and he kisses her on the lips. She is soothed by the embrace as she missed him so.

They walk back together toward Emily and see David also sitting there near the terrace windows. He too had rushed from the study, but for a different reason. David was oblivious to his son's conversation with Lilith as he became immersed in his own conversation of the past.

46
Emily and David

"Is that orange and jasmine scent coming from you?" asks David.

"Yes. How astute of you," replies Emily.

"Adeline wore it. I suspect so did your mother and it was fitting that you would too."

"Ah. Well, I'm still impressed that you remember the fragrance."

"Don't be. I purchased a bottle before returning to Philadelphia the first time –I wanted to give it to Adeline as a gift. I've kept it all these years and every so often I spray some of it in the air so I can breathe in her memory," he confesses.

"How romantic. No wonder Adeline was smitten with you." She smiles.

"Well, I've matured a lot since then, I assure you." He leans forward and rests his elbows on his knees. "Why did you never marry? You're obviously a lady and ... oh, would you listen to me? I'm no gentleman. This is none of my business."

"It's all right. This appears to be a day for honesty. When I first moved to Delton, I knew that if I met anyone, the truth about my situation would one day come out. As time went on, I was sure that if any respectable man found out about my father's destructive behavior or the business I worked for, that he would distance himself from me. So, why invite heartache?"

"Surely, if a man fell in love with you, he would understand. He could take you away from all that nastiness and provide you with the standard of living that you were born to."

"Like you tried to do with Adeline? I guess I was too young to think that possible. I convinced myself that no one would want me, so I made sure to not meet anyone worthy of my affection. I was afraid to love if I would only end up getting hurt so I never let anyone get close."

"How sad and how terribly lonely for you. I'm sorry about that, Emily."

"I lost my mother to a physical illness and my father to an illness of the mind and heart. But when I lost Adeline, I gained Daniel. I was too busy to grieve for her like I needed to. It took me years to come to grips with her death—and my part in not getting her to safety sooner. Then the tragedy of Daniel's death made me want to give up on living altogether. Lilith was very soothing to have around and I can only say that I hope she decides to live with me in this big house. I don't want to become like Delilah."

"No, I don't think you could ever become like Delilah. She was harmed by her mother's depression and her father's aloofness—which is typical in a lot of rich families. Furthermore, she was considerably damaged by her parent's lack of love for her. Even she remembered that her father cared more about her mother's feelings than her when she was struck down to the floor and in pain." David clenches his fists and then releases them. "I swear I'd punch him in the mouth if I could."

Emily doesn't comment on his compassion, but clarifies, "I don't know that I couldn't become bitter. I may also be negatively affected by my parent's actions, you know. Not by my mother, as I'm sure she didn't want to die, but because of her death, my father became locked in his grief and guilt. He couldn't move forward nor backwards. He was stuck there. Adeline and I had to go on living somehow even though we just had our world turned upside down. We didn't know how to live outside that mansion, especially without parents. It was a horrible awakening. However, I suppose, where Delilah's abuse from her parents began with her twin sister's death, mine and Adeline's only surfaced with mother's death."

She pauses upon hearing footsteps. Looking up, she says, "Oh, here comes Lilith and Graham."

"Would you mind if we carried on this conversation another time, alone? I would like to get to know you better, Emily. You don't know how excited I was to know that I'd be meeting someone connected to my past. Because of our relationship through Daniel and Adeline, I feel that I don't have to explain myself to you or to pretend I'm just a happy, rich landowner like I always do when I'm around strangers. At least you know things about me that I don't have to explain. I feel that I can be myself when I'm with you."

"Funny you should say that, David. I feel that way too."

47
January 23, 1868

For their first evening meal shared together, the foursome changed into formal attire. The two handsome men wore dark grey, single-breasted jackets over starched, high collared white shirts and meticulously tied cravats. Emily and Lilith wore their new evening gowns. The purple, or English violet, satin material of Emily's dress was heavily edged with an embossed fleur-de-lis pattern in gold, while Lilith's was royal blue adorned with black lace trim. The fullness of the skirts, known as the Rococo Victoria style dress, entered the room before them.

Emily had asked the staff to place them in the more comfortable and intimate tea room rather than the larger dining room and is not disappointed with her surroundings. The square table with its ornately decorated wooden legs showing beneath the light blue cloth, is meticulously set for four guests with silver cutlery, fine glassware and gold-trimmed plates.

The gentlemen help the ladies sit facing each other and have hardly swooped into their own seats when the footmen serve hors d'oeuvres consisting of two wheat crackers each holding a sliced pear topped with melted white cheese, adorned with sprigs of rosemary. Water glasses are filled and wine complimenting the cheese is poured.

Emily is taken back to a time when she sat at such a table, dressed up in the latest fashion, and served a delectable plate of food by men wearing white gloves. Lilith also reminisces of a time when Aunt Rosanne was teaching her proper etiquette at a dinner table.

Graham asks, "How is it that you're here Father? I mean, how were you informed?"

"I received a letter at the same time you did. I knew yours couldn't possibly say the same thing mine did because you didn't have a history in Philadelphia. When you so innocently opened yours in front of me and read it, I was even more curious. Why would you be included in this Will? That's why I encouraged you to come here. There was no way I'd be missing out on whatever was going to be unfolding in the past couple of days, and I wanted us both here to find out the answer to the mystery. I kept my letter from you on instructions by Mr. Trolley. It was certainly convenient that I was already to be in Philadelphia on business myself."

"So, we would have come to Philadelphia regardless?" asks Graham.

"Yes." David stops eating. With a faraway look, he says, "I felt sure it involved Adeline and I hoped that I would be seeing her again." David forces a smile on his face and takes another bite.

He continues, "My arrival here a couple of days ago was very late at night. Even so, Mr. Trolley met with me to ask that I show up at nine-thirty the next morning to make sure I would remain undetected until it was time for my part of the story to be revealed. He believed my appearing to the three of you before that time would force his hand and reveal Mrs. Neustat's plans in a hurried way and not how she had orchestrated it."

David changed the subject, asking, "How was your meeting with Mr. Trolley this afternoon, Emily?"

She puts her wine glass down and her eyes glisten when she turns to speak to him, "Eventful. We've accomplished so much in just a few hours, but only because Mrs. Neustat was prepared and well organized.

I've agreed to keep all the staff in my employ and I've already heard that they are overjoyed by my decision."

Lilith asks, "So that's why you got the master bedroom."

Emily smiles and nods.

A lull in the conversation is cause for the appearance of the next course—cream of celery soup is ladled into cup sized bowls.

"So, what's next?" asks Graham.

Emily replies, "I'm leaving for Delton day after tomorrow. I have to release my new apartment. As I don't have any other business there, I won't be gone for more than two days."

"What about you Lilith?" asks David.

She inhales, puts her spoon down and breaks off a piece of rye bread before answering. "Nothing is more important to me than family especially when all I have in the world is one person. I'm going home to Delton with Emily to quit my teaching job and release my apartment as well. I've decided to move here. It was the easiest decision I've ever made."

"How about you, David. What's next for you?" asks Emily.

He replies, "I'll soon be done with our business here in Philadelphia. Graham and I sold two businesses when we were in New York, but they were small properties compared to the land in Delton. So, we'll be going back to England some time this spring, I suppose. We haven't really firmed up our plans."

Graham quickly looks over at Lilith and repeats, "No, we haven't made firm plans. Some things are still undecided."

David adds, "That's right. I've engaged Mr. Trolley to work with my lawyers in New York and Delton. We have several meetings with him lined up for next week."

Nobody is listening. The realization that their worlds and lives are an ocean apart causes stomachs to fall. Emily lets her spoon circle the bowl of soup before putting it down on the saucer underneath.

Bowls are then replaced by plates for the main course consisting of beef sirloin, yellow beans, and seasoned roasted potatoes. Wine glasses are replenished. However, the mood and appetites around the table have changed.

Emily says encouragingly, "Well, I would hope that whenever you find yourselves in Philadelphia that you would consider staying here with us. Starting right now, please be our guests here for the next few weeks while you settle your business matters in America. I would be happy to see you both here when we return from Delton. Won't you too, Lilith?"

"Yes, of course. That's a marvellous idea, Emily. Please say yes."

"That's very generous ... " David starts by saying.

"I say yes," Graham interrupts.

David smiles, "As I was saying, that's very generous, Emily. Thank you."

All four now look forward to another month or two of spending time together. David wants to revisit the Philadelphia of his youth and see what has changed on Michigan Avenue since he was last here, decades ago. Emily wants to do the same except her curiosity would bring her to North Sedgwick Street, where she grew up. Lilith wants to explore her new city and Graham wants to go wherever Lilith wanders.

Appetites restored, the balance of the five-course meal is devoured. The fourth course is a cold salad which is followed by French ice cream. Emily has never tasted this dessert and is pleasantly surprised by its cool sweetness.

Gathered in the family room after dinner, Graham asks, "Brandy?"

"Yes please, son."

"Will you please pour me one as well?" asks Lilith.

"Certainly," replies Graham, surprised and smiling.

"I might as well join in too, then," says Emily choosing to sit by the fire. She feels a chill and thinks it might have been caused by the cold dessert.

Graham serves the ladies first.

David says, "Thank you," when Graham hands him the small round goblet. He tastes it and sits back to extend his long legs. "Emily, will you please tell me more about Daniel?"

"Of course." She tells a couple of stories that she hadn't revealed in the past couple of days. Her daughter-in-law has heard them all and sighs, remembering Daniel's humor that Emily's stories highlight.

"Lilith!" Emily exclaims, "I just remembered a story I haven't told even you. Daniel was old enough to speak, so he must have been about three. Deborah never stopped trying to make him say 'I love you, too.' when she'd say 'I love you' to him. He just wouldn't play along. He'd say 'Thank you' or nothing at all.

"Then one day, that boy's humor must have been extra polished. Deborah said, 'I love you' and he said, 'I love you.' He didn't include the word too, so she tried something new and said, 'I love you more.' To which he promptly replied, 'I love you less.'" They all laugh.

David pours himself another shot of brandy and offers it to the others. Only Emily declines a refill. When he sits back down, he asks, "How about you Lilith, is there anything else you would like to share about his life?"

There's no stopping Lilith. Her mind and heart have been filled with Daniel lately. Her eyes, her smile, her whole face lights up with love. She goes so far as to tell them about the time he grabbed her foot that was sticking out of the tub and how they had both laughed at their surprised reactions.

As the re-telling of Daniel's sad and tragic end brings three adults to tears, they don't notice Graham has stood, replenished his glass of brandy and left.

He is jealous. His own father is learning about a lost son and is obviously falling in love with this deceased soul. It's also apparent that this dead man still warms Lilith's entire being. Jealousy is a new experience for Graham but feeling like he's in competition with a dead man is unacceptable. He shudders to think, *Will she compare me to my half-brother? Will I be able to fill her heart too?*

:

Emily does not have a restful sleep and determines it is due to her misplaced attraction to David. She felt it the moment he came out from behind that book shelf and even before he spoke. He is of an appropriate background and the right age for her. He is very handsome, but mostly, he is the only man who has ever made her instantly feel this way.

When David told his story, she discovered that they had a similar upbringing—one of wealth and privilege. She felt empathy when he spoke of distancing himself from his parents and hometown—although his had been voluntary, she had still felt a kinship.

She continues to defend her emotions and then stops abruptly. Had Adeline lived, her sister would be reunited with David. Attraction or no attraction, David would have ended up being her brother-in-law.

She struggles with her sense of responsibility and duty. *I can't let myself be more than fond of David, can I? Isn't it wrong to think of him beyond friendship?*

48

Lilith and Graham

At the breakfast table the next morning, Lilith perks up when she sees Graham enter the room. "You left early last night. I never even had a chance to say goodnight," she says as she scoops a spoonful of strawberry jelly onto a scone.

"I didn't want to interrupt just to say I'd had a long day and was heading upstairs," he replies, trying to sound pleasant.

"I would've asked you if you have time for a walk today before I leave tomorrow. So," she chuckles, "I'm asking now. Do you?"

"I don't know. I'll have to check with Father," he replies, still sounding chipper.

"Were you there when Emily told your father about Daniel's 'I love you less' story?"

"Yes, I was," he said, with a smile that didn't reach his eyes. He thinks, *She is obviously still in love with Daniel. So much so, that she hadn't even noticed that I left.*

Graham notices the Philadelphia newspaper on the sideboard and grabs it before sitting down with his coffee and pastry. He is briefly skimming an article about the upcoming election—it is the first one to be held since the ending of the conflict between the northern and southern states. It goes on about issues concerning Reconstruction of the South and suffrage for the newly freed slaves.

David walks in next and says, "Good morning. Graham, where did you go last night? You went to fill your glass and then you were gone."

"Oh, I was just telling Lilith that I'd had a long day and didn't want to interrupt just to say goodnight."

"I see. What are you doing today?" David asks him.

"I was waiting to see if you had any specific plans, Father."

"Not really. It promises to be a nice day outside and I would like to go for a long walk. Then I'll spend the rest of the morning going through papers. If you would like a good stretch of the legs, you're more than welcome to join me. I promised Emily I'd spend time with her this afternoon. She has questions about running a house like this. We're including Mr. Reynolds and Mrs. Harper in our meeting. I'm sure they'll provide Emily with all the help she needs but perhaps my presence will reassure her, so I'll be there."

"What are you doing, Lilith?" David asks.

"I was hoping to spend time with Graham. Perhaps a walk."

"Splendid. Then that's settled," David says.

Graham craves Lilith's company but he's confused by his emotions and discerns he needs more time to figure out why he's feeling this way. Spending time alone with Lilith before resolving his issues may confuse him even more. Nevertheless, he flashes her a smile over the edge of the newspaper he is no longer reading.

He puts the paper aside and gobbles down his breakfast, finishing his coffee before anyone else asks him questions he doesn't want to answer. He passes the newspaper to his father and says, "There's a good article about the tax on page three, Father. Perhaps we should speak to Mr. Trolley about referring us to a lawyer who specializes in tax issues on the sale of land holdings."

Resolving his feelings won't be done by closing himself up with paperwork. He nods towards Lilith. "Well, I think I'll change into warmer clothes for that walk, Lilith. Let us meet in the garden in half an hour?"

"Your father's right, it's not that cold outside today. I love this garden. I can't wait until spring to see it in bloom," says Lilith pleasantly.

"Lilith," he waits until she stops walking ahead. "Do you still love, I mean, do you, ah, are you … ?" he stumbles on his words.

"What are you trying to ask me Graham? I don't mind answering whatever question is on your mind."

"It's just that I see how much you love Daniel. I can't use the past tense, because I really believe that you still love him."

"Yes. I'm sure I'll love him for the rest of my life. He was a wonderful man and husband."

"Oh, I see."

"No, you don't see. I don't want to spend the rest of my life alone Graham, pining for a dead man. I want to be with someone who can make me feel again. One who can love me and want to share our dreams together. I think I deserve that."

"Yes, of course you do."

They continue their walk along the flagstones in the garden.

"Father and I have to go back home and make concrete decisions about business and such. After that, I don't know what will happen so I won't ask you to wait for me. That wouldn't be fair to either of us," Graham continues, walking with his head down.

Lilith turns and pokes him in the chest. "Oh, well! You do what you have to do!" Then quieter, "But I would wait if you asked me, Graham."

"No, I really don't think that would be fair, Lilith."

She nods and looks away, disappointed. *That's it then. He won't be coming back to America or to me.*

Graham is convinced that no man can ever replace Daniel. Hurt and at a loss, he says, "I don't want to just leave things like this, Lilith."

He takes her by the arms and pulls her closer to him. She looks up into his big brown eyes and her lips part. He moves a hand to cup her cheek, bends his head and kisses her. She clings to him and moves her arms to hold him closer. He does the same, embracing her hungrily. He kisses her thinking he might never have another opportunity ever again. She feels his desire, and reciprocates.

Abruptly, he tears himself away, "I must go. I'll see you and Emily off tomorrow." Defeated, he leaves in a hurry, his eyes blurring with tears by the time he closes the door to his bedroom.

Her arms are not done with him, but she lets them fall to her side. She waits for him to turn around, but he does not.

Graham is very quiet at dinner that evening. Lilith blushes every time she thinks of his kisses, but Graham misinterprets her blushed cheeks and ascribes her flush to memories of her lost love. They both retire early, leaving Emily and David alone.

49
Emily and David

"So, Emily, tell me how you felt about the meeting this afternoon." David asks while pouring two brandies as they stand near the window looking out into the dark garden.

"You were right, David. I'll have absolutely nothing to worry about except meal plans. As long I manage to keep all my excellent staff, that is." She reaches for the glass he has extended.

"Good. I'm glad for you."

"I do want to thank you for being available."

"Nonsense. It was my pleasure. I've not had weeks to observe, but you seem to have just waltzed right back into the lifestyle you were born in." He paused. "I must say that I'm very fond of you. I hope you don't find that statement offensive, considering my time with Adeline."

"You mean how the two of you became parents?" she smiles.

"Oh, well. Yes. I guess I mean that," he replies, shocked by her blunt question.

"Please, David. I've seen many things in my life that I would never have seen if Mama hadn't died or if Papa had overcome his grief. I've seen people waste their lives away because they never spoke their peace. I'm not young and naive anymore. I don't want to let people talk on my behalf because I'm meek. I don't want to fade away like Delilah Neustat or Deborah Seevers whose long lives were empty, void of true love and companionship."

She takes a risk spilling her thoughts like that and hopes it will pay off. She also thinks that she can't help her feelings for David and that Adeline would likely have done exactly what she is doing had the roles been reversed.

David looks at her anew and is happy to discover that she isn't meek, nor defenceless. He says, "Having said that, you make me wonder why you asked me to join you for the meeting this afternoon."

"Because I enjoy your company and wanted you there. I rather like you, very much," she replies, almost nonchalantly, directing her gaze back to the shadowy garden.

Brazen, he thinks.

"Emily."

She looks away from the window and turns to face him.

"I'm more than fond of you. I've tried to reason with myself that it's not possible because we've just met but I feel like I've been waiting my whole life for you. And, here you are."

"It's very comforting to hear you say that, David. I too wondered how I could feel like this so soon after having just met. Then I stopped questioning it and just accepted. I've long ago determined that life is too short to leave some things unsaid. Tell me, do you think we are being irresponsible or wrong?" Emily obviously still has a doubt or two but mostly, she needs to hear what he will say now.

"It can't be wrong to feel what we're both feeling. No, Emily, I don't think we are being irresponsible or thoughtless or anything like that," he says reassuringly.

David approaches her and puts an arm around her waist and lifts her up to his lips. He swings her a little before realizing that brandy is being spilled on the carpet.

He lets her go and reaches for her glass and puts it back on the tray with his and asks, "Have I offended you?"

"No, I'm not offended. Why would you say that?" she asks, even though she can guess why. She is behaving like a young girl. She blushed—at her age!

"You should see your face!"

"My dear David. This is my first kiss."

"Oh! Yes, I guess I knew that. May I kiss you again?"

"I was hoping you would ask me that," she replies, smiling blissfully.

He picks her up and swings her around again. She puts her arms around his neck this time. They kiss all the while they are going around. They laugh out loud and kiss again, and again.

"We'll be here for at least a month after your return from Delton. I think what needs doing in London will take about four months, five at best. Emily, I'm not sure I have the right to ask ... "

Emily's heart skips a beat.

" ... but will you wait for me?"

No longer a youthful woman with decades ahead of her, she is deflated, and answers, "Why, David. You surprise me. I'd like to think about that before I reply, if you don't mind."

"No, of course not." His hopes fall to the pit of his stomach when he sees the jubilation on her face change to a frown. They have just met, what other question was she expecting?

"Well, goodnight then." Emily takes her glass of brandy, bows her head down and leaves in a hurry.

"Goodnight." David clenches his square jaw as he watches her leave the room too soon.

50
January 25, 1868

Four adults cautiously withhold emotions at the train depot the following day.

"See you on the 28th."

"See you then."

"Goodbye."

"Godspeed."

David is upset with Emily's aloofness after he kissed her gloved hand at the train station. He doesn't notice Graham's gloominess until the young man speaks up. Grateful for the distraction, David listens carefully to his son's story about his summer months spent with the lovely Lilith and even he is shocked by Graham's outburst at the park.

David's only reaction when he hears of Graham's apology is a loud inhale and exhale. "I don't understand Graham. Do you love Lilith?"

"Yes, I do, Father. I don't want to be without her."

"So, what's holding you back?"

"Really? You have to ask?"

David gives him a befuddled look.

"Daniel! That's what's holding me back. She's still in love with him. I can't compete with a dead man and I can't be compared to my half-brother. I can't deal with this, Father. I don't know how."

David lets Graham rant until he exhausts all his doubts. Finally, he asks his troubled son, "Have you talked to Lilith about that?"

"I tried, but I don't think it went well. I have no words to explain fully what I feel and I'm afraid she won't tolerate indecisiveness. I need time to set myself straight."

"That's a good counsel. Do that, son. I'm afraid you'll have to figure this out yourself. No matter how much I want to help, I probably can't do more than give you my full support."

A snow storm delays the women's return by two extra days.

As he watches the man load the closed carriage with luggage, David asks, "How did it go?" The rest of the women's crated items that they decided to bring to Philadelphia were being shipped separately so it didn't take long for the luggage to be loaded and for them to depart the train station.

"Splendidly," replies Emily. "How did it go here?"

"Excellent. Mr. Trolley is very efficient. I can see us being ready to return to England by the end of next month. The sooner we go, the faster we will return," David says to Emily by his side. He hopes that she has warmed to the idea to wait for him but she practically ignores his statement.

"Where's Graham?" asks Lilith, sitting across from them.

David lies when he replies, "He's off running an errand for me. I thought he would be back in time to accompany me to meet your train." He had suggested to Graham to stay behind in the hopes that he could study and discern Lilith's feelings for his son better if he wasn't present. Alas, it doesn't. Emily takes hold of the conversation and updates David on the events of the past few days. David cannot observe Lilith as he's genuinely interested in Emily's every word.

Graham greets them at the door. "Quickly. Come inside where it's warm. I can't believe how cold it gets here in Philadelphia."

"Unfortunately, this city is well known for drastic weather," explains Emily.

The ladies go upstairs to rest before supper. After the meal, the four gather in the parlor where the absence of staff gives them the freedom to openly converse.

David decides to convince Lilith that they have something in common and hopefully play on her sympathies and help her see Graham's struggles. He begins, "I remembered something about Adeline the other day and I wanted to share it with all of you." He lets a smile come to his lips and his thoughts wander to the treasured love of his youth.

If David was trying to help the young couple realize something, he hadn't succeeded. He did, however, stir new feelings in Emily—curiosity on learning something new about her sister—and confusingly, jealousy!

"It was an afternoon when Adeline was caring for my cousins. She was determined to help them find a craft that they could love doing for the rest of their lives. Teaching them to sew was a disaster and shopping couldn't be considered a craft. But when Adeline took out her painting supplies, she had done the right thing.

"They spent the better half of a week exploring their talents and as a lark, they put a few of their pieces, along with several of Adeline's, out on display for my parents to judge. It was a game, but I later found that my parents had one painting framed and they even hung it in their bedroom as a keepsake of their nieces' well spent summer with them. Little did they know, Adeline had painted it. Of course, I took it after my parents passed."

David feels a renewed re-connection to Adeline and Emily can eerily sense the hold her late sister still has on him.

David hopes, *Can Graham see that speaking and reminiscing of the dead is perfectly normal and healthy? Can Lilith feel Emily's jealousy, even for a moment, and understand that Graham feels like second best, never to be first?*

Even if Lilith is unaware, she is not unfeeling when she asks, "You love her still, after all these years, David?"

"The love never goes away Lilith, as I'm sure you know perfectly well. Nor do the happy memories, but my time with Adeline was so short that it never had the chance to grow beyond our attraction, I'm afraid. I've forgotten more about her than I knew."

"You were satisfied with that brief love?" Lilith asks.

"No."

Lilith is painfully aware of Emily's feelings for David and yet, she feels compelled to add, "Even so, you've never married. Have you even courted someone special?"

He can see that his plan has backfired when he gazes upon Emily's stoic face. He replies, "No. Over the years, I was introduced to many possible connections, but none that developed into that special relationship."

He doesn't disclose that the women he has known on an intimate level are not suitable for marriage especially to a respected gentleman like himself. And the women who were socially acceptable, he would unjustly compare to Adeline and inevitably find them wanting.

51
February 1868

Prior to her death, Mrs. Neustat fed the Philadelphian rumor mill with intriguing stories of her heirs in the hopes of establishing curiosity. It worked. Anybody who was anyone wanted to be seen talking to the Breat women or one of their male guests. It didn't take long for invitations to balls and soirees and dinners to start showing up at the house.

Seated at her desk in her new study, Emily peruses the dozens of envelopes and finds four of the same size and with the same penmanship, personally addressed to each of the new occupants. She opens hers, reads it and calls for Lilith.

While she waits, she writes a quick message.

"Shut the door behind you, please."

"What is it, Emily?" asks Lilith, a bit out of breath.

"Nothing serious but I think I found a solution to our stagnant problem."

"What problem?"

"The two men in our lives."

"Oh? How's that?"

"Well, see these invitations?" she asks, handing Lilith her invitation.

Lilith reads hers and nods.

Emily continues, "Their return address is that of the first home ever built on Michigan Avenue. That means they are from the Clarkson family who is the most prestigious, wealthiest family in Philadelphia."

"So?" asks Lilith, encouragingly.

Emily smiles, "We need to go shopping, but first I need to send this by messenger."

Lilith reads the note and gives Emily a quizzical look.

Mrs. Lilith Breat and I have received your gracious invitations and very much want to accept. We would be pleased to meet you beforehand for tea so that we may feel less like strangers and more like neighbors on the night of your ball.

Please reply, favorably, if possible, by return messenger, on your availability, where we will be sure to schedule it in our calendars.

Mrs. Emily Breat
Mrs. Lilith Breat

Emily says, "I'll explain on the way."

Emily places the two invitations addressed to the men in the top drawer of her desk, to be delivered to them the following day.

The late Mrs. Clarkson's granddaughter-in-law replies favorably to meet mid-morning of the next day. During the rendezvous, she agrees to engage her husband in a small ruse.

That same afternoon, at the lawyer's office downtown, David and Graham are leaving the establishment when they notice a man approaching them.

"David? David Lestor? Is that really you?" the man asks.

"Yes, it is. My apologies though, I'm afraid I don't recognize you," replies David.

"Hal Clarkson!"

"Well for goodness sake. It's been more than thirty years. How did you recognize me?"

"Truth?" He points to Graham. "Your son looks just like you did at that age."

They laugh.

"Listen, I would love to reminisce but I'm late for an appointment. Are you coming to our party on the seventh?" Hal asks.

"What party?"

"Look through your invitations. I know we sent you one."

"I'll be sure to do that and accept."

"Bring your son."

"Will do." Father and son have an occasion to look forward to.

The soiree on Friday the seventh of February, begins at seven. David and Graham are greeted by their hostess who warmly welcomes them into her home. She leads them down the hallway and leaves them in a room full of men, where they will find refreshments and conversations of sports, politics, and business.

Hal notices them, excuses himself to the three men he is talking with and extends his hand out to David and Graham.

Forty-five minutes later, Graham has exhausted his interest in the topics and drifts toward the music coming from the room across the hall. David sees him leave and follows. They both enter the ballroom at the same time.

"How typical," remarks David out loud. Graham gives him a quizzical look, so David elaborates, "You see how one side of the room is filled with women and the other with men?"

"No, not evenly. There are men and women everywhere."

"Yes, but they outnumber each other from one side to the other. Don't you see?"

"Yes, now I do. What's typical about it, Father?"

"What's typical is that every dance I've ever attended has the same pattern. In this room, north is where single men gather, and south is where the debutantes and single women are. East and west are a mixture of the married or promised couples. North and south are hoping to move east and west by the next ball."

Graham smiles. "Where do you want to stand?"

David forces a smile and announces. "I've asked Emily to wait for me."

"What did she say?"

"She needs time to think on it," he frowns.

Suddenly, both are chagrined as they observe Emily and Lilith being led to the dance floor by a couple of men from the north side of the room. Graham and his father didn't even know that the women would be in attendance this evening and although they should have anticipated their attendance, wonder why neither spoke of it at dinner the night before.

Graham turns his head in support for his father and says, "Maybe an ocean is too far and it has come between you and your future. I'm sorry to say that her answer appears to be negative, Father."

David is hurt and returns a look of pity toward his son, "Don't be like me and wait for the world to make decisions that concern your heart. If you love Lilith, tell her. For heaven's sake, don't let a dead husband stand in your way! You can be sure that no other man in this room tonight would be stopped by that, especially if Lilith is even slightly interested in him."

Graham nods and whispers, "Don't you give up yet either," and moves to the north side of the room. David follows and lines up to ask Emily for a dance when she is next free.

Twenty minutes of waiting agitates David beyond his gentle nature. He doesn't mean to squeeze Emily's hand so hard when his turn to dance is up, "That hurts, David. Are you angry with me?"

"I'm sorry, Emily. It's very crowded in here. Do you mind if we dance toward one of the entrances and end up in the hallway where it's cooler."

"No, I don't mind."

"It's quieter for conversation too."

"I came here to dance, David."

But by now they are near the exit. "Emily Thordeaux-Breat, have you something to tell me?"

"Here? You want my reply here? Right now? Standing in a hallway?"

"Yes. I must know."

"Fine. My answer is that even though I care about you very much I cannot wait any longer to start living, David. I hope you understand."

David is deflated and hopeful at the same time. After all, she did say she cared. He releases his hold around her waist and gets down on one knee. "Emily, will you fill my empty life and marry me?"

"David, do you love me or a memory of a sister I'm fulfilling?" she bravely asks.

That's not an answer, so he rises. "You. Why would you think otherwise? Have I offended you?"

"That evening last week, you spoke of her and looked like a man very much in love when you shared that story."

He tilts his head back, "My answer to that is two-fold. One, I did that for Graham with the hope that Lilith would see how her love for Daniel is keeping my son at bay. I assure you that I've not felt such love for Adeline as I do for you. I've come to realize that I knew so little about Adeline, and that the time we did share together was perfect, but only because it was so new. But it clouded my judgment and I've unjustly compared all other women to her."

"Even me? Or is being her sister like a pass?"

"One of the things that has surprised me is that I've not compared you to her. And I must add, nor am I trying to replace her with you. I am intrigued by you and your wisdom."

"Did it work?"

"Did what work?"

"Has Graham come to realize that there is nothing to fear?"

"I don't know. I did my best."

"What's the second part?"

"I have uncomfortably, for the first time in my life this evening, been jealous. I can't stand to watch you dance with other men."

She smiles, "In that case, my answer is yes. I will marry you."

Lilith is pleased that Graham wants to dance with her. She had wondered since the day they met if they would have the occasion. She would gladly erase all the names on her dance-card above his, but Emily had counseled her earlier on that day to be sure to make him wait. If he truly wanted her, he would have to prove it. She knows Emily is right.

In Graham's arms now, only they exist. She tried hard to not let him enthrall her, but her heart won't listen to her brain. He is as agile on his feet as she is light. Graham hopes that the blush on her cheeks is because of him and not the heat.

He says, "I was right. You are a good dancer."

She replies, "On the contrary, I'm a good follower. I was wondering if this dance would remind you of when I stepped on your foot when we first met."

"Well, have you stepped on my toes? If you have, I didn't feel a thing."

She laughs, "That's because you're holding me up. I'm hardly touching the floor, Graham!"

He leans down to whisper in her ear, "I love you."

"How can I know that is so? You confuse me, Graham. In the garden you said goodbye and then you kissed me with such passion ... "

"I know," he interrupts. "I'm sorry that I didn't tell you then that I was jealous of your love for Daniel. I've never been in love before and it hurt when I found out that you're in love with someone else. Knowing that he is gone doesn't ease the jealousy because I want your whole heart and love and I'm not sure you can give it. I couldn't ask you to wait for me either, especially when you said that you would love him for the rest of your life.

"That night that Father told us about his memory of Adeline, even I could recognize Emily's jealousy. You know, Father never went out of his way to meet someone special. He spent his life alone and I've come to realize that he didn't want to find someone to replace her. I hope I'm wrong, but I thought that you didn't want to as well.

"I've been protecting my heart by not telling you that I love you. But you must know—I want to spend the rest of my life with you, Lilith. If you'll have me. Marry me. Maybe someday you can love me as much as you love Daniel. Can you love two men—two brothers—at the same time?"

Epilogue

My dear Noreen,

I was surprised how quickly I became comfortable wearing my new wedding ring. The day before Graham and I wed, I put aside the ring Daniel gave me, tucking it into a small wooden box and placing it with my other treasures.

The trip from England back home to Philadelphia was especially difficult for me. The motion of the ship wreaked havoc with my morning sickness. Gratefully, walking on land settled my upset stomach.

Most sincerely, your friend,
Mrs. Graham Lestor

Book Club Questions

1. Maggie lives little more than hand to mouth—the responsibility of providing for another person is an additional burden. When you learn of Deborah's history and how she began a nomadic life with Maggie, do you wonder about Maggie's motives? Was it more than getting revenge on Beatrice? Or did she make a decision she regretted?

2. Deborah's menstrual cycle is once every six months; Elizabeth had an apparent huge weight loss before the diagnosis of "nothing can be done"; Delilah's misfortune of becoming barren—did you note other medical aspects that were just accepted as-is for this historical time period?

3. Deborah considers James as her first love. His behaviour does align with what many of us would consider love. Why do you think Deborah would say or believe this?

4. Writing the book involved researching elements of the time (daily wages, Napoleon, concept of quasi war, clothing, food menu items and course selections). Did any of these details cause you to be curious enough to research further?

5. In present day, do you think Victor would have forgiven Delilah's lies and stayed married? Why or why not?

6. Historical Note: Ships that crossed the oceans in the early 1800s did not have cabin numbers. Nor could passenger ships accommodate first-class travellers as guests with their own private one-room sleeping arrangements. This detail has been changed for the flow of the story in *The Three Heirs*. Do you think that it is important that authors note when a detail is chronologically out of place. How should they do that?

Would you like a drawing of that red dress?
Find it at my website www.moniquedesrosiers.com

Acknowledgements

I thank my loving family—my parents and siblings—for their antics and talents at recounting great stories.

An enormous amount of credit goes to my Beta readers—Angela Michalick, Joanne Raimbault, Loni Eskildsen, and Rachel Bradet—whose sharp eyes and questions enriched the final product of this manuscript.

Endless gratitude to Jeanne Martinson, Publisher and Senior Editor of Wood Dragon Books, who faced so many challenges in the past several months while we tackled the finishing touches on this book.

Thank you to Jeanne's countless colleagues and reviewers that she tasked with reading the first couple of drafts. Their recommendations on the changes that could be made to improve my story were spot on.

I am in awe of the talented artists involved in the finishing touches. I love the cover of my book, designed by Callum Jagger, the inside design by Christine Lee, and new chapter page pen graphic by Celine Peter.

Much appreciation to the newest member of the team, Carlene Clark. She is my Social Media Manager and the bulk of her work begins now.

I thank God, every day, for everything else.

About the Author

The Three Heirs is Monique Desrosiers' second novel. Her debut novel, The Cartwright Men Marry, published in 2020, is about love and adventure in the Nevada historical west.

Monique loves playing cards and is an avid collector of Joker/wild cards. She enjoys teaching the basics of the card game Bridge to her condo neighbors and plays the game as often as possible. The freedom to travel once more gives Monique opportunities to gather material for good story telling.

When home, she lives in Winnipeg, Manitoba, Canada.

The Cartwright Men Marry

Have you ever wondered what happened to those Cartwright men of the Ponderosa plains? Did they fall in love? Marry?

This book explores the possible connection between the Cartwrights of today and those four men of the past as Cartwright descendants try to solve a family mystery and, in the process, introduce us to the women the four Cartwright men meet and fall in love with. These women seem perfect for Ben, Adam, Hoss, and Joe - but will avalanches, cattle rustlers, criminals, and wily women keep them apart from true love?

Available in eBook, hardcover, paperback, audiobook and large print.